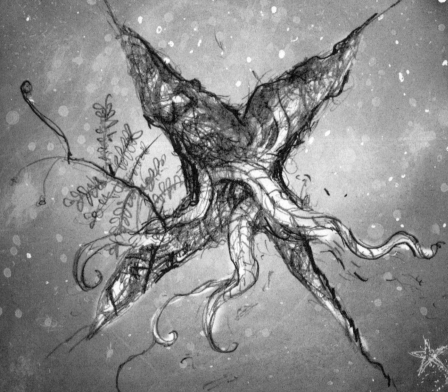

Hold your breath.

We're going in.

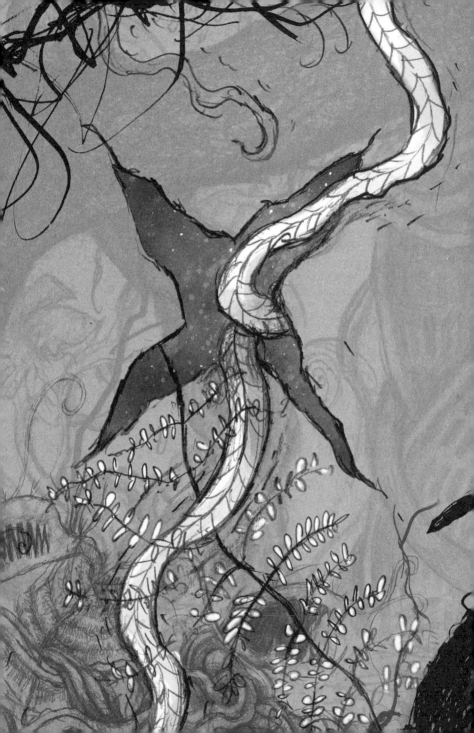

To the freelancers:

Belinda Jones

Maurice Lyon

Lisa Davis, Emma Zipfel.

As Waterstones Children's Laureate until
very recently, I want to say a wider thank-you
to all the book-y world heroes: librarians, booksellers,
literacy organizations, teachers, journalists, and
book advocates online. Every child has the right
to read for the joy of it, because reading is magic,
and magic is for everyone.

And most important of all...
Simon, Maisie, Clemmie, and Xanny
The Best Family in the World
Because...True Love and Beyond,
and Family really is Everything.

Because a family should be built on
KINDNESS,
and kindness has no limits

ACKNOWLEDGMENTS

A whole team of people have helped
me write this book.

Thank you to my wonderful editors,
Ruth Alltimes and Naomi Greenwood, and
my magnificent agent, Caroline Walsh.

A special big thanks to my brilliant designer,
Samuel Perrett, and to my incredible Publicity
and Marketing team, Rebecca Logan,
Camilla Leask, and Naomi Berwin.

And to everyone at Hachette Children's Group,
Hilary Murray Hill, Dominic Kingston,
Katy Cattell, Alexandra Haywood, Inka Roszkowska,
Laura Pritchard, Nicola Goode, Katherine Fox and the
Sales team, Tracy Phillips and the Rights Team.

IMAGINE...

Imagine somewhere unlike anywhere your human eyes have ever seen before.

I know this will be hard for you because it is difficult to imagine any other world than your own, particularly if you are a grown-up and your imagination has become stiff and hard and slow. So remember what it was once like to be a child, if you must, to help you imagine this other world. This other planet.

This planet is called Excelsiar and it has three moons: one pale orange, one a beautiful turquoise, one purple and green. The sun is redder than your own sun, and many of the mountain ranges are striped, almost as if they are made out of candy. And, oh, the jungle in that world! A jungle so green it makes your eyes ache, with rivers that burn and smoke.

Most of this planet is covered in an ocean that can be black as ink and red as wine, and the creatures in that ocean glow starlike in the glorious darkness as they swim lazily through the seas. Many of these animals you will recognize from worlds all across the universe: whales, porpoise, jellyfish... but in the enormity of this particular dark ocean, the jellyfish can be large as islands, drifting ominously with their tentacles hanging down.

There are great continents with land masses that are either sinister wastelands of dust-blown desert or tangled jungles brimming with life. Every now and then, the forest is punctuated by the stripy mountains that climb up into the violet clouds, and there are floating cities built on gases, populated by all sorts of creatures that perhaps you thought were just myths. The skyscrapers and the trees have twisted around each other in spirals; the roads can be rivers all on fire; the buildings are growing, very slightly, every day, like big bamboos.

Now, calm your breathing, for there are truly terrible things in this planet's jungle who hunt by the smell of fear, and they hate human beings with a hungry, bloody hatred. They can sniff out fear from a distance of several miles, and you do not want to draw the attention of these creatures. You do not want them to sense that you are here. The instant you find yourself becoming anxious, the sweat beginning to form on your forehead, the first flutterings in your stomach, make your heart slow down.

HOLD YOUR BREATH.

Are you ready?

Hang on to the sides of this book very tightly.

Sharpen your wits.

Open your eyes, clean those smears off your glasses, prick up your ears.

Cling tight to the hairs on the back of my neck.

Chapter 1
THE HUNTED BOY

On the planet with three moons, a young human boy was running through the choke of a vividly tangled jungle, heart pounding, chest heaving with sobs, absolutely petrified.

The boy was called K2 (pronounced "Kay Too"), and he was rather ordinary-looking, thin as a twig, covered in grazes, his clothes in rags and ruins about him, his glasses so scratched and broken he could barely see where he was going.

K2 was right to be so terrified.

For *this* was a planet where human beings were hunted to the death.

Above K2's head there was a whirring, flying robot, about the size of a small dog. The little robot was called Puck, and he was in an even worse condition than the boy. One of his rotary wings was bent so he was flying lopsidedly and a

whole chunk of his left-hand side had been shot off.
It was a miracle he could still fly at all.

"We is being chased by people-eating plants...,"
said Puck.

"Yes, Puck, I know," panted K2.

All around K2, the jungle was alive and
waking up.

"And hunted by that thing I ab*squo*lootely cannot mention...," said Puck (but he *was* unfortunately mentioning it, nonetheless). "That hairy, scary unbemaginably terrifying *BEAST*...with its grabbers and its stingers and its big...What's the white pierce-y unloving bits on the ends of the gnashing things called?"

"Teeth," gasped K2. "But *please* don't talk about it, Puck! That Beast and those others all hunt by the smell of fear, and the more you *talk* about them, the harder it is to stay calm."

But K2's stomach had already liquefied with terror, and the vegetation must have caught the smell of his fear, for nearby vines unwrapped themselves from tree branches, reaching out long tendril fingers, growing in front of K2's eyes.

"Is...there...anything...you...can...do?" cried K2 as one long, curling python of a vine whipped out languorously and tripped him up. He squirmed out of its grip, staggered to his feet, and ran on, limping even more than he had been before.

13

"Lasers would be good!" said Puck enthusiastically.

"You've got *lasers*?" said K2 in excitement.

"I HAS got lasers!" said Puck, always keen to please.

"*Use the lasers, Puck!*" squealed K2.

"I *has* got lasers," Puck admitted sadly, "but I's afraids my lasers gots jammed up with sand in that dessert."

I think he means "desert," thought K2, *because that would make more sense.*

"Let me see...what's I sqwat in here instead?" Puck put out a little robot arm with an array of attachments, like a more sophisticated version of a Swiss Army knife. "Fork?...*No*...Can opener?...*No*...Ice-scream scoop?...*No*...Egg whisk?...*No*."

Egg whisk?

WHEEOOOOOOOOOWWWWWW!

K2 ducked just in time as a great harpoon shot above his head and straight into a tree trunk ahead of him. The area around where the harpoon had struck turned a great spreading black, as if the tree were bleeding.

The tree let out an enormous scream that made K2's ears ring with the sound of it.

"Sorry, tree...," said K2 as he stumbled past the poor shriveling sapling. "I'm so sorry..."

"*I's sorry* too, K2!" wailed Puck. "I's got nuffink helpful!"

"Don't worry, Puck, that's not your fault. You've done your best..."

K2 was in Big Trouble, but he knew that his robot was in dreadful danger too.

"You hide in my backpack," he recommended. "They hate robots nearly as much as human beings. Go in there and keep quiet and maybe they won't find you. That's an order, Puck!"

The little robot dived down into K2's backpack, for robots have to obey orders, even if they don't want to.

K2 could smell the Beast that was chasing him now, a rich, hot stink that reminded him vaguely of the scent of lion, for he had breathed it once before when he visited a zoo. But this was a far more powerful, angry stench, and it exploded the memory of the poor weak reek that came from the caged lion he had inhaled before and replaced that faint echo with something far more scary.

All around K2 the trees were reaching back their branches to comfort the stricken, poisoned tree, murmuring soothing noises, and he knew that underneath the ground where he could not see, they were stretching out their roots through the sluggish soil, and at any moment, the roots would push through that mud and vegetation that was already bulging up in leaf-quakes underneath him and catch him by the ankle...

And if they caught him, the Beast would be on him.

WROOOOOOUUUUAAAEERRRRRR!

The astonishing roar reverberated around the jungle and around K2 as if he were being turned over like a big ocean wave, and as the sound drummed right into the heart of his body, he no longer knew whether he was running *away* from the Beast or *toward* it.

And the Beast caught him.

Or more precisely, another great tendril of vine came licking around K2's ankle, tripping him up, and although he shook it off, he stumbled, and that slight hesitation enabled another tendril to get a good hold of his other foot, and he was tipped over onto the ground and in five seconds flat, wrapped all around with vines and stems as thick as curling ropes...

...and dragged across the jungle floor to face the Beast.

No wonder this boy's mother was getting such terrible headaches...

Perhaps this was a little too scary an opening...

And I've just realized, it isn't really the start of the story.

So save your very reasonable, heart-beating, stone-cold terror for a moment, for we will not carry on in that dangerous world right now. We will wait until you are more prepared.

I'll just leave K2 being dragged to who knows WHAT dreadful fate, while I go back and explain how and why he was so very far from home in the first place.

For K2 was a long, long, LONG way from home.

Let me just check my tablet, where I have the official guide to all the worlds in all the universe... Yes, I'm right.

Soooooooooooooo many *long*s, there isn't room to put them all here.

I do not know where you are, dear reader; you could be literally *anywhere* in the numberless galaxies, so this planet may be very familiar to you or you may have to travel quite a distance to get there. But as you fall into the strange rectangular portal of this book, imagine you are falling through space, mile after soft black mile; think of a number and times it by a billion.

From morn to noon you will fall... until suddenly you arrive at K2's home, a small and unimportant blue planet called Earth.

Once there was Magic here on Earth.

Once there were dragons.

The earth you are currently walking on is in fact built on thousands and thousands of years of human intelligence in the form of stories, like layer upon layer of limestone and chalk and clay and basalt.

Many of those stories described Magic in all its glory and manifestations.

It is only here on this thin little layer of the present where human beings DON'T believe in Magic, as opposed to millennia upon millennia of human existence when they DID.

All I am asking you to imagine *now* is...

What if some of those stories were true?

This is a story of a Very Modern Magic that is not buried faraway in the darkness of the Bronze Age nor in the shifting mists of the Viking past, but is hiding in plain sight, right underneath the tip of your nose, so close that you can touch it.

For the people who now live on Earth are totally unaware of the multitude of species and worlds and incredible creatures having their spectacular wars and their loves and their lifetime business just out of sight of the limits of the people of Earth's own comprehension.

Isn't that funny?

We need to go a little closer, to an unexceptional, wet, and windy bit of Planet Earth on the edge of one of its shores.

Because we're visiting Earth at a very bad moment, when one particular family has unfortunately come to the notice of the most ruthless and imperious and dreadful minds in the Infinite Galaxies.

And, as a result, the lives of *every single living being* on Planet Earth are now in danger, even the lovely birds and the quiet sea creatures, who most certainly haven't done anything at all to deserve such merciless attention.

So the stakes are already rather high at the beginning of this story. Particularly if you happen to come from Planet Earth yourself, because you may just be rather fond of it.

So, cling tight to my wings.

Adjust your thinking caps.

Make brave your heart, make clever your fingers.

We're going in.

Hold your breath.
We're going in ...

Chapter 2 FOUR UNLIKELY HEROES GET SOME OUT-OF-TOWN ATTENTION

hen K2 woke up the previous morning in his bedroom, he had never even *heard* of the planet on which he was going to be fighting for his life. He hadn't met the little robot that would be accompanying him. And he didn't yet know about the existence of life on other worlds.

So when K2 was stomping to school through a witch-cold wind that was blowing across the soggy, forgotten part of the Planet Earth countryside, burning the tip of his nose and making its way through three layers of clothing to chill his stomach and freeze his heart, he was worrying about math tests and PE lessons and if his lunch was going to get stolen again.

When what he OUGHT to have been worrying about were the eyes that were following him.

Two pairs of very strange eyes were watching K2 and three other children making their way along that frozen, muddy country road, doubled over against the force of the wind.

The eyes, and the creatures those eyes belonged to, shouldn't have been there.

You might even say they were eyes-that-were-out-of-this-world.

One set of eyes belonged to *me*, so that's all right.

But the other eyes—ah, the *other* eyes—why, *they* were a different matter entirely.

The second set of eyes was watching from behind a nearby hedge.

These children, you see, were being *tracked*, and they did not yet know it.

The children were all making their way to the same school. But two of the children had crossed to the other side of the road, as if the other two had some sort of nasty disease.

Because these two sets of children, whose parents had married each other, and who were now expected to be all joyful about it and jumping around holding hands and skipping like merry little lambs, making a newly blended, happy-ever-after, ever-so-modern stepfamily together...

...did not really get on.

In fact, just between you and me...

Some of them *absolutely LOATHED each other.*

Let me introduce you to these children, and you can decide which one is going to be your favorite.

You've already met K2 O'Hero.

He had been named K2 after the second highest mountain in the world, because he was from a family of world-famous, very clever adventurers and explorers.

So this really ought to have been a good Heroic name.

But if you are looking for a Hero with film-star good looks, massive charisma, and amazing physical prowess, well, K2 is not the Hero for you.

He was a rather unremarkable kid who was always trying his utmost not to stand out in any way. Which was tricky when he had a not-very-ordinary name, lived in a not-very-ordinary house, and for the moment he was having to wear a not-very-ordinary pair of glasses with one blacked-out lens to correct his lazy eye, which made him resemble a small, earnest, worried-looking pirate.

But this isn't just a story about K2, even though you've met him first.

It's a story about the whole family.

Izzabird was K2's sister, and his twin. She was small and chatty and incorrigibly optimistic with a lot of sticky-outy hair and a very determined expression indeed.

Most people would have described Izzabird as the most disobedient, cheekiest twelve-year-old they had ever met, but K2 knows her best, and he would say: "Izza is the most wonderful person in the world. She's clever and funny, and she can't decide whether she's going to be President of Everything or an astronaut. She talks all the time, which is great because it means that I don't have to."

The other two children were called Theo and Mabel, and they had been living perfectly comfortably in the capital city before their father, Daniel Smith, took a job in Soggy-Bottom-Marsh-Place and extremely inconveniently fell in love with Izzabird and K2's mother.

Of all the children, Theo had the most *obvious* potential to be a Hero. He was the same age as Izzabird and K2, and he was intelligent and quick, and already considered by the whole school to be a Hero because he was top in all the academic subjects and so great at sports. Theo managed to look smartly turned out at all times, even when a witch-wind was howling about his carefully styled hair and trying unsuccessfully to turn his hoodie inside out. Mabel was three years younger than Theo, and K2 might have liked to talk to her if Izzabird would let him. She was kind and quiet and small and shy, and maybe those are Hero qualities too? The story will no doubt tell us.

There's nothing like an adventure to find out whether you are a Hero.

All four children had something important in common. They were all sad and rather angry, and for very similar reasons. Two and a half years earlier, a couple of years after their parents had divorced, K2 and Izzabird's father had disappeared on a very dangerous scientific expedition, missing presumed dead. And a long time before that, Theo and Mabel's mother had died.

Losing a parent is enough to make any child sad and angry, whatever family they are from.

"This is *Witch* weather," said Theo darkly. "Maybe your weird mother summoned it up..."

"OUR MOTHER IS NOT A WITCH!!!" (Izzabird had to HOWL this above the roaring of the wind.) "*You're* just jealous because *our* father was a Great Explorer Hero, and *your* father is as unheroic as anything!"

Theo was just as cross as Izzabird, but he had one of those faces that didn't change expression much, and his apparent coolness made Izzabird even more annoyed.

"She *is* a Witch...," said Theo.

Now, there were thousands of years when people on Earth had believed in Wizards and ghosts and giants and sprites and all sorts of extraordinary things. But nobody here had thought such things were real for at least a century or so. Science had disproved the existence of Magic, apparently.

But K2 and Izzabird knew otherwise. They knew that Magic did exist as they were from a family that had a strange Magical history. One they were under strict instructions from their mother to keep a secret from everyone, including the Smith children.

So, Theo and Mabel weren't supposed to know about all this.

But Theo was the kind of person who thought for himself.

The fact that everyone in his world thought that there was no such thing as Magic only made Theo all the more determined to believe in it.

And Theo was *especially* suspicious of the O'Heros.

He turned to Izzabird with narrowed eyes. "They're *all* Witches, your mom *and* your great-aunts, and I'm going to prove it one day. This isn't a suitable family for Mabel to be living in."

"Leave, then!" yelled Izzabird. "I don't *want* you in my family. I HATE you!"

Theo gave a glittering smile and strolled off down the road, pretending he didn't care, pulling Mabel after him.

Ah, *hate*. That's a very bad word to come out of the mouth of a child on such a storm of a day.

I can tell you right now, hatred isn't going to get any of them anywhere, not with the tornado that is about to engulf these children. They're going to need something better than hatred to help them deal with *that*.

"There's nothing strange about *US*!" raged Izzabird, shaking her fist at the backs of Theo and Mabel.

Izzabird was so busy shouting about how deeply NOT strange she and K2 were, that she hadn't noticed something going on that *most* people would have considered extremely strange indeed.

A large toothbrush with some of its bristles falling out had hopped from Izzabird's pocket and was now jumping up and down on one of her shoulders, trying to get her attention above the shrieking of the wind.

This isn't regular behavior for a toothbrush, not on Planet Earth anyway.

Watching from the shadows, even *I* caught my breath when I saw that Magical toothbrush.

Because ALL MAGIC WAS SUPPOSED TO HAVE LEFT THIS PLANET.

Hmmmmmmm.

This was a very interesting family indeed.

Luckily, the two Smith children were walking some way ahead, trying to ignore the yelling of Izzabird, so they didn't see the excitable toothbrush.

"It's only because you Smiths are so RIDICULOUSLY ordinary that you think there's anything odd about us at all!" shouted Izzabird as the toothbrush jumped even more wildly on her shoulder.

"Izza!" hissed K2 in alarm, tugging on Izzabird's coat as he spotted the toothbrush.

The jumping toothbrush had been joined by a baby toothbrush and a very smart electric one that turned its buzzer on with such urgency that little sparks came off it in the rain. Desperately, K2 tried to catch hold of the toothbrushes to hide them.

"You are the MONARCHS of Ordinary!" yelled Izzabird.

Suddenly she noticed the toothbrushes too. She gave a small squeak of surprise and started grabbing at them as well.

And then, something even odder happened.

A shock of rooks burst up from the trees around them, cawing raucous cries of alarm.

The toothbrushes jumped up and down on Izzabird's shoulder for a few more seconds in frenzied agitation, and then hopped down her body, through the puddles and the driving rain, to behind the hedge.

The wind took on an even more menacing high-pitched whine, howling as if to summon the ancient peoples who had lived there long ago.

"Something's wrong…," whispered K2, looking up and around him. "Something's spooked the toothbrushes…" He thought he saw movement in the lane behind them.

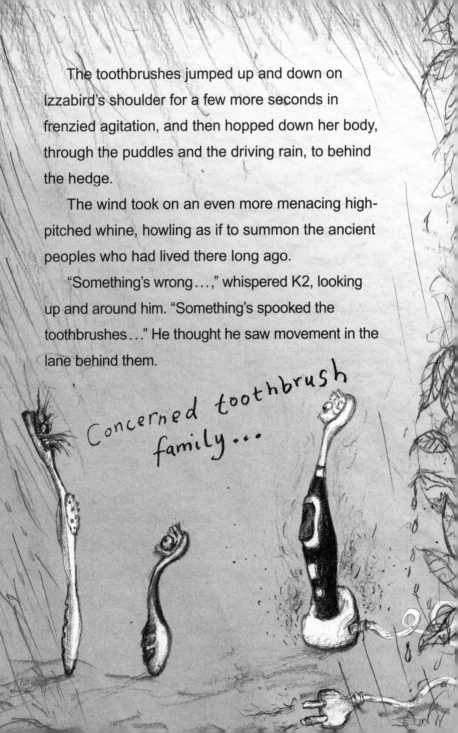

Concerned toothbrush family…

"Get behind the hedge!" K2 yelled.

Theo and Mabel were so far ahead they didn't seem to hear.

"Get behind the hedge!" echoed Izzabird, running to catch up with Theo and Mabel, and grabbing Theo's backpack to get his attention, so that the zipper opened and some of his books fell out into the mud.

"Get off my backpack, you annoying girl!" snapped Theo, spinning around.

And then he felt a little chill going down the back of his neck as he saw K2 and Izzabird scrambling into the undergrowth.

What on earth were those O'Heros DOING?

Theo stood in front of Mabel, trying to protect her.

"Didn't you hear what we said? *Get behind the hedge!*" hissed Izzabird.

Something about the urgency in her voice made Mabel and Theo obey her. Theo grabbed Mabel's hand, and they scrambled into the undergrowth too.

They could hear each other breathing, *in* out, *in* out.

"What are we DOING here?" whispered Theo, furious that he was getting dirty in the mud.

"Shhhhhhhh...," hissed Izzabird.

K2 had a good hold of all three toothbrushes now, and their little plastic sides were trembling with fear in his hands, in a way that made his own palms slippy with sweat.

Something truly strange was going on.

Down the road, SOMETHING came bounding.

The Something was the owner of one of those pairs of eyes that had been watching the children without them realizing, and it was the kind of thing that I was perfectly familiar with, but then *I* have wandered around a bit in the vast and starry paths of the endless dusty universe. It would have been most unusual to the eyes of those children.

The Something was wearing a huge hooded brown cloak, like Death itself, and it was at least seven feet tall and running much faster than an ordinary person.

In five bounds the SOMETHING was right in front of them, and then it stopped, and the children's hearts stopped too, in terror.

Peering through a ragged hole in the hedge, K2 could feel himself nearly passing out with fear.

Theo's math book was lying in the mud.

The immense cloaked figure seemed to be studying the book very intently, as if wondering where its owner had gone. Tears pricked at the edges of K2's eyes.

The brown cloak shifted a little, and there was a flash of something underneath that was an extraordinary silver in color, but unlike any silver they had ever seen before. It was a silver so bright it was almost luminous, shining out like a fierce aluminum sun.

WHAT was under that cloak?

K2 could feel his own hot blood flooding fearfully into his cheeks, and he pressed his cold hands on to them to cool them down.

All four children were frozen stiff, trying to still their rabbit-speed beating hearts, desperate not to draw the attention of this possible predator.

It did not work.

From underneath the cloak came the unmistakable sound of an almost-human sniff.

Almost human.

There was a small clicking noise, and Theo's math book burst into flames.

And then slow-ly, slow-ly, the head of whatever-it-was turned toward them, and oh my goodness, oh my goodness!

What they saw was quite clear now, even through the drenching rain.

A vision from a dream, or a nightmare.

Buried in the depths of the brown cloak, a head in the form of a human skull, brilliantly stamped with diamonds in the shape of stars, turned to look straight at them. Very, very beautiful it was, the stars imprinted on the silver bone of the skull, blinking and shining, winking with a soft, bright light that might have belonged to the planets that their shape suggested.

And those eyes!

No human eye was ever that gorgeous shifting rainbow of colors and patterns, like the movement of clouds across a troubled night sky.

But as the not-human eyes burned through the sad, dripping vegetation that wasn't really shielding the children and focused on them, the pupils shot pinprick small, the emotion within them changed to pure fury, and a blaze of light shot out like a laser and incinerated the bit of hedge in front of them.

A visitor from
Out-of-this-World

Chapter 3 A VISITOR FROM OUT-OF-THIS-WORLD

What might have happened next could have been very messy, but at that moment, the children were saved by—well, it was by *me*, actually, but they did not know that yet.

To the children and the brown-cloaked silver SOMETHING standing in the road, it sounded like a car approaching very fast, and whoever or whatever was underneath that cloak made a strange noise, as if they were swearing in an unknown language.

And then to the children's infinite, gasping relief, the cloaked figure bounded off, in immense strides, and the car came shrieking around the corner, way too fast, and disappeared in pursuit of whatever-it-was.

The children waited, trembling, petrified. And when they felt it was safe, and no one was coming back, they crept out from their hiding place.

"Are you all right, Mabel?" said Theo, trying to

hide his own fear, brushing the mud off the front of his little sister's jacket.

"What ON EARTH was *that*?" said K2, shivering.

Theo picked up the burnt remains of his math book. "I wouldn't have thought they'd have an advanced robotics company working out here in the back-end of nowhere...," he said thoughtfully, his mind buzzing with alarm and excitement and questions.

"Which just shows how ridiculous you are," said Izzabird, who was looking very thoughtful too. "In the middle of nowhere is *exactly* where they'd put an advanced robotics company."

"We should tell the police," said Theo. "That *thing* could have really hurt Mabel. We've got this as evidence." He held up his math book as he hurried Mabel ahead.

K2 would have followed, but Izzabird was looking at the ground where the truly scary SOMETHING had been standing.

"Izza, what are you *doing*?" said K2 anxiously. "I really don't think we should be hanging around here…" The toothbrushes had wriggled out of K2's hands and were hopping behind Izzabird, trying to shoo her away, like three tiny plastic sheepdogs.

"And why did you bring these toothbrushes to school?" scolded K2. "You PROMISED Mom you wouldn't use Spells anymore, especially outside the house…"

"Well, if *she* won't teach me Magic," said Izzabird, "I'm just going to have to teach myself, aren't I? I merely *borrowed* a bit of animation-y potion-y type stuff from Aunt Trudie's workshop and put it on the toothbrushes to make Annipeck laugh…"

Annipeck was their baby sister.

"*You stole stuff from Aunt Trudie's secret workshop?*" said K2 in horror.

"Yes, well, that's not the point," said Izzabird hurriedly. "I left the toothbrushes locked in my cabinet waiting for the potion to wear off, but they must have broken out, probably because they wanted to be with me. Which is quite sweet, don't you think?" she added. "It's lucky they warned us about that *thing*. I think it's in the toothbrush nature to be protective, since they've been made to look after teeth."

K2 breathed heavily. The toothbrushes were marching up and down in the puddles more and more urgently.

You didn't have to be an expert in Toothbrush Behavior to know these toothbrushes were saying *Let's get out of here NOW...*

"I'm looking for clues," said Izzabird excitedly. "But I can't find any."

K2 shivered in relief. "In which case, send the toothbrushes home, and let's get out of here."

But the toothbrushes would not leave them. Izzabird had to put them in her backpack next to the bottle marked "Animashun Poshun" and various other magical spells Izza had "borrowed" from Aunt Trudie.

The dark and warmth made them curl up together and fall asleep, the stems of the two adult toothbrushes wound protectively around the baby one.

Even though it was still raining and K2 was dying to go, Izzabird opened up her Plan Book.

She marked OPERATION END LOVE: *PLAN TO GET RID OF THE SMITHS* as "Super Urgent," and then above the plans called FIND DAD and GET

MYSELF EXPELLED she added: WHO IS THAT
WEIRD CLOAKED GUY?

"Why do you want to get expelled?" asked K2.

"Because then they'll have to homeschool me,"
said Izzabird. "And Mom and the aunts will have to
teach me how to use Magic properly and find out my
Magical Gift.

"They should be doing that anyway. Look at me!"
she grinned. "I'm completely out of control!"

Here I had to agree with wild little Izzabird. The
adults in these children's lives really ought to be
teaching them how to use Magic correctly. Even
non-Magical people can use a Magic potion, but it
might go wrong for them. Magical people use sticks
or wands to concentrate the effect of that potion or
spell, and many Magical people have an extra
"Gift" that tends to come in when they're
about eleven or twelve. The "Gift" could be
powers of hearing or teleportation or if
you were unlucky, something
a bit less useful, such

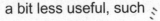

Izzabird O'Hero (the GREAT)
PLAN BOOK
House of the O'Heros
Which Way Crossing
Soggy Bottom Marsh Place

Planet Earth

SPACE

OPERATION END LOVE: ✔. **※ Super Urgent ✦**

PLAN To Get Rid of the Smiths

FIND DAD I know they are
lying to us !!!

??? WHO IS THAT WEIRD CLOAKED GUY ???

GET MYSELF EXPELLED ✓✓✓

Progress report today

Me	Theo
Put stink bombs in Theo's backpack	Poured juice over my history book.
Sneaked into classroom and wrote rude things about teachers and signed it: Love, Theo Smith.	Made rude noises behind Mr. Hargreaves's back and said it was ME, but Mr. Hargreaves did not believe him. HA.

2 - 1 to ME. And 2 extra ticks
for Plans to Get Myself Expelled.
Very Good !! ✓

Some things I took from Aunt Trudie's workshop

1. Animashun Poshun. Try out on toothbrushes? ✓ ~~Try out~~ Good plan.

to shrink his head

2. Shrinking Loshun. ← Put in Theo's shampoo bottle !! Maybe not.

3. Powders of Forgetfulness. Apply to Mom directly after she reads my school report.

4. Tablitts for the Growing of Love. Hmm. Try on Aunt Violet? DANGEROUS,

Best Before Date 15-11-15

Shrinking

Powders of Forgetfulness

Animashun Poshun

Tablitts for the Growing of LOVE

as turning into a jellyfish. Whatever it was, you needed good instruction in Magic to use your "Gift" appropriately. What on earth were these adults thinking?

Izzabird closed the book and put it back in her backpack next to the sleeping toothbrushes.

"*I* think," said Izzabird energetically, "that this is something to do with our dad!"

Their father had disappeared two years after their parents divorced. He had been on a highly important and slightly hopeless mission to reach the bottom of the Mariana Trench, which is the very deepest part of the whole of the oceans...

...and he never came back.

Look at me! I'm completely out of control!!

Ever since, K2 and Izzabird had an ache in their hearts that felt like they had swallowed a stone. A great stone. A closed door.

"Dad is *dead*, Izza," K2 whispered back. "Don't you understand? That's why Mom wants to protect us. She doesn't want us to end up DEAD like our father. She wants us to blend in and stay safe."

"He *isn't* dead, K2," said Izzabird obstinately. "And *I'm* going to find him one day. They've never explained HOW he disappeared, have they? Why is Mom lying to us? Why did she land these SMITHS on us, rather than trying to find our wonderful Hero of a father?"

"I don't know, but I'm more worried about this robot skeleton thingy," said K2 anxiously. "I have a feeling it's something to do with us, even if it's not Dad. And what if Theo tells everyone and people start asking questions about our family?"

"Oh, Theo!" said Izzabird, with a contemptuous snort. "Pooh! I can deal with Theo... You worry too much, K2."

"That's because I'm worrying for both of us," said K2 glumly. "It's hard work, worrying for two."

They ran the rest of the way to school.

Ah, yes, the children were in trouble.

Out-of-this-world trouble.

And even *I* might not be able to help them out of it.

Chapter 4 A STRANGER ENTERS THE STORY, AND THE STORY GETS STRANGER STILL

As I peered through the rain-bashed windows of the school, it became clear that the day was going to give K2 a whole lot more about which to worry.

Firstly, Theo *had* gone to the head teacher to get him to call the police about the robot skeleton they had seen on the way to school.

But the head teacher had not believed him.

Because Daniel Smith was not only the head teacher of Soggy-Bottom-Marsh-Place Primary and Secondary School. (It was a very small school.) He was also Theo's father.

That was how he had met Freya O'Hero, who taught math at the very same school.

Daniel Smith did not want to become a laughingstock in front of the police.

So K2 and Izzabird and Mabel were summoned to Daniel's office, where Izzabird denied everything.

"I mean, really, a 'robot skeleton' with a grudge

against Theo's math book?" scoffed Izzabird. "How likely is *that*? Theo hadn't done his homework, so he set fire to his math book and lied about the rest, and Mabel is backing him up because she does everything Theo says. Isn't that right, K2?" She stared fiercely at her twin.

K2 nodded reluctantly.

This seemed a whole load more believable to Daniel Smith than a robot skeleton rampaging around the countryside.

And that meant Theo got told off for lying.

So, when they left his father's office, Theo's mouth was a pencil-thin line of crossness. "*You two* are the *liars*, not

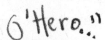

"You Better WATcH OUT, Izzabird O'Hero..."

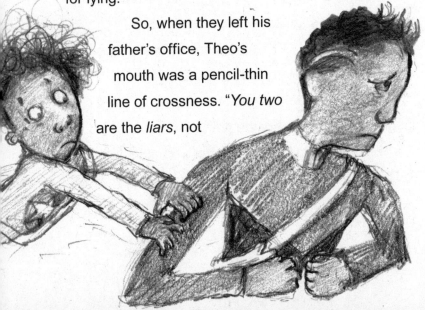

me," said Theo. "K2, you shouldn't let Izzabird boss you into doing everything she wants you to do, isn't that right, Mabel?"

"Um—" said Mabel.

"You better WATCH OUT MORE, Theo Smith..."

"K2 is *always* thinking for himself, aren't you, K2?" hissed Izzabird.

"Er—" said K2.

"You better *Watch Out*, Izzabird O'Hero," taunted Theo.

"You better Watch Out MORE, Theo Smith," Izzabird retorted.

And the day went downhill from there.

Izzabird and Theo spent the whole morning getting each other into trouble, deliberately. Izzabird put Shrinking Loshun on Theo's PE top and Theo hid Izzabird's English and math and chemistry homework, and Izzabird crushed "Tablitts for the Growing of Love" onto Theo's football cleats so they became magnetically attracted to each other and Theo could not pull them apart however hard he tried. They both got sent to the head teacher's office many times.

K2, on the other hand, wasn't getting into trouble, but he was having a tricky morning nonetheless. K2 sometimes found school frustrating because he had such great ideas but he couldn't write them down quick enough or spell them the right way. And then he accidentally shot an own goal that lost his team the match in PE, so Angus McDognut gave K2 a dead arm, and K2 had to hide in the bathroom for a bit.

This is what learning to be a Hero is all about, thought K2, giving himself a stern talking-to as he dried his eyes. *I bet if this happened to MY FATHER, he would pretend nothing had happened.*

K2 blew his nose and squared his shoulders and marched out of the bathroom, immediately bumping into Angus McDognut again, who stole K2's packed lunch, so K2 had to share Izzabird's sandwich at lunchtime.

But things were about to get a whole lot worse.

The weather was getting wilder and wilder, and stranger and stranger.

And, talking of strangers, it wasn't their usual teacher, Ms. Foremichael, who turned up to class 7D's last lesson of the afternoon, but a tall stranger wearing long black gloves, who had a smile with too many teeth in it.

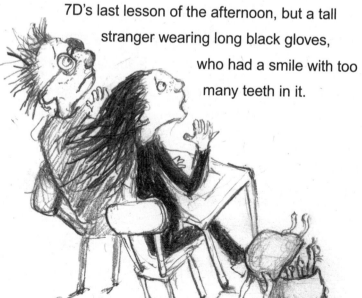

"I am going to be your substitute geography teacher for the day," smiled the stranger. "Because, unfortunately, Ms. Foremichael had a little accident. Her hand slipped on her can opener while making her lunch in the teachers' lounge. There was a terrible amount of blood, but we are hoping that she will live, thank goodness…" The stranger put his hand to his heart and closed his eyes in pious relief.

Class 7D gave an *OOH* of surprise.

The stranger opened his wicked eyes and smiled at them again. "Luckily, I turned up just in time to call the ambulance. And as I am a Poor Wandering Geography Teacher who came to this school in search of work," explained the stranger smoothly, "I was able to offer my services as a substitute teacher. Effective immediately."

Hmm. How fortunate.

"My name is Professor Cyril Sidewinder," said the stranger, and he whirled around and wrote *PROFESSOR CYRIL SIDEWINDER, POOR WANDERING GEOGRAPHY TEACHER* in huge letters on the whiteboard in such furious haste that the pen made the most hideously unbearable

Professor
Cyril Sidewinder

A stranger
with a smile
with too
many teeth
in it...

screechy noise until its tip broke on the final "R"
and the stranger muttered what sounded like a filthy
swear word under his breath, and his sleeve fell back
to reveal a skull and crossbones tattooed on his wrist.

"But capital cities...and...er...rivers and
everything are so BORING," sighed Professor Cyril
Sidewinder. "So I thought we would start with a fun
project. You like fun, don't you, children? I want you
to create..." He turned back to the whiteboard and
with a new pen wrote in big, bold, swirling capitals:
AN ALTERNATIVE ATLAS.

Izzabird stiffened, and K2 was so surprised that he let out a small gasp of astonishment.

The professor spun around. "Have you HEARD," he asked penetratingly, "of an Alternative Atlas?"

Have you HEARD
of an Alternative Atlas?

K2 tried to make his mouth say "No," but when he opened it nothing came out.

Professor Cyril Sidewinder came right up to K2 and looked straight at him. He had the most peculiar, hypnotic eyes. "What is your name, child?" said Cyril.

K2 couldn't say anything.

"Take no notice of *him*, sir," said Angus McDognut, shooting K2 a dirty look. "That's just K2. He's a bit odd."

"Kay Too?" asked Cyril, peculiar eyes positively SNAPPING with thoughtfulness. "Is that 'K2' as in the second highest mountain in the world?"

K2 nodded.

"In-ter-esting...," mused Professor Cyril Sidewinder. "Well, child, what do *you* know about an Alternative Atlas?"

"Nothing," whispered K2.

"Don't LIE to me, little subatomic particle," hissed the professor, still smiling, but his eyes had turned as cold as two icy pebbles. "I can smell out little liars at twenty paces."

"DON'T YOU DARE CALL MY BROTHER A LIAR!" shouted Izzabird.

There was a horrible pause.

The professor turned white, then red, and he yelled: "SILENCE! OR I WILL SPELL YOU SO HARD YOU WILL BLAST *INTO THE NEXT GALAXY AND BEYOND!!!!*"

"*Cy-ril...*," warned a barely audible metallic-sounding voice that seemed to come from the professor's briefcase, which was sitting on the teacher's table. "Calm down. Remumber. No unnecessary violence."

Cyril gritted his teeth. "Dear, oh dear," he sniggered, wiping angry perspiration from his brow. "Don't worry, dear little children! I am only joking, of course..."

Class 7D stared at the professor and his talking briefcase in absolute horror. They had made up their minds. This teacher was neither nice nor nasty.

He was completely terrifying.

Cyril gave an unconvincing giggle.

"You may have noticed that I am wearing gloves," said Cyril. Class 7D had noticed. "It is because I am most unfortunately allergic to children. It is a terrible thing to love children as I do, and yet to be allergic.

"Now, where was I?" Cyril was smiling amiably again. "Ah, yes. 'What *is* an Alternative Atlas?' I hear you ask."

He paused for effect and lowered his voice as if he were telling them some dangerous secret.

You <u>may</u> have noticed that I am wearing gloves...

*It's a terrible thing,
to love children as I do,
and yet be allergic...*

"An Alternative Atlas," whispered Professor Cyril Sidewinder, *"is a collection of maps of imaginary and real places...a gorgeous and entire and complete geography of worlds that no one has ever seen before...*

"...and the best place to create an Alternative Atlas is in the mind of a CHILD, because even *I* have to admit that children are the most creative people in the world, because they don't know the rules yet," finished Cyril.

"Now, some examples!" he said briskly as a great map appeared on the whiteboard. "Treasure Island...," said Cyril, "my favorite..." and then he flicked through map after map very quickly. "Narnia, Rivendell, the London Underground, Neverland, Hundred Acre Wood, the City of Gotham, forests of Borneo..."

Izzabird had her hand up.

"Yes?" said the professor through gritted teeth.

"The London Underground isn't imaginary," said Izzabird. "And nor are the forests of Borneo. Some of these places are made up and some of them are real. What do you want us to draw, a real place or an imaginary place?"

"A piece of paper has two sides, doesn't it?" barked Cyril. "I want you to draw *both*. On ONE SIDE of the piece of paper draw a map of your imaginary world, but not just any old map... I want you to draw *A MAP THAT LIVES!* Maybe your map will have mountains with winding rivers full of strange winking jewels..." Cyril licked his lips appreciatively. "Or an island with mysterious coves and beaches where someone buried treasure a long time ago... Make it somewhere delicious or somewhere awesome or somewhere gloomy. Make it smell of the blossoms of infinite flowers, or as stinky as rotten eggs and sulfur... Let your little imaginations run riot... whatever comes into your rascally, ratlike minds," spat Cyril.

He paused and held up a black-gloved finger.

"But on the OTHER SIDE of the piece of paper you must draw a map of somewhere *real*, a place that you know well. Your house, for instance. This school. The wood at the end of your garden. And don't forget to put a small 'X' somewhere on the map, and draw it VERY DARKLY so you can see where the 'X' comes out on the other side...

"...or the Alternative Atlas won't work."

Izzabird already had her hand up again.

"Yes?" said Cyril irritably. His hands made involuntary strangling motions.

"WHAT won't work?" asked Izzabird. "HOW won't it work? WHY won't it work?"

"Never you mind! None of your business! No more pesky questions!" snapped Cyril. "What are you waiting for? Get out your geography books! MOVE! DRAW! NOW!!!!"

Chapter 5 DRAWING A MAP THAT LIVES

lass 7D started making their maps, chattering excitedly, for although the teacher was a bit scary, drawing imaginary islands or unbelievable mountains or impossible ice caps was an enjoyable thing to do.

What would YOU draw, reader, if YOU were asked to draw an Alternative Atlas?

James Cartwell drew forests where sweets grew wild on every tree. Chocolate bars blossomed huge and scrumptious on the branches, and curly fries twirled temptingly in the grasses, showing off to each other.

Scarlett-Marie's was a far fiercer world, where robots with a hundred eyes slumbered deep underneath the city and put up periscopes with claws to drag down unwary travelers.

Professor Cyril Sidewinder paced up and down in between the tables, shouting, "Make a map that LIVES, children, make a map that LIVES!"

Izzabird's map was dark with dragons, flying across

skies with twenty moons in them; Theo's was covered with mazes of such intense intricacy and complication that Theo was even beating *himself* in the game of trying to get out of them.

K2 was the only one who wasn't enjoying the lesson, and he was trying to get away with drawing as little as he possibly could.

The professor's eyes fell on K2's empty paper. "So, boy-who-is-named-after-the-second-highest-mountain-in-the-world," said Cyril, eyes narrowing. "You haven't got very far.

"Let's start with something simple," he purred, reaching in his pocket for a big dark marker pen and holding it out to K2. "Just draw me an 'X.'"

K2 hesitated.

Cyril's tone hardened. His hypnotizing eyes stared into K2's. "DRAW," he said.

K2 put down his pencil and picked up the professor's pen. He drew a rather shaky "X."

"Bigger," said Cyril. "Darker."

K2 went over the "X" to make it larger and heavier.

"Excellent," smiled Cyril. "I'll take that." He tore the page out of K2's geography book.

The bell rang for the end of the school day.

"Everybody, tear the page out of your book and give your map to me!" said Cyril. "We can carry on with this assignment in our next lesson..."

Class 7D wasn't in the habit of tearing pages out of their schoolbooks, but what a teacher wants, a teacher gets, so they obediently did as Cyril asked.

"This is our little secret," said the professor as he gathered in the torn bits of paper. "I don't want anyone to know we've been playing GAMES in our geography lessons..."

As soon as they left the classroom K2 turned to Izzabird. "We HAVE to get my map back," he said.

"You mean, your map that had just one big 'X' in the middle of it?" said Izzabird, eyes bright with excitement and interest. "Excellent, you can tell me why later."

They ran around the outside of the building to their classroom window. The gale was really getting going now, so it was hard work to scramble up and hold firmly on to the slippery window ledge with their forearms, their legs dangling.

The substitute
geography teacher
was marking those books
in a WEIRD way...

Izzabird rubbed the window with the edge of her sleeve so they could see into the classroom.

Cyril was standing by the door, looking into the corridor as if checking that no one was there. Then he walked to the teacher's desk and sat down to look at the pile of maps.

"*Puck*, make yourself useful!" they could just hear Cyril snapping. "Come out and tell me if one of these could have been drawn by the child we are looking for!"

To K2's astonishment, Cyril's briefcase snapped open and out flew a little, lopsided thing that looked like a toy helicopter, about the size of a small dog.

It buzzed into the air and hovered above Cyril's head.

"Wow...," whispered Izzabird in fascination. "What IS that? Maybe Theo was right and there really IS an advanced robotics company around here. Oh...it's so sweet!"

"It can't be sweet," K2 whispered back with a shiver. "It belongs to that man...How do we get my map?"

"Don't worry," said Izza. "I have a Plan."

She opened her backpack and out hopped the toothbrushes, well-slept, perky, and eager to help. Izzabird whispered the Plan to the toothbrushes and they headed to the window, which was slightly ajar.

Izzabird pried it open farther, and they both ducked down quickly as the gale rushed into the classroom with such force that K2 nearly lost his grip on the window ledge.

The wind sent the pile of maps whirling around the room.

Cyril cursed loudly and tried to catch them.

The three toothbrushes hopped bravely over the window ledge and into the chaos of the wind-and-paper-filled classroom. Puck was trying to be helpful by catching the papers, but as soon as he got near any of them, his rotary blades sent them swirling up into the air again.

In the pandemonium, neither Cyril nor the little robot noticed the toothbrushes hopping around the classroom seeking the paper with K2's "X" on it.

When the toothbrushes finally located it, wedged under a chair leg at the back of the room, they pinned the piece of paper in between the head of the big toothbrush and the electric one, and hopped in unison back toward where K2 and Izzabird were waiting, with the baby one bouncing along behind trying to be helpful but actually just getting in the way.

The two big brushes hopped together onto a chair, and then the electric toothbrush hung its plug and electric cable down to the floor and hauled up the baby toothbrush, the cable wrapped around its middle like a minimountaineer. Working as a team, they made it back out to the ledge where Izzabird and K2 were dangling.

"Mission accomplished," grinned Izzabird with satisfaction as the toothbrushes and the paper plopped into her bag.

Meanwhile, Professor Cyril was so cross with Puck for getting in the way that he picked up a chair and attempted to club the little robot with it, which was not a great idea because the robot buzzed out of reach and Cyril lost his balance and knocked himself out on the edge of the whiteboard.

He swayed drunkenly for a moment and then crashed to the floor, the hand-drawn maps drifting down around him like snow.

Izza forgot where she was and started laughing.

Puck spun around, his eyes swiveling toward the sound, and flew in their direction so quickly that K2 and Izzabird barely had time to slam the window shut, drop down, and run for it before the robot thumped against the glass.

K2 and Izzabird sprinted home, looking over their shoulders the whole way.

Chapter 6 THE PLAN TO GET RID OF "THE STEPFATHER"

t was so dark and wild out that it was as if night had decided to come early. To get back home, K2 and Izzabird had to battle through winds that seemed to be trying to blow them out of their shoes and bowl them in cartwheels back to school.

I am tracking the children with more intention now, for I know I am on the right path. This is not an ordinary Planet Earth family. These are not ordinary Planet Earth children. I know it in my bones. I can feel it in the twitching of my twiglike fingers.

The House of the Heros

The house where the children lived was built on an ancient Crossing of the Ways, where people had been walking since way before the Bronze Age. Above the door it called itself "The House of the O'Heros," with a picture of two hands pointing in different directions and the O'Hero motto underneath: "An O'Hero Knows No Limits! The Sky Is Just the Beginning. No Rivers Can Stop Us. No Mountains Can Stand in Our Way."

It would have been a grand house if large parts of it hadn't fallen down, and trees and brambles weren't growing over the rubble.

But it was a surprisingly friendly building, especially considering it was a place where chairs moved around unexpectedly and doors slammed in unseen winds and there were whispering noises that could not be mice in all the walls.

It had four towers like a castle, one of which had partly collapsed, it was so blasted by holes. The other three towers housed workshops belonging to Aunt Trudie and Aunt Violet and K2 and Izzabird's mother, Freya, and it was absolutely forbidden to enter them—although Izzabird had disobeyed this on many occasions.

The house was stuffed from top to bottom with things that had been collected from all over the globe and from all human history, which had then been upended all higgledy-piggledy and on top of each other, in a big, once-grand-and-now-falling-apart mess.

And everywhere there were maps. Enormous, exquisite, detailed maps, beautifully painted by O'Heros, of the extraordinary islands and forests, cities and rivers they had seen on their travels.

However, by the time K2 and Izzabird's grandfather and great-aunts and great-uncles had grown up, it was becoming harder and harder to find wild parts on this Earth to explore. One of the great-aunts studied the flora in rain forests, but just as fast as she came across fascinating plants that might be useful as medicine, people were chopping down the forests the plants were growing in, so it became rather difficult to carry on with her job.

So K2 and Izzabird's father, Everest, had become an expert on OCEANS and SPACE because when you have run out of wilderness on land, there are still the unexplored regions of the seas and the infinitely vast untracked regions of the sky.

The house was littered with pictures of him posing nobly in front of his rather eccentric "diving machines" and telescopes, all built for him by his Aunt Violet. Some people thought he was crazy because of the incredible voyages he made with really very unsuitable equipment.

But K2 and Izzabird thought he was marvelous.

K2 could still remember the excitement in his father's voice as he described coral reefs and black holes, the Milky Way, the glorious, star-studded limitless universe...

...but he was beginning to struggle to remember his own father's face.

The children had arrived home now. I was unable to get into the house, because it is protected by Deep Magic and nobody had opened a door into it for me yet. But I was close enough to hover and peer through the windows, and use my super-senses to see what was going on in there.

It was a house that had too many people in it.

And the atmosphere was a little...*tense.*

Theo and Mabel were in the kitchen having a snack along with their stepmother, Freya; Aunt Violet and Aunt Trudie; and their baby sister, Annipeck; and their father, Daniel, who Izzabird called "the Stepfather."

The kitchen was the only truly warm room in the house when a gale was blowing. Even the bits of the house you *could* live in were full of holes, and the wind blew right through them in weather like this. And for a kitchen it had a lot of vegetation in it, because Aunt Trudie liked to grow things, and she had brought in all her dahlias to shelter from the storm.

Annipeck, the children's seventeen-month-old baby sister, greeted K2 and Izzabird delightedly, waving around her spoon, covered in mashed potato.

Annipeck was the one thing that both families of children could agree on.

How Freya and Daniel could ever have had such a wonderful baby together was beyond all of them.

Annipeck laughed at K2. He leaned in to give her a kiss, and she very generously shoved a carrot covered in mashed potato in what she meant to be his mouth but accidentally turned out to be his *ear*. She had been saving it especially for him because she knew he loved carrots.

"*Thank you*, Annipeck." K2 smiled, taking it out of his ear and eating it anyway, so as not to hurt her feelings.

"Yer wor war wor *YAR*!" sang Annipeck, beaming.

Annipeck constantly babbled away in a sing-song stream of chat that made complete sense to Annipeck herself but was less clear to her listeners.

"*HEL-LO*, K2! *HEL-LO*, Iz-bird!"

In front of Annipeck's seat there was a small plastic dinosaur and some Lego bricks. The dinosaur got to its feet and waved merrily at K2. The Lego bricks built themelves into a minitower entirely of their own accord.

Aunt Trudie

Aaargh! thought K2. *Izzabird's used the potion on Annipeck's toys as well! We're going to be in SUCH TROUBLE...*

But Mabel and Theo were busy eating their snacks, and one of the things about grown-ups is their ability to willfully ignore things they don't want to see.

Aunt Violet

Annipeck saw K2 frowning at the Lego bricks.

The dinosaur fell over on its side. The Lego tower collapsed.

The baby put her head down and hid her face in the mashed potatoes, giggling.

Phew, thought K2 in relief.

Aunt Trudie

saluted K2 and Izzabird with a friendly wave of her wooden spoon, and Aunt Violet grunted and raised an eyebrow. Aunt Violet was cracking her knuckles while watching the television, which was turned up really loud. She was a heavily muscled, wildly tattooed old lady with a mean look in her hooded eyes.

Their mother, Freya, was small, frenzied, determined, and, in Izzabird's opinion, way, *way* too anxious. She gave them a warm but slightly distracted smile because she was trying to feed the baby, catch that can of baked beans before it fell off the shelf, mark class 8R's math homework, and work out what was going on with the unusual weather that was giving her these terrible headaches, all at the same time.

"Hello, darlings!" she said, trying to hug Izzabird as she sat down, but Izza shook her off furiously. "I hope you all had a good day? K2...you didn't bump into any...*large animals* or anything, did you?"

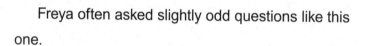

Freya often asked slightly odd questions like this one.

"Not unless Angus McDognut counts as a large animal," said Izzabird.

"Oh, thank goodness, and nobody got sent to Daniel like I was expecting?" said Freya.

"I'm afraid they did, and I simply can't understand it, Theo," said Daniel, staring as fiercely as he could through his glasses. "How can you be top of the class in all of your academic subjects, but still get sent to my office so many times for bad behavior?"

"*Izzabird* got sent to you too," said Theo with a glittering smile. Only Mabel could tell, from a slight narrowing of his eyes, that he was hurt by his father's disappointment.

"Oh! Yes! I'm sure she did...," said Freya hastily, giving Daniel a warning look.

Theo was pleased for a moment before reminding himself crossly that Freya wasn't his *real* mother, so she shouldn't be interfering.

"Why don't you tell *Izzabird* off for once, Dad?" suggested Theo. "She might get less full of herself."

"It was a setup!" cried Izzabird buoyantly, going into her Automatic Defense Mode, punching the air and speaking through a mouthful of snack. "I was framed!"

Daniel looked even more harassed. "Can you explain *this* then, Izza?"

He handed a piece of paper to Izzabird. On it was written: *List of Ways to Get Rid of the Ridiculous Stepfather and His Ridiculous Family.*

Uh-oh, thought Izza. *That beastly Theo.* He

must have found her Plan Book and torn that bit out. Izzabird handed the piece of paper back very quickly. "I've never seen this before in my life," she said.

Daniel sighed.

It had all seemed so simple.

Freya was practically perfect, of course, a fairy princess disguised as a math teacher. And his children would have a mother; her children would have a father. They would marry and live happily ever after.

What could be more straightforward than that?

Even Daniel's misty, love-blinkered eyes had vaguely noticed the chaos, the scary aunts, objects mysteriously moving around the house, and worst of all, Freya's ex-husband's weird machines all over the place and that enormous portrait of him holding his diving helmet in the hall, which Aunt Violet refused to take down.

"This list says *'By me, Izzabird O'Hero,'* in the top right-hand corner," Daniel said sadly. He drooped and ran his hands through his neat, correct hair so it stood all on end, and pushed his glasses miserably up his nose.

Mabel put out a hand and rested
it gently on her father's sleeve.

"Oh, Izzabird!" sighed Freya. "This
is so disappointing…Why are you
doing this?"

Aunt Violet gave a big sniff.
"Well, Everest
was quite a
Hero, wasn't
he? It's hard for
Izzabird. Daniel is
very *different*."

Freya held her head as
if it were going to explode.

Theo quietly went on eating his snack,
delighted to have set off this argument. The more
confrontations there were, the more his father was
going to realize this marriage of his was never going
to work.

Daniel could see all this wasn't helping Freya's
migraine. "Okay, everyone needs to do their
homework before supper," he said soothingly. "I'll
bathe Annipeck. Freya, you go and have a little lie

down, and we'll all let Trudie and Violet get on with the cooking…"

Theo and Mabel followed Daniel and Annipeck and Freya out of the door.

Izzabird and K2 were left finishing their snacks with Aunt Violet and Aunt Trudie.

"Violet and Izzabird, you were both very rude," said Aunt Trudie.

"I'm sorry, Aunt Trudie," said Izzabird. Thinking about it, she could have worded her Plan a little less insultingly. Izzabird tended to act first and think later. But she was always genuinely sorry when she made a mistake. Which was often.

Aunt Violet grunted. *She* wasn't going to admit she had behaved badly.

Aunt Trudie looked at K2 sympathetically. "Was school bad again, K2?"

K2 nodded miserably.

"You have to remember," said Aunt Trudie, "you're just a late developer. You're biding your time, very sensible. The longer your powers cook inside your warm heart, the greater they'll be in the end."

Lovely Aunt Trudie! K2 could feel himself

unfurling like a flower in the sunshine. He sat a little straighter. He pulled back his hoodie. "And my Animation Potion seems to have gone missing. I hope it's nothing to do with you, Izzabird?" added Aunt Trudie.

With a sigh, Izzabird reached into her pocket and took out the little bottle of liquid marked "Animashun Poshun" in Aunt Trudie's rather creative spelling-and-handwriting style. She handed it back.

"You shouldn't steal my things!" scolded Aunt Trudie.

"*You* shouldn't leave them lying about, Trudie... *scatterbrain*," said Aunt Violet with a grin, winking at Izzabird.

"This is really important, now, you two," said Aunt Trudie, putting the little bottle of potion in her coat. "The weather is rather unpredictable at the moment, so if you see any strangers, you have to tell us. And on no account should they suspect there's any Magic going on here."

"Be grateful they don't have the, er, geographical Gift... you know...," Aunt Violet said shiftily to Aunt Trudie.

"More like a Curse, you mean? Yes, that would be exceptionally dangerous," Aunt Trudie whispered back. "But we shouldn't be talking about that in front of the children. Freya wouldn't like it."

"A geographical Gift?" asked Izzabird excitedly.

"You would tell us if either of you suspected you might have a Gift like that, wouldn't you?" said Aunt Trudie.

K2 opened his mouth to tell Aunt Trudie about the interesting six-and-a-half-foot geography teacher wearing black gloves who wanted them to make an Alternative Atlas. And the other even more interesting (and terrifying) stranger with the silver-and-robotic air and the star-stamped skull.

But Izzabird gave him a look that quite clearly said *Shut up.*

Obediently, K2 closed his mouth again.

"Absolutely, Aunt Trudie," said Izzabird, opening her eyes innocently. "Both K2 and I are really bad at geography. And if we see any strangers we'll tell you straight away. And now we need to do our homework. Come on, K2."

Izzabird dragged K2 out of the room.

• • •

Theo was hiding in the hall when Izzabird and K2 came out, and then he crept back to look through the keyhole of the kitchen door.

"You worry too much, Trudie," said Aunt Violet.

"But I think this weather is trying to *warn* us about something," said Aunt Trudie, uneasily looking out the window. "I checked the Atlas this morning and it's showing that *someone* crossed a Which Way in the last couple of weeks without using Stealth Mode..."

"That Atlas has been playing up a bit," said Aunt Violet. "Maybe it was a mistake. Don't overreact."

"Mistake or not, could the illegal Crossing have come to the attention of the people from Out-of-Town?" said Aunt Trudie.

"I'd have spotted it," growled Aunt Violet, cracking her knuckles and narrowing her shotgun eyes menacingly like a Mafia boss. "Nothing so far. Relax."

"You don't think...could this be something to do with...*Everest*?" said Aunt Trudie, putting down the tea towel she was fidgeting with and lowering her voice, as if Freya might be able to hear through the ceiling.

"Why? Have you heard anything?" snapped Aunt Violet, suddenly very unrelaxed indeed.

"No, but you know when he left with the Cure all those years ago..." Aunt Trudie paused. "I think I *may* have, er, accidentally given him the wrong potion!"

"Whaaaaaat?" said Aunt Violet.

"I must have got the bottles mixed up," said Aunt Trudie guiltily. "With all the strange things happening, I decided to check this morning. It's very easily done..."

"Oh, for the black holes' sake!" exploded Aunt Violet, jumping to her feet. "Then of COURSE this is something to do with Everest! You SCATTERBRAIN! Have you at least got the right Cure *now*?"

"Yes, yes!" said Aunt Trudie, patting the top pocket of her coat hanging on the back of the chair, where she'd put the Animation Potion too. "Right here! Oh dear, whatever should we do?"

Aunt Violet shrugged into her motorcycle jacket.

"Everest would have been in mortal danger with no Cure to bargain his way out of it!" said Aunt Violet grimly. "If there's even a *chance* he's still alive, we need to get out there RIGHT NOW and try and rescue him!"

Outside, there was a loud crack of thunder that sounded remarkably like a slightly exasperated seal of approval for their belated understanding of the trouble they were in.

BOOOOOM!!!

"What? You think we should go *traveling*? Aren't we getting too old for that sort of thing?" said Aunt Trudie. "I'm not sure I've got the knees for it anymore."

"Speak for yourself," snapped Aunt Violet, flexing her muscles. "I'm a very young seventy-eight."

"We'll need the Power of All Three of us working together to rescue him...," Aunt Trudie pointed out. "But Freya might refuse to come if she knows Everest is involved!"

"We won't tell Freya about Everest," barked Aunt Violet, military style, briskly hitching up her trousers. "But we *will* say we need to go on this quest to prevent possible Out-of-Town attention that might put the children in danger. *Of course* Freya will come to sort *that* out!"

"I don't like to leave the children unprotected," worried Aunt Trudie.

"The house will protect them, and the Smith stepfather is here," said Aunt Violet. "We can't take the children with us, can we? Not where *we're* going..."

Aunt Violet's fierce blue eyes lit up with excitement. She slapped her thighs and stomped briskly toward the door, limping a little, but game. "One last journey, Trudie! One last quest, and then we will be done. Come on! Get packing...Wet-weather gear! Lotions and potions! Leaving in ten minutes, no excuses..."

Theo whisked away from the keyhole and hid behind the banister as the aunts hurried out of the door. And then he tiptoed back into the kitchen, went through the pockets of Aunt Trudie's coat that she had left hanging on the back of her chair, and removed the bottle of Animation Potion and another one that was in there, and replaced them with two bottles of spices that were sitting on the kitchen shelf so she wouldn't notice immediately. He zipped up her pocket again and slipped away like a ghost.

Ah, Aunt Violet. She was Cunning, all right, but her Cunning was a little out of date. She hadn't spotted *me*, curled up on her windowsill, had she, for all her so-called Gifts. And not only am I most definitely from Out-of-Town, there were far worse than *me* out there, and they were slowly closing in on the house.

The Cunning old women may already be out of their depth.

One
last
journey,
Trudie!

Chapter 7 SOMEWHERE A VERY LONG WAY AWAY INDEED

Now, before we carry on with the story, I'm going to take you out of this boringly unimaginative bog-wet little world where they don't believe in Magic or Cunning or other worlds, or any of the other perfectly reasonable things that we in the rest of the universe take for granted.

It is quite hard to pick out one separated family in the head-spinningly enormous expanses of endless dusty space, but now I know who K2 and Izzabird's father is.

And Izzabird was quite right: The grown-ups HAD been lying to her.

Everest the Great Explorer Hero had not died exploring the bottom of the Mariana Trench. He had traveled rather farther than that. In fact he had gone...

...*to the exact same planet where we saw K2 in such danger in chapter 1.*

No wonder Freya had been having such terrible headaches.

Let me take you back in time to just a fortnight ago, and across distances...well, quite a lot. Distances that it would take an ordinary human being several hundred lifetimes to cross in "rockets" or "shuttles" or whatever they used to call those lengthy forms of travel. Which involve going into comas, and hoping not to age too much along the way, and waking up with dreadful eye bags and terrible problems with *rust*...and that's before we get to the eye-watering expense of it all.

It is infinitely more convenient, and considerably cheaper, if you happen to have about your person an Alternative Atlas.

Yes, they ARE a real, rather special thing.

Cling tight to my wings and I will take you back to that world I mentioned in the beginning, the one where you have to be very, very quiet, for they hate human beings there with a hungry, bloody hatred.

So, as we enter this world of truly terrifying creatures who would tear you limb from limb if they got just a whiff of your scent, a rustle of your clothing...

Don't forget to HOLD YOUR BREATH.

We're going in.

About two weeks earlier, on that very same planet with those beautiful three moons, there was a floating city in the sky.

This was a very great city indeed, a place of harmony, with twisted buildings, where the architecture and the trees hugged each other as if they were kissing in a long embrace.

The city was humming with people dashing about their business, but there was something about the way they moved—hunched over and nervous, as if they thought that at any moment something might swoop out of the sky and swallow them up.

When I say "people," I mean humanoid species you may not have come across yet, dormindrads, for instance, half-human, half-winged-horse...gergashes, taller and slimmer than your regular human being, long of leg and yellow of eye...boggles, shy with see-through ears, useful gills and

golden hearts,

along with those with which you

may be more familiar: elves, but of the whispering

kind, and dreamy one-eyed cyclopes.

A rather handsome man in his late middle age,
called Everest, was running down a side street in this
city, heart pounding, absolutely petrified.

Take note, young K2, if you ever read this: Even
Great Heroes get scared sometimes. Because
even a very pleased-with-himself Hero, the kind of
happy-go-lucky human being who acted first and
thought later, like Everest, gets terrified when they're
being pursued by lions redder than sunsets. And
dormindrads armed with lasers.

Above Everest's head there was a small whirring
drone, about the size of a small dog and, you
guessed it, the little drone was called . . .

...*Puck*.

Both the Hero and his robot were very battered about the edges, and Everest appeared to be wearing some sort of broken security tag around one of his ankles and very tattered coveralls in a brilliantly luminous yellow.

"I thought you said you knew Excelsiar like the back of one of your little robot *hands*, Puck?" panted Everest as he ran.

"Yes, I is SO SORRY!" squealed Puck. "I does get confused. This planet has done lots of changing since we was last here. Diamont mines *sounded* so pretty but they weren't very nice, those diamont miners, were they?"

"NO, THEY WEREN'T!" shouted Everest, with understandable resentment, because the diamont miners had been really Not Very Nice at all, keeping Everest imprisoned, and he'd only just managed to escape.

Everest rounded another corner, and a boggle ducked into a building, gill flapping anxiously, slamming the door behind him.

"But they're *ever so* welcoming to humans in the cities you said." Everest spotted some more dormindrads flying toward him, and doubled back on himself again. "Once we get to the city we'll be FINE, you said...Look, there's a Which Way in this city that we can go through NO TROUBLE, you said..."

"Well, they used to be so LUVVERLY in the cities!" protested Puck. "Offcourse, I remember the cities as less FLOATY...And those dormindrads were triffically friendly back then..."

"Would you say they were friendly *now*?" asked Everest as he tried to run and take out the ragged remains of an Atlas at the same time.

NEENORRNEENORR.

Dormindrads

Dormindrads are a highly intelligent species, half-human, half-winged-horse, who organize life in the cities. Normally peaceful, the situation of conflict on Excelsiar has led dormindrads to take up arms so they can defend themselves, and the shy, gentle boggles and gergashes, from attacks from both Warlock miners and from the Abhorrorghast.

The city's horn started blaring—they clearly considered themselves under attack.

"It is odd," mused Puck, looking about himself as the boggles and elves started to scatter, terrified. "I'm beginning to wonder if it is something about your diamont miner outfit."

"Well, yellow has never been my color, but this is no time for fashion advice," howled Everest, "not when they're trying to kill me! *Intercept the lasers!*"

"Pardon me?" said Puck politely.

"*Hail of lasers!*" bellowed Everest, looking up from the Atlas and pointing as the lasers came screeching toward them.

"Hail?" said Puck, eager to help, flinging out a small umbrella from the end of one of his arms.

Luckily, the umbrella was made of metal, so the lasers bounced off it, but unfortunately one hit the remains of the Atlas along the way, and it burst into flames.

"*I meant with your LASER DEFLECTORS!*"
roared Everest, desperately trying to put out the fire.

"Ooh, yes, forgot about those!" said Puck,
hurriedly changing the umbrella for his laser
deflectors.

But it was too late for the
Atlas pages. The flames had
consumed them, and Everest
dropped them to the ground.

"Whoops," said Puck.

No Atlas.

This was a disaster.

Now they didn't even know
where the Which Way in the city
was.

WHOOPS.

"Hang on!" Puck dived down and picked up the
last, half-burnt page. "Look! There's one tweedly bit
here that still has a Which Way on it!"

"Brilliant!" Everest tore it out of his hand and
ducked into a doorway.

The last page showed a Which Way back to
Earth that wasn't far. But it wasn't in the floating city.

It was down below in the forest.

"Ooh, we don't want to go back *there*..." Puck shivered.

As the sirens blared again, one of the gergashes abandoned the flying scooter she was traveling on.

Everest picked it up and shot off in a humming cloud, just above street level. He wove and turned as screaming boggles threw themselves out of the way. With a dreadful, hissing, snakelike noise, bits of vine unwrapped themselves from where they were winding around doorways, buildings, and bridges, and reached out toward the man on the scooter, stretching and chasing after him.

"Oohh..." Puck sighed. "When the vegetation attacks I absquolootely DEPLORES it..."

But Everest had reached the perimeter of the city. Below him was a cloud-filled drop.

The jungle below was very beautiful, as well as terrible, if Everest had been in a state to admire it.

With one trembling hand Everest steered the
scooter straight off the edge of the city walls...

...into the forest below.

It was the frantic leap of a truly desperate man.

Down...

Down...

Everest flew, the scooter sputtering, complaining,
but carrying on, until a sleepy jungle vine unwrapped
itself from a nearby tree trunk, this time catching one
of the wheels in a lazy lasso and tipping Everest onto
the forest floor.

Everest stumbled onward on foot, bleeding. "Are
we nearly at the Which Way?" he panted as he ran
as fast as he could through the forest.

"I *thunks* so," replied Puck uneasily.

A terrible sound came booming out of the
darkness in front of them. It was a wild, horrifying
howl that sent the hairs prickling up on the back of
my neck.

Everest knew that sound.

He stopped abruptly.

"They're there before us...," he
gasped, clapping his hands over his

ears because the roar throbbing through his skull was giving him a headache. "They'll be guarding the Which Way. If the Beast is with them, we'll never get through."

Now the trouble that Everest was in had turned from Big Trouble to Absolutely Gigantic Trouble. He was stuck.

"Change of plan," said Everest hurriedly. "Again. I'll distract them and you'll have to go back through the Which Way without me, Puck. You're small enough to go unnoticed."

Every warning light on Puck's metallic body lit up like a Christmas tree. "You can't let me go, NO!" wailed Puck.

"LEAVE!" said Everest. "You're supposed to follow orders."

"Don't you love me, Everest?" begged the little robot.

"Of course I love you, Puck," said Everest. "But now you need to do what I tell you. You must go back through the Which Way that leads to the

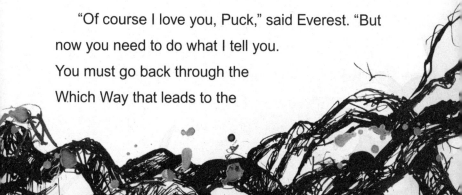

House of the O'Heros, quickly, before the worlds shift again . . . *but you will not let Freya know you are there.*"

"Why not?" asked Puck.

"Because if I get my family mixed up in this," Everest gave a shaky laugh, "Freya will be cross. She's always had this extraordinary impression I get everyone into trouble. I have no idea why; it's terribly unreasonable . . ."

A few more lasers passed over the head of the well-meaning, non-trouble-attracting Hero, missing him by inches as Puck absentmindedly lobbed them back with his laser deflectors.

"You will go into the house in secret," continued Everest. "You will find Aunt Trudie. You will tell her she gave me the wrong potion. I need the Cure for the Plague of the Silk Trees, and she has given me something to cure WARTS. Return to me with the real Cure and a copy of the Atlas as soon as you can.

"Avoid the children. Neither of them are the Child-with-the-Atlas-Gift," said Everest. "Don't let Freya and the aunts come after you . . . And DO NOT ON

ANY ACCOUNT let Cyril Sidewinder track you when you are there…"

"That's easy," said Puck, with a shiver. "I don't like Cyril…he's an absquoloot weasel-meaner of a human being…"

"Quick!" said Everest impatiently. "Repeat back to me what you're going to do!"

"*One. Go through the Which Way,*" repeated Puck obediently.

"*Two. Find Aunt Trudie, and don't let Freya and the children see you.*

"*Three. Ask her for potion.*

"*Four. Bring a copy of the Alternative Atlas.*

"*Five. Don't let Cyril Sidewinder track me.*

"*Six. Come back through the Which Way and give Everest the potion and the Atlas…*

"*Seven. Don't let Freya and the aunts come too…*

"Easy-peasy, lemon-squeezy!"

"Very good," said Everest. "And I will do my best to survive until you get back."

"But how will you survive without ME?" wailed Puck. "I is *indistructiFENSIBLE!*"

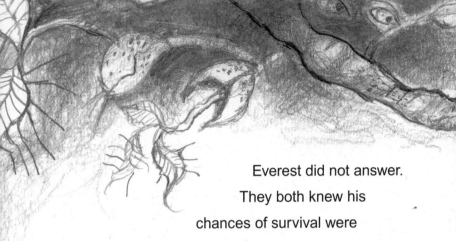

Everest did not answer.
They both knew his
chances of survival were
vanishingly slim.

"GO!" said Everest sternly. The undergrowth
had begun to move in gentle undulations beneath
his feet, like waves gradually swelling on an ocean.
He started to run back the way he'd come. *"DON'T
FORGET TO USE STEALTH MODE!"* were the last
words Puck heard before he was out of range.

And then Puck buzzed up and away with a high-
pitched wail of despair...

For the first time since his creation, the little robot
was entirely alone.

Now, I'm afraid such a wild and ridiculous Plan,
thought up by a Hero in a state of most dreadful
desperation, was bound to go wrong, wasn't it?

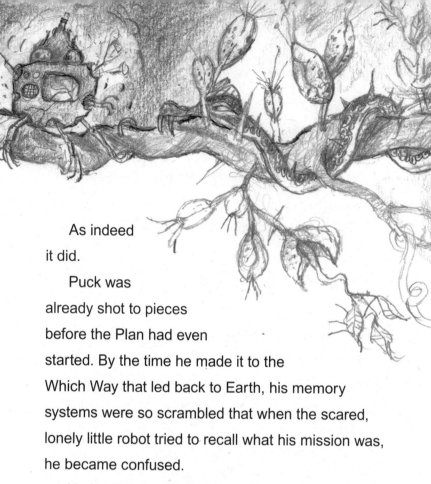

As indeed it did.

Puck was already shot to pieces before the Plan had even started. By the time he made it to the Which Way that led back to Earth, his memory systems were so scrambled that when the scared, lonely little robot tried to recall what his mission was, he became confused.

He landed on a branch to collect his thoughts. He did not notice keen eyes in the forest that had been tracking him, quick wings that had been following him, sharp ears that were now listening to him in the darkness.

The followers of the Beast.

"Now, what was I doing or supposed to *be*?" said Puck to himself. He checked his crossed wires. "Yes, I know! Was peasy-lemony-squeezy, oh, no...I mean, yes. It was:

"One. Go through the Which Way...Yes, I'm nearly there...

"Two. Find Cyril Sidewinder...Ooh dear, not sure about that, but Everest must know best...

"Three. Ask for the Child-with-the-Atlas-Gift.

"Four. Bring the child to Cyril with a copy of the Alternative Atlas.

"Five. Don't let Plant Foodie track me...

"Six. Come back through Crossing and bring Everest the Atlas and...something else?"

"*Bring us the Child-with-the-Atlas-Gift...,*" came a longing, sighing whisper from the forest darkness all around Puck.

"Oh, yes, *thank you!*" said Puck gratefully to the unknown voices in the darkness. "*Bring the Child-with-the-Atlas-Gift...*and...

"Seven. Don't let the Bear and the Ants come too...

"Now, who on earth are the Bear and the Ants

and Plant Foodie? Never mind. I cans do everythinks else."

Oh dear.

The little robot had muddled his instructions, and in a very alarming way.

And once he'd made it through the Which Way Crossing, instead of buzzing off to find Aunt Trudie, he flew in entirely the wrong direction to find the appalling Cyril Sidewinder instead.

A big mistake.

To make matters worse, Puck had forgotten to use Stealth Mode. So anyone who was interested could see that someone or something had made an illegal Crossing through the Which Ways between the worlds.

That was what had drawn the Out-of-Town attention to that particular little spot.

Including myself.

And what of Everest?

The forest creatures caught him.

They took him somewhere dark.

And now Everest, also known as World-Walker, the Uncatchable One, who had once tracked the motions of the stars beyond the Outer Limits, the great discoverer of so many of the Hidden Planets, the Darer of the Lost Black Holes, the Trickster, and the Storyteller of the known Cosmos, whose very name was a legend in the Sentient Galaxies, now this gargantuan man's world had contracted to a tiny prison of darkness with a little blue monkeylike creature in it.

Everest shrunk away from it into the corners of his prison, but there was nowhere for him to escape.

"Greetings, Everest O'Hero," said the monkey pleasantly. "Where is the Child-with-the-Atlas-Gift?"

Everest's heart sank but he smiled his most charming smile. He fixed the monkey with his twinkling eyes, and drawled casually, "I think you may be under a misapprehension. No one has had the Atlas Gift for thousands of years, and I do not know this 'Everest' you are talking about. Perhaps, good monkey, you could release me?"

But Everest's Magical Gift of "Excessive Amounts of Persuasion" was never going to work in this case, because by sheer bad luck the monkey had a very similar one. The two Gifts would cancel each other out on neutral ground, but Everest was in the monkey's territory and that gave the monkey the upper hand.

The monkey stared back at Everest with his own hypnotic stare, and Everest was forced to drop his gaze. The monkey put one of his hands on Everest's chest.

Everest froze, solid as rock, even though he was willing himself to move. *By the dusty trail of asteroid tails. Move!*

On the monkey's right hand was a long, long finger, and he put that finger in Everest's ear.

"Your thoughts will tell me what I need to know," said the monkey.

Everest was generally very good at hiding what he was thinking, but he was tired and frightened, and one slippery thought popped into his weary

mind before he
could catch and
snuff it.

*Freya DID have a
vision that one of our
children might be the
Child-with-the-Atlas-
Gift . . .* , thought Everest.

"*AHA!*" said the monkey, in triumph.

But Everest was back in control, and he kept his
mind blank.

"Keep your secrets then." The monkey gave a
gleeful giggle as he took his finger out of Everest's
ear. "It doesn't matter now. Your little robot told us he
will bring the child here."

"You can't believe *PUCK*; he's always muddling
things up!" protested Everest, now cold with dread.
"I tested both my children thoroughly and they don't

have the Atlas Gift. *Freya's Gift of 'Seeing Into the Future' is extremely unreliable…"*

"You are tricky, Everest O'Hero," said the monkey. "And you will say or think anything to save your children. But your robot will bring us the Child-with-the-Atlas-Gift nonetheless."

The monkey's voice turned nasty. "Which means the Abhorrorghast does not need YOU anymore. *You* have no Atlas."

Everest knew that could only mean one thing.
He was going to die.

Oh dear, oh dear, oh dear, oh dear.

I think it is already too late to rescue Everest.

And very, very dangerous to try and go where he has gone.

But the story did not listen.

"The Abhorrorghast does not need You any more. You have no Atlas."

117

Chapter 8 THE ALTERNATIVE ATLAS

Back in the House of the O'Heros, Izzabird took K2 by the arm and dragged him to their bedroom.

She took the crumpled piece of paper with K2's "X" on it out of her backpack and stared at it. "Okay, K2, what are you hiding from me? You might as well tell me everything."

K2 put his hoodie over his head in a last-ditch, desperate attempt not to tell her. But now that Izzabird knew there was a secret, she wouldn't let go until she knew what it was.

"It's something our father gave me before he left," K2 sighed through his hoodie. "I promised him I wouldn't tell and I don't like to break that promise."

"Tell me!" raged Izzabird. "I already know about the Alternative Atlas anyway. I just didn't know YOU knew too..."

So K2 pulled down his hoodie and told her.

"Okay, K2," his father had said kindly, "I know you're not very good at football or climbing or any of these

other things, and I'm completely understanding about that…"

Even little K2, only seven years old, knew that this wasn't quite true.

Everest thought that explorers had to be strong and fit and handsome, just like him.

"But maybe you have other gifts…," his father went on, his merry eyes looking straight into K2's. "I think you're a lot cleverer than they all think you are. I mean, you're my son, aren't you?"

K2 remembered the warm fuzzy feeling this gave him. K2 didn't get much admiration, so it was like a drink in a desert.

Everest handed K2 a book. It was a book with blank pages. Around the cover, Everest had wrapped more white paper.

K2 turned the pages. They were so white they were intimidating. It was like a book filled with snow.

K2
drawing
in
map
age 7

"What is it?" asked K2.

"It's an Alternative Atlas," explained his father. "You write down the name on the cover."

K2 shook his head fearfully. He wasn't keen on writing, particularly a long word like "Alternative."

"Don't worry," sighed his father. "I'll spell it for you."

So K2's father said the letters, and K2 wrote them down carefully, concentrating hard, filled with pleasure as his father applauded each shaky, wandering, daddy longlegs of a letter.

The "e"s appeared to have trouble knowing which way around they should be facing, but K2's father didn't seem to mind.

"Inside the book," said Everest, "you fill the white spaces with your own maps. But you must never, ever tell anyone this . . . it will be our secret. Come and show me what you are doing every now and then and we can talk about it . . . IMPRESS me, K2. I want you to impress me."

K2 had brought the Atlas to his father in secret every week.

And every week his father wasn't impressed.

In fact, his father had seemed to be rather disappointed with K2's progress. K2 had seen it in his eyes, although Everest tried to conceal it.

But then his father had suddenly left in a hurry. And K2 had no idea where he had gone.

Since then, K2 had practiced and practiced, in secret, in the hope that one day his father would come back and be impressed with what he'd done.

Izzabird stared at her brother, open-mouthed. "He did exactly the same with me!" she said. "But I got bored of drawing maps and turned the book into my first Plan Book..."

The twins were both a little annoyed that what they thought had been their own special link with their father wasn't so special after all.

"Well, go on...," said Izzabird eventually. "Where

is it? Show me. This could be our clue to finding him again!"

K2 opened the window.

I was listening outside and had to climb quickly on top of the window casement so he didn't bump into me.

K2 balanced on a chair and leaned out perilously far. Underneath the eaves there was a small space behind a loose slate that did not get wet. K2 had wrapped an old jacket around something hidden there.

"The thing is," said K2 uncertainly, bringing the package inside and opening it up to reveal a great big book, "I used to like drawing in it, but I'm not sure I want to anymore."

The book had its title written in large decorated letters by a younger K2.

"Well, go on, open it!" urged Izzabird.

Reluctantly, K2 opened the book. Inside was a great scrapbook of maps of imaginary worlds, extraordinary islands, and unseen-before mountains, but also maps of real places, the woods around their town, playgrounds they'd visited, but mostly the House of the O'Heros and its large, messy garden.

"Why is this so important?" said Izzabird, very puzzled. "It's just a book of silly kids' stuff... And let's face it, they're not even brilliant maps..."

"Well, I was only seven when I drew those ones," said K2, already regretting showing her and slamming the book shut.

"I didn't mean it like that, K2," said Izzabird, coaxing him to open it again. "It's just a bit odd, you have to admit, that scary Cyril would be interested in your... *really fascinating*," she added hastily, "map collection..." But then Izzabird turned the pages more thoughtfully. "Actually, these later ones are really quite good."

Something very odd was going on. Why had their father asked them to draw an Alternative Atlas and why was Cyril Sidewinder looking for the very

The Alternating Atlas

by K2OHERO

Jiant Mushroom Forests

singing Lake

← K2's drawing in the Atlas from when he was seven years old

same thing? And why had Cyril thought K2's "map" might be important, when all it had been was one big "X"? Did it have something to do with the family "geographical" Gift that the aunts had been talking about?

Izzabird handed K2 a pencil. "Show me...Draw in it."

K2 shook his head. "I told you, I don't want to. I was getting a bit obsessed, as if the book was...controlling me, and it gave me nightmares. Anyway, I can't do it inside."

"Why not?" asked Izzabird.

"I think it's the noise of all the ghosts in this house," said K2. "They keep whispering together about how useless I am, and what a disgrace to the name of the O'Heros, and it puts me off."

"So, where have you drawn all these maps?" asked Izzabird.

"Outside," said K2, pointing to the roof.

"Well, come on!" urged Izzabird. "Get out there and do some drawing!"

K2 sighed.

He climbed carefully out of the window and put the jacket down on the little ledge outside. It had stopped raining for a moment, and the clouds above had parted. The wind was trying its best to blow him off the ledge, but somehow that wasn't scary, because this was K2's safe place. He often came here to think, as well as draw.

Izzabird stood behind him in the window and pretended to be looking in the other direction. "Go on, then! I'm not watching! I'm not judging!"

K2 looked up at the starry, starry sky above, so endless, so uncritical.

He took a deep breath.

He began to draw.

Getting the pencil in his hand was a lovely, powerful feeling.

He had forgotten how good it felt.

He began slowly, hesitantly, writing the name of the imaginary world he was drawing in careful

capitals as it came to him: EXCELSIAR. And then he became more and more confident as the map came to life beneath his hand, in darker and darker pencil lines. He was concentrating so hard and was so absorbed in what he was doing that he was almost lost in the paper.

Izzabird watched in astonishment as K2 appeared to go into a sort of trance. She even managed to shut up for a second and stop fidgeting.

As K2's drawing got more intense and complicated, she gazed at him in ever increasing amazement. K2 was the person she knew better than anyone else in the world, he was her *twin*, for goodness' sake. How could this be the same K2 that she knew, drawing so astoundingly well?

K2 drew jungles on that map, dark, tangled forests with strange animals and birds that Izzabird had never seen before with names like "tiger-griffs" and "unideer" and "cackling bluebirds" lurking in the undergrowth, and paths through the greenery made by huge drowsy mammoth-like creatures with five heads and gigantic twisting red-and-white tusks.

Singing lakes, sky rivers, diamont mines that formed great empires underground, sprawling secretly for miles and miles. Cities floating in the air that appeared to be fleeing the growing, groping forests, for what was that tendril of greenery *doing*, snaking, unfurling, reaching out like a thorny finger as it stretched up from the tree canopy toward the flying cities as if to tear them down?

K2 drew and redrew, in a fever now. Izzabird began to think that she could actually *smell* the tiger-heat of the heart of that forest as well as see it, *hear* the animals and birds singing and calling to each other, *taste* the honeysuckle sweetness of the heavy windless air trapped in the curl of the thick forest leaves, *touch* their bumblebee furriness, and as each movement of the pencil got more and more fevered, it was as if each stroke was an act of conjuring that entire world into existence.

One, two, three more strokes of K2's magician's pencil and she might actually *be* in that jungle—or think she was.

The trees were moving, walking, growing up

and out of the page...the smells, the sounds, the songs felt real...*and something was moving in there that all in the forest were afraid of, even the big catlike creatures with tusks, even the slowly sliding multicolored Leviathan snakes smoothing through the undergrowth, tongues flicking in, out, in, out, with warning hisses.*

A sweating, trancelike K2 was beginning to draw the utmost tip of the tail of *something* grander by far than all these, *something* that might be in there too, hidden deep in the tangle and the vines and the wildness of the vegetation, and starting to move and slouch into dangerous life...

...and Izzabird was seized by sudden terror.

"SHUT THE BOOK!" she cried, and she dragged K2 inside and slammed the covers shut on K2's picture, snapping his pencil.

K2 started and came to.

"The Gift!" said Izzabird in absolute astonishment. "The family geographical Gift! The one that is sort of a Curse, the one that the aunts were talking about!"

Her sensible, practical little forefinger was shaking as she pointed straight at K2. "I can't believe it," whispered Izzabird, scared, exultant, jealous. "*You* have it, K2...

"*You* have the Gift."

Chapter 9 A PIECE OF PAPER HAS TWO SIDES

nd you're right," finished Izzabird with round eyes. "Whatever it is, this Gift, it's absolutely terrifying."

Above them, outside on the window, invisible-but-there, I sighed.

I'd found him.

The Child-with-the-Atlas-Gift.

And he was now in the most terrible mortal danger.

I hate it when the story takes this sort of direction. But what can I do?

Izzabird licked her lips; she could taste the fear on them.

They both stared at the cover of the book, now quiet, and not remotely alarming-looking.

"But although it's scary," said Izzabird at last, with reluctant respect, "I have to admit, it's also kind of cool."

K2 gave a shy smile.

It was a nice feeling to have her admiring something that HE did, for a change, rather than the other way around.

"Do you think Dad would be impressed if I could show it to him?" said K2 hopefully.

"Probably..." Izzabird shivered. "But you mustn't do that on your own," she added. "It was getting out of control."

It was starting to rain again.

Izzabird swallowed hard. "What happens if we open the book again?"

"It only goes crazy like that when I'm actually drawing in it," said K2.

Apprehensively, as if the book might bite her, Izzabird opened the Atlas and turned to the page K2 had been drawing. It now looked like a perfectly normal map.

"Look, you've drawn a cross! Just like Cyril said." Izzabird suddenly pointed out a small cross in the middle of a jungle K2 had drawn.

"That's the weirdest thing about it. I'll draw a cross in one place and then when I open it again it will be in another place. They just move of their own accord; even the maps themselves seem to sometimes," K2 whispered.

As if the map could hear them, the paper started humming with heat, and when Izzabird put her hand on the page, it was as warm as bread just coming out of an oven.

And then she pulled her hand away in shock as the cross got larger and larger, burning so blue-bright that the edges curled up as if they had been lit by a match, and the paper split, and you could see through the open cross to a drawing on the other side.

The odd Magic fire put itself out as quickly as it started.

Trembling, Izzabird turned the page.

On the other side was a map of the House of the O'Heros.

"You've drawn another cross in our garden, in exactly the same place as the cross on the other side of the page!" gasped Izzabird. "Just like creepy Cyril told us to! How did you know? How did *he* know? What is going on?"

Diamont Mine

GRATE SILKLESS

DESERT

the World of

EXCELSIAR

THE FORREST of the ObHo Rhargast

The Sea of Cress

River of Fire

Beware!!!

The Prison of the ObHorrargast (Beast)

No Man's Land

Spotted Lake

Freya
My mother's
workshop

Aunt Trudie's
Workshop

Everest
My father's
workshop

Aunt
Violet's
workshop

The House
of the
O'Heros

K2 grabbed the Atlas out of Izzabird's hands and slammed it shut again, panting hard. K2 didn't normally stand up to his twin, but this time he was too frightened not to.

"We need to tell the aunts and Mom about this...," he said, feeling thoroughly sick. "I told you, this jungle has given me some REALLY SCARY nightmares...

"The trees don't just grow, they MOVE...there are these huge snakes that can swallow a human whole...there's a weird monkey-creature that takes out your thoughts with its finger...But the worst is the BEAST...who is known as the Abhorrorghast!"

K2 swallowed. He'd been trying to forget about the Beast. "Don't ask me how I know, but he REALLY doesn't like humans..."

Izzabird could feel her heart beating in double-quick time, because she'd just realized something far more exciting. "*Excelsiar!*" she whispered with shining eyes. "The name of this world you just drew is EXCELSIAR! Wasn't that the name of the place in the song that Dad used to sing to get us to go to sleep?"

"Yes...no...I don't know...," said K2, anxiously

hopping from foot to foot, hugging the Atlas to his chest.

"Maybe that's where he's gone!" said Izzabird.

"Oh, goodness! *Yes*...No!...Maybe...But Dad is DEAD, isn't he?"

"What if he *isn't* dead?" argued Izza. "What if he never went to the Mariana Trench? What if all along he's been exploring places like this 'Excelsiar'? And the 'geographical Gift' secret that Cyril was looking for and the aunts and Mom have been hiding from us...What if that's how he's doing it?"

"That's a lot of 'What ifs,' Izza...*What are we going to do?*" said K2, knowing he wasn't going to like the answer to this question.

"We're going to find out how to use this Alternative Atlas," said Izzabird, determinedly punching the air. "And then we're going to find Dad and bring him home where he belongs, and put our family back together again."

"*But we don't know what we're doing!*" objected K2.

BANG! There was a very loud noise from outside the window.

K2 and Izzabird ran to see what it was.

Chapter 10 WHAT THEO DID

About half an hour earlier, Theo had crept out from his hiding place in the shadows, into the kitchen, taken something from Aunt Trudie's coat, and then run up the stairs, quivering with excitement.

Mabel was supposed to be sitting at Theo's desk doing her homework, but in fact she was playing with Clueless, the O'Heros' little black-and-white dog. (Clueless had taken a particular shine to Mabel, much to Izzabird's irritation.)

Theo's genius for creating order wherever he went meant that his room was the only neat place in the entire house. He'd even managed to arrange the bowls he had to put out for leaks in the ceiling in a tidy, structured, and color-coordinated fashion.

"I knew it! They ARE Witches! I knew it!" said

Theo as he entered his room. He hadn't been able
to hear everything, but he'd heard enough through
that kitchen door to feel sure now that his hunch
about the O'Heros was correct.

"Oh, Theo, no!" said Mabel.

"They were talking about Magic and potions and
powers and all sorts of weird stuff!" said Theo.

Mabel was a quiet, noticing sort of child, and
having lived for a while now in the O'Heros' house,
she knew perfectly well that something very strange
was indeed going on here.

Once, for instance, she had opened the door to
the linen closet to find it already occupied by a long,

lean, see-through gentleman in old-fashioned dress and a large Viking hat keeping warm in there. She wasn't frightened, only a little sorry for him, because the ghost was weeping gently and was very polite, requesting she find him some sort of "Cure," before handing her the pillowcase she was looking for with one trembling, skeletal hand.

She hadn't mentioned this to Theo, however, because he disliked the House of the O'Heros quite enough already, and ghost stories would not help.

"You're way too little to be mixed up in this, Mabel," said Theo determinedly. "There's been a lot of odd things happening recently, and I bet it's something to do with these Witch aunts!"

"So what are you going to do?" asked Mabel.

"I'm going to collect evidence and take it to Dad and the police, and then we can go back to the city where we belong," said Theo confidently.

Mabel's heart sank. She had fallen in love with the excitement of this house, even though it was haunted (by *friendly* ghosts, at least) and crumbling down. And although she was terrified of Aunt Violet and a bit scared of Izzabird, she loved Clueless and Annipeck, and she had secretly grown fond of Freya and K2 and Aunt Trudie as well, although she wouldn't have dared tell Theo that. In her heart of hearts too, Mabel thought Theo was less numbly unhappy here than he had been back in the city. At least here he was enthusiastic about his war with Izzabird. Theo loved a project. But Mabel kept that opinion to herself.

"What about Annipeck?" she objected.

"Dad will get custody," said Theo.

"But the O'Heros might be put in jail!" worried Mabel. "Or... into some laboratory or something... Weren't people who practiced Magic persecuted in olden times?"

"I'm sure it won't come to that," said Theo vaguely.

Secretly he didn't like that idea either, but he was so obsessed with his quest that he put any possible unpleasant consequences of his plan to the back of his mind.

Triumphantly, he whipped out the two little bottles he had stolen from Aunt Trudie's coat. One of them was a very small bottle, so tiny that Trudie hadn't had room to write the whole name of its contents on it, so it was just marked with tiny capital letters: *C.4.P.S.T.*

Great.

He couldn't take *that* to the police. It might be a Spell, but the initials could just as well stand for: "Cobnuts for Poppy Seed Tart," or "Croutons for Pumpkin Soup Toast." And that would be embarrassing, because nobody was going to take perfectly ordinary cooking ingredients as evidence of witchcraft.

The other one was more promising. In Aunt Trudie's loopy handwriting, with her rather creative spelling, the label read *Animashun Poshun*.

"Let's see if this works...," said Theo. The bottle was about half-full—enough for him to test it and still keep some as evidence.

Theo put on a pair of swimming goggles as a precaution and made Mabel stand well back.

What should he try it on?

Theo's eyes landed on his blow-dryer. Gently, he poured the liquid on the blow-dryer handle and backed away quickly.

Nothing happened.

"It's not working...," said Theo, hugely disappointed.

Knock! Knock! Knock! Daniel put his head around the door. He had Annipeck in his arms, bathed and in her pajamas.

"I'm just putting Annipeck to bed," Daniel said. "She wanted to say good night."

"Night-night, Feo! Night-night, Mabel!" said Annipeck, waving her hands at them and blowing them a kiss.

"Night-night, Annipeck...," said Theo and Mabel,

blowing kisses back, but rather distractedly, because they were staring so fixedly at the blow-dryer.

For in front of their astonished eyes...

The blow-dryer was trembling, even though no one was touching it.

Theo and Mabel froze breathlessly, in shock, as slo-owly the little blow-dryer reared onto its handle and up into the air, balancing on its cord. It turned its head this way, that way, like an aerial seahorse.

"NEIGH!" said Annipeck in delight. She pointed at the vertical blow-dryer, levitating just above ankle level.

But Daniel didn't seem to see it.

Why is Theo wearing SWIMMING GOGGLES? Daniel was thinking before shaking his head at the unfathomable

nature of young people in general, and Theo in particular.

"It'll be supper in five minutes," said Daniel, turning to leave despite Annipeck still trying to draw his attention to the funny little blow-dryer by saying, "Neigh! Neigh! Neigh!" repeatedly as Daniel shut the door behind them.

"Oh!" gasped Mabel, enchanted, once they'd left. "The blow-dryer has COME ALIVE!"

Theo's heart was beating so hard he thought it would burst. He was secretly thrilled. Even though he was thoroughly against the whole idea of Magic in principle—it was odd and messy and he knew his wonderful, sensible mother would have disapproved

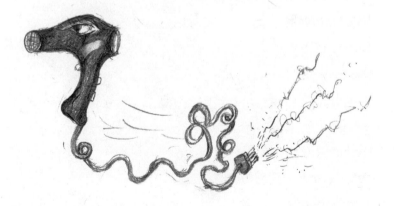

of it—still, it was pretty impressive that he, Theo, could get this potion to work...*

Clueless the dog yawned. She had seen plenty of stuff like this before in this house. It would take more than an animated blow-dryer to impress *her*.

Theo ran quickly to his desk drawer, took out his mobile phone, and started filming. He had it! His father and everyone would *have* to believe him now...

Startled by Theo's sudden movement, the little blow-dryer shot forward, propelling itself with a twisting side-to-side snakelike motion of its cord, its head rocking through the air in a very horselike fashion, and head-butted the door repeatedly, as if it were trying to get out of the room.

---

*Theo was only half-right about this. Anyone can use a Magical potion, of course—but it was true this had gone unexpectedly well for Theo's first time.

Theo grabbed at it to try and stop it hurting itself, but that only alarmed the blow-dryer, and it rocketed off, wiggling around the room, plug flailing wildly, accidentally knocking over Theo's chair.

They had just cornered the trembling blow-dryer underneath the desk and Mabel was making soothing noises to calm it down when Daniel barged back into the room, without knocking this time. "Will you SHHHH?!" he hissed in exasperation. "It's impossible to get Annipeck to sleep when you're making so much noise in here!"

There were distant sounds of Annipeck wailing in her room.

"Dad!" gabbled Theo. "Freya and the aunts are practicing MAGIC. *Look!*" He pointed at the blow-dryer, but at that very moment there was a loud boom of thunder that distracted Daniel and covered the noise of the blow-dryer shooting out from under the desk, between Daniel's legs, through the crack of the door, and out into the corridor.

"At *what*?" blinked Daniel, staring down at the empty floor. "I haven't got time for these childish games, Theo."

"But Dad, see, I filmed it!" said Theo, trying to find the video on his phone. "And these are SPELLS!" He grabbed the little bottles and waved them at his father. "I found them in Aunt Trudie's coat! They're *Witches*, Dad!"

Daniel drew himself up to his full height. He gave Theo his strictest look as he took the bottles and put them in his pocket. "You should not be looking through Aunt Trudie's coat, young man. And the idea that Freya and the aunts are 'Witches' is preposterous."

"Why do you never *listen* to me?" asked Theo in distress, shaken out of his normal composure.

"I'm *trying* to listen, Theo, but you're not making a lot of sense," said the exasperated Daniel.

"But—"

Daniel strode out and closed the door.

Theo and Mabel looked at each other and then went to the door and opened it again.

Daniel was walking quickly back along the corridor.

The blow-dryer was standing upright with its head leaning against the door of Annipeck's room. It was motionless.

151

Has it run out of potion, or is it playing dead? wondered Mabel.

Daniel stopped in front of the blow-dryer with a confused expression on his face. He shrugged, picked it up, and took it into Annipeck's room with him.

BANG! Another, much louder sound came from outside that didn't sound like the storm this time, more like a car backfiring—or a gunshot.

Theo and Mabel, nerves jangling, ran to Theo's window. *What could that be?* The strange, scary robot skeleton from the morning sprang straight into both their minds.

They looked through the glass.

Something shot out of the kitchen door below like a great big bullet, as the rain gathered intensity.

It was an aunt on the back of a Hoover.

Aunt *Violet*, in fact, sitting astride an ancient model from the 1970s that belched out smoke like a polluting old motorbike. It was her vacuum cleaner that was making the noise like a car backfiring. Helmet jammed low over her eyes, she zoomed straight for a gradually decreasing circle of clearness in the clouds.

Freya came
shooting out next
on a skinnier, more
modern vacuum cleaner. She
had a more scattery approach, up, down, blowing this
way and that way on the wind.

And Aunt Trudie took up the rear, bolt upright,
riding her vacuum cleaner sidesaddle with as much
dignity and solemnity as if she were a queen riding a
horse. The increasing wildness of the rain and wind
caught her cloak and made it fly out behind her. Like
Freya, she was moving rather erratically, because
she was trying to map-read some photocopied pages
at the same time.

From the back and forthness of their progress,
they didn't seem entirely sure where they were going.
Clearly Aunt Trudie needed a new pair of reading
glasses.

Three windows along, Izzabird and K2 were

peering out of K2's room at the very same spectacle.

"Wow," breathed Izzabird in envious admiration. "They're like those hover-thingummies in spy movies! Why don't they let *me* ride one of those things?"

"*Witches...*," whispered Theo with a slightly hysterical gasp, three windows back the other way. "I *knew* they were Witches...riding Hoovers instead of broomsticks!"

That was Aunt Violet's idea, of course. She could perfectly well have engineered their flying machines to look more like those hover-thingummies from spy movies, or broomsticks for that matter, but vacuum cleaners appealed to her sense of humor.

Theo took lots of videos with his phone.

"Where are they going?" said Mabel.

As the three flying figures disappeared up into the closing clouds, Aunt Trudie's Hoover let out a smaller, politer *bang!* and the resulting white smoke turned into Gift-writing, clearly defined, if a little hard to read as it was so far away.

WE'LL BE BAK TOMMOROW LUNCHTIME
DON'T LEEVE THE HOWSE
DON'T OPEN THE DOR TO ENY STRANGERS

How did Aunt Trudie know they were looking?

And then they were gone.

Yes, thought Theo. *They're Witches all right.* That was what they were. *Thoroughly modern Witches.*

"They've left us…" K2 gulped.

The house, without any aunts and mother to protect it, suddenly felt very vulnerable.

"Don't worry, K2, I have this feeling they're going to wherever Dad has gone, and we're going to follow them," said Izzabird excitedly.

Well, *that* didn't make K2 feel any better.

Theo put his head around K2 and Izzabird's door just as Izzabird was hiding K2's Alternative Atlas back in his sock drawer.

"Supper time, creeps," said Theo.

"GET OUT!" yelled Izzabird.

Theo shut the door again, grinning. He waited in the bathroom while Izzabird and K2 went downstairs and then double-backed into their bedroom.

Theo opened the top drawer of the chest of drawers. He pushed aside K2's socks and picked out the book hidden beneath them.

Theo's heart skipped a beat, his stomach lurched queasily, and he could feel an unpleasant sensation not unlike beetles crawling over his tingling scalp.

There was something spooky going on.

Theo needed to get to the bottom of it, and this book was even more evidence. He was going to take everything to the police.

If his father was too weak to protect Mabel, well, Theo was going to have to do it himself.

"THEO! The Stepfather says supper is getting cold!" Izzabird shouted up the stairs.

Theo would have to look into this later. Where could he hide the book in the meantime? Where would horrible Izzabird not find it?

Theo tiptoed into Annipeck's room and gently slid it under her mattress. They'd never look there.

And then he went downstairs.

And *I* watched him go.

Ah, thought I. *Interesting. I now have a Way In.*

Chapter 11 THE "X" THAT K2 DREW HAS A LIFE OF ITS OWN

Nobody but *I* saw what happened next in K2 and Izzabird's room.

Something forgotten on the floor gave a mouselike rustle.

In her excitement at opening the Atlas, Izzabird had dropped the map that K2 had been not-drawing in the geography lesson.

The "X" K2 had drawn in the center of the map was pulling up, up, as if it were the body of a bird, and the two sides of the paper stretched out like wings.

There were a few attempts at launching off the ground, for the map was just learning to fly. It batted about, bumping into things, having a little explore underneath K2's bed, before emerging again, crumpled and covered in dust. Until, determinedly, it flew under the crack of the door and off down the corridor, like a small white seagull.

On the landing it paused a second, hovering with slow wingbeats to listen to sounds coming from downstairs in the kitchen. The noisy hum of people having supper was drifting up the stairs.

And then it turned right, into the big family bathroom.

Down K2's map flew.

It got a little entangled with some clothes hanging above the dryer, before blundering toward the door of the washing machine.

As it *flat-flit-flutter*ed through the room like a confused bumblebee, I could see, when it turned, the very faint outline of the beginnings of a map drawn on the other side of the "X," which K2 had tried to rub out. I zeroed in on the names on that map to give me a clue as to what world it was.

O-ho, thought I. *O-ho.*

The map turned a last time, growing in confidence now, soaring around the room as if showing off its newly acquired flying skills, before plastering itself against the door of the washing machine, *SPLAT*, like a fly against a windshield.

And there it stuck, as if glued, caught.

With the "X" right in the center.

"X" marks the spot.

Chapter 12 EVERYTHING IS JUST FINE

hen Theo walked into the kitchen his father had that fixed, bright smile on his face that an adult always has when they are trying to pretend that everything is *just fine* when it isn't.

"Where are Freya and the weird aunts?" asked Theo innocently, as if he didn't know perfectly well that they were somewhere out in the thunderstorm, seated on flying vacuum cleaners.

"They seem to have just popped out for a moment," said Daniel, elaborately casually. "Sit down and eat your supper—"

BOOM! A particularly loud crack of thunder exploded outside, and the rain smashed like hailstones against the window.

"Oh yes, *lovely* weather for popping out for a moment," said Izzabird sarcastically.

She tried to read the note addressed to Daniel in her mother's scrawly handwriting that was lying on the table. But it was upside down so all she could make out was *DON'T CALL THE POLICE!* before Daniel reached out, scrunched it up, and put it in his pocket.

Theo sat down at the table next to K2 and Izzabird.

K2 was feeling too sick to eat.

"What are you going to DO?" said Mabel, looking up at her father with big, solemn eyes.

"I'm going to look after you," said Daniel with false cheerfulness. "I *am* qualified to do that, you know, Mabel. I'm forty-five. It's FINE."

On that last, very firm FINE, there was a blast of thunder so loud that K2 jumped out of his skin.

"We should call the police," said Theo.

"Nobody's calling the police," said Daniel, trying to laugh. But he walked over to the kitchen door and pulled both bolts shut. "Eat up and then you can find something to watch on the TV."

"What are YOU going to be doing?" asked Izzabird.

"I'm going to make a few phone calls," said the Stepfather.

"To the police?" asked Mabel hopefully.

"No!" said Daniel, very rattled. "Why does everyone keep saying that? I told you, we're not calling the police. Everything is JUST FINE!"

And that's how you know that it isn't.

As soon as they finished washing up, Izzabird
grabbed her rain boots and ran up the stairs, with K2
trying to keep up.

"We're going to work out how to use that Atlas
of yours to follow the aunts and Mom!" said Izzabird
in excitement. "Absolutely TYPICAL of them to go
on an adventure searching for Dad and to leave us
behind!"

"How do we know that's what they're doing?"
puffed K2.

But when they opened K2's sock drawer . . .

His Alternative Atlas was GONE.

"Where is it?" hissed Izzabird. They looked
everywhere in the room.

NO ATLAS.

They couldn't go anywhere without an Atlas.

"Draw another map, K2!" ordered Izza.

"No way!" said K2 obstinately.

"This is Theo's fault for putting ideas into your
head—normally you'd do what I say!" raged Izza.
"And I BET he's the one who took our Atlas!"

When Theo came up to his normally beautifully

tidy room he found Izzabird turning it upside down. And then there was a row that rivaled the storm outside for loudness and temper.

"Give us back K2's book!" shouted Izzabird.

"It's not stealing. It's gathering evidence," Theo retorted, holding up his mobile phone. "I've got *photographs* of what those odd aunts and mom of yours have been doing."

Izzabird grabbed the phone and smashed it into the wall, once, and then twice, to make absolutely sure it was broken.

Theo blinked. Once, twice.

"My phone. You smashed my phone...," he said, taking it out of Izzabird's hand and staring at it disbelievingly. "My mother gave me that phone."

"I'm sorry, Theo...," stammered Izzabird, instantly regretful. She put out her hand toward him, but he leaped away as if she were poison. "Aunt Violet can mend it...Aunt Violet can mend *anything*..."

But Theo was beyond listening. "You evil, wicked, malevolent...*thing*..." Theo couldn't think of a word bad enough to call her. "I wouldn't give my phone to that *Witch* to mend..."

"Wah ah yah MOMMY!"

Annipeck had woken up.

Daniel, who had been phoning everyone he knew to try and find out where Freya had gone, came running up the stairs two at a time and shouted at them both. "Theo and Izza, will you stop it! You're not even *trying* to make this family work!"

Which was very unlike him.

"I WISH I DIDN'T EVEN *HAVE* A FAMILY!" yelled Izzabird.

Even I, used as I am to loneliness, gave a shiver at this. What were the adults teaching these children?

"YOU CAN'T WISH THAT MORE THAN *I* DO!" Theo yelled back. "ANYTHING WOULD BE BETTER

166

THAN
HAVING TO BE WITH
YOU LOT!"

Dreadful, dreadful words
to say on a howling horror of
a night, and in a house of ancient Cunning too,
brimming with magic, swimming with ghosts, where
the tables walked and the pictures talked and where
there were people like *me* listening at the doors who
could give you your wish in a blinking.

Yes, you have to be careful what you wish for.

It may come true.

SLAM! Izzabird slammed her door.

SLAM! Theo slammed his door.

Silence, apart from the loud wails now coming
from Annipeck's room. "Mommy! MOMMY! OW OW
OW!!"

"It's fine, Annipeck," said Daniel, stroking her back.

And when that didn't work, K2 sang her the lullaby that Izzabird had mentioned earlier, the one their father had sung to them when they were babies.

It went like this, to the tune of "Twinkle, Twinkle, Little Star," but the words were slightly different:

"Twinkle, twinkle, little star
Heading to Ex-cel-si-ar
Way beyond the distant Poles
Watching out for great black holes
Wander, wander, little star
Heading to Ex-cel-si-ar."

Surely there isn't REALLY such a place as Excelsiar? thought K2 as he sang the lullaby over and over, with Mabel and Daniel joining in once they knew the words, until finally Annipeck fell asleep. And then K2 and Mabel went to bed, and Daniel went downstairs and sat in an armchair in the hall, staring at the front door, willing Freya to open it.

Portraits and photographs of Everest smiled down at him from the walls and the sideboards: Everest smugly hanging off some mountain; Everest standing nobly on top of a dangerous-looking diving machine, or was it a rocket? It was hard to tell.

Daniel put his hands over his face.

Where was she?

Everest

Chapter 13 WHO OR WHAT LIES BEHIND THAT DOOR?

Later, deep in the heart of the night, when Daniel had fallen asleep in his chair, the witch-wind raging over that boggy part of Planet Earth got sharper and colder and angrier. If you were a fanciful person, and you believed in such things, you might even say that it was as if ghosts from the past were lifting up the lids from their coffins and walking abroad.

Be that as it may, some things that were definitely NOT ghosts, but as solid as you and me, were approaching the O'Hero house even now, in the slow dropping of the darkness, and the gathering howling of the wind.

The three toothbrushes were on patrol on baby Annipeck's windowsill.

Up down, up down, this toothbrush patrol marched. The electric toothbrush was making a low, alarmed growling noise, and sparks were exploding anxiously out of its plug. The baby toothbrush was doing little cartwheels like an animated jelly bean.

The toothbrushes were built to be protective, so they were acutely aware of any approaching danger.

And I am the Story Maker, so, circling above the scene, I can see it all.

There were things out there looking for K2's Atlas.

And they were prepared to do *bad things* to get it.

But perhaps more alarming still...

There was a door *inside* the house that was trying to open.

The door of the washing machine where K2's map was stuck was trembling, humming, as if it could see into the future and knew that it was about to become important.

Who or what lay behind that door?

Watch out for the washing-machine door, readers.

You might think that the big front door with the heavy bolts that have been there since 1752 is the one you should be keeping an eye on.

But there is more than one way into a house.

Trust me, the washing-machine door is the one you really should be watching.

Chapter 14 AN UNEXPECTED VISITOR

When K2 had fallen asleep that night, Izzabird had still been awake, her light on, furiously writing in her Plan Book.

It seemed like only a minute later when K2 was woken by a baby toothbrush in a state of high agitation.

Izzabird's bed was empty.

And then, heart racing, K2 realized there was a loud noise, and it was coming from *inside* the house.

He was immediately, electrically, awake.

There it was again.

Knock! Knock! Knock!

It was coming from the family bathroom.

He met Izzabird, Clueless, and the other two toothbrushes on the landing.

Izzabird was carrying a heavy iron poker.

Where did she get THAT from?

Her eyes were huge and wide.

They tiptoed down the hall and into the bathroom, holding their breath.

Knock!

Knock! Knock!

Plastered onto the
washing-machine door was
the map that K2 had drawn in the
geography lesson. It was making a slight
buzzing noise, as if some electric energy
was animating it.

Knock! Knock! Knock! came the sound from right
behind K2's shakily drawn "X."

Oh dear, oh dear, oh dear.

It sounded horribly like somebody or some*thing*
was knocking on the *inside* of that door.

Not possible, surely?

Nobody could fit inside a washing machine.

But there it was
again: *Knock! Knock!
Knock!*

"Open the door of the washing machine," hissed Izzabird to K2.

"Whaaaaat? No!" whispered K2.

Clueless gave a little whimper and bravely tried to stand her ground.

"It might be Mom or Dad, trying to come back," said Izzabird.

"Come back from where?" shivered K2.

"From wherever," said Izza. "From the places you drew in the Atlas."

"But they're not *real*...," moaned K2.

However, this didn't sound convincing anymore, even to himself. "It could be a vampire...or worse," K2 added. "Things like that have to be *invited* into this house. As long as we don't open the door, it will be fine. Remember what Aunt Trudie said: 'DON'T OPEN THE DOOR TO ANY STRANGERS.'"

"She meant the *front* door, didn't she, not the door of the washing machine," argued Izza. "We can't never open the door of the washing machine again. How will we do any washing?"

Both of them knew that this was beside the point.

"There could be something bad in there!" wailed K2.

"That's why I'm carrying the poker," said Izza. "*Both* our parents are missing now, K2. We can't do nothing. We can't just sit here and let things happen to us. We have to take charge of our own destiny."

Outside, the storm, still battering the house, seemed to agree with her, howling with that extra edge of carnivore menace.

Oh, for goodness' sake. Izzabird was right. Sometimes you have to act rather than let the storm of events swallow you up and carry you away.

With trembling fingers, K2 opened the door of the washing machine.

And then stepped back in terror, as a hand reached out of it.

Izzabird kept the poker ready, shaking.

The water flooded out of the washing machine, and with the water...

...a second hand came out of the washing machine drum and gripped the edge of the open door.

Like he was in a nightmare, K2 tried to scream, but no noise came out.

And then a slim, graceful figure in what looked like a wet suit followed the hands and swam out on the tide of the gushing river of water, getting to its feet like a ballet dancer, shutting the door, and standing there looking at them, dripping, ankle-deep in water and sodden clothes.

There was far more water in the room than could ever have been in the washing machine in the first place, and it was an odd color, almost shinily fluorescent, and little stars of light seemed to be breaking off it.

But at least it was pleasantly warm, for K2 was up to his ankles in it, the bottom of his pajamas completely soaked. Izzabird, practical as ever, was wearing her rain boots.

Drip, drip.

Izzabird thrust the poker toward the figure in front of them in what she hoped was a menacing manner.

Whatever-it-was was wearing a hood with breathing apparatus, a bit like Darth Vader. It reached to the back of its neck and removed the hood.

Both the twins stepped back, ready to run.

It wasn't, sadly, their mother.

But if it was a vampire, it was an extremely pretty one.

It was a girl, in her late teens maybe, so about six years older than Theo and K2 and Izzabird.

The girl shook out her hair and gave them both a charming, reassuring smile, as if she were meeting them at a party rather than swimming out of their washing machine unexpectedly in the middle of the night.

She looked calm and rather pleased with herself.

Quite rightly.

Because really, I just have to say it again...

She was very, very lovely.

"Don't shoot!" smiled the girl, gesturing to the poker. "Though goodness knows *how* you could shoot with that thing. Couldn't you find something better?"

"You don't shoot with it," said Izzabird. "You bonk people on the head."

"Really?" said the girl, with interest. "How crude. But if you *do* shoot—or try to bonk me on the head (I'm sorry, but that's *primeval*)—I *may* have to shoot back. And I'm on your side."

"How do we KNOW you're on our side?" hissed Izzabird crossly.

"Good point," the girl admitted cheerfully. "You have no idea. Don't trust anyone, that's my motto."

"Who ARE you?" asked Izzabird.

"I'm Horizabel Delft," said the girl, humming happily. "And this is Blinkers." She waved vaguely to her right.

Where there was nothing.

K2 coughed politely. "Um...there's nothing there."

Horizabel gave a start. "So there isn't. Where is she?"

Horizabel opened the door of the washing machine and put her head into it, shouting, "BLI-I-I-I-INKERS!"

The sound of her cry was nothing like the muffled echo that happens when you shout into a small enclosed space, like the inside of a washing machine. It was the sound of calling out in a great open wood where the noise is carried away on the breeze, and K2 could feel a great rush of warm wind blowing out of the open door. It lifted Horizabel's hair with it so that it streamed out behind her.

"Oh, there you are!" said Horizabel with relief. "Do keep up..."

On the blow of the wind, a little flying object that looked rather like a small, huggable balloon, came shooting out of the open door of the washing machine, followed by a couple of even smaller ones.

"As I was saying, this is Blinkers...and—I'm so sorry, what are *your* names?"

Something tells me that Horizabel already knew their names but asking is always polite.

"Izzabird," said Izza, her mouth dropping open in amazement and delight. "And this is K2...Oh, they're so adorable, your little drones! I love them!"

Horizabel

The little mechanical objects made offended mechanical noises, and the one called Blinkers sent out a laser jet of light that incinerated the collar on Izzabird's pajama top.

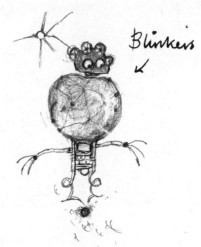

Blinkers

"You mustn't call them 'drones'—it's very rude," said Horizabel. "They prefer to be called 'robots.'"

Blinkers was the largest, the size of a small cushion. The smaller robots were the size of insects, resembling little mechanical daddy longlegs, or dragonflies.

"But who ARE you?" Izzabird asked. "And where are you from?"

"Excellent question," said Horizabel. "But a hard one to answer in a way you will find believable. I've been called so many names over the years. Fairy,

Fate, a Dryad, and Genie, but people generally know me as 'Horizabel the Grimm'...

"But I'm also a bounty hunter. And mostly I suppose I'm what you might call an 'alien,' although I hate that word because it brings to mind green people with trumpetlike ears. Very nice, I'm sure, but not really *me*. Let's just say, I'm from another world. More romantic."

"I knew it!" said Izzabird triumphantly. "What did I tell you, K2? I *knew* there were other worlds out there. Welcome to our world, Horizabel!"

Horizabel was a little surprised. "That's very open-minded of you," she said approvingly. "When I tell most people I'm an alien from another world they tend to scream and run away."

"*Bonjour? Hola? Namaste, salaam, googleplig?*" Blinkers squeaked enthusiastically, delighted by this welcoming attitude.

"ENGLISH, Blinkers," Horizabel recommended. "They speak English here..."

"OOH, ENGLISH!" said the little robot enthusiastically. "I LOVE English! I LOVE the new peoples! How beauteous mankind is! O brave new world, that has such people in it!...How ist thou? Ist thou goodings?"

Horizabel frowned and sighed. "Blinkers sometimes sounds a little old-fashioned," she explained. "We have no idea how she learned English but we think it was partly from a copy of *The Complete Works of William Shakespeare*—"

"It wast!" said Blinkers happily.

"Whereas *I* am absolutely tip-top and up-to-date, and I can blend in anywhere," said Horizabel enthusiastically. "I've got this clever instant translation device that allows me to understand and speak like a native. You'd never guess I hadn't been brought up here all my life, would you?"

Hmmm. Neither Izzabird nor K2 liked to hurt her feelings, but it wasn't *entirely* likely that she had grown up around these parts. Also, there was something rather odd about her eyes. They were a color you couldn't quite identify. And her arms were elegantly beautiful, but one was robotic and the other was shaped curiously like the five-twigged branch of a tree.

All in all, Izzabird and K2 weren't absolutely sure that she wouldn't stand out in a crowd on Planet Earth. Perhaps if she wore gloves?

"Yes, gloves would cover the arms," said Horizabel, airily waving away any possible blending-in difficulties.

She sniffed the air, putting out her tongue to taste it as well for good measure, and wrinkled her delightful nose in disgust. "This house smells unhappy," she said. "In fact it *reeks* of it. It's giving me a headache. I wonder you can live in such a gloom-smell of an atmosphere."

"Children don't get much say in where they live," said Izzabird. "But maybe you can help us with that."

"I was rather hoping you could help *me*," said Horizabel. Perhaps her smile grew a little colder for a second and the door of the washing machine closed with something of a snap, and maybe it was K2's imagination, but he thought there was a small locking noise.

"But you told us not to trust you," K2 pointed out.

"Quite right, don't tell me anything, let me guess …," said Horizabel. "House full of magic? Parents and aunts disappeared? Orphans, all alone in the world and unprotected just like me?"

"Yes—apart from the orphans bit…," said Izzabird. "We're not orphans…"

"A pirate posing as a geography teacher has recently entered your life," continued Horizabel, "and a rather splendid robot assassin. Am I right?"

"You *are* right," said Izzabird, staring suspiciously at Horizabel. "What on earth *is going on*?"

"Well…there are people who are in charge of keeping order in the universe," Horizabel explained.

"Really?" said Izzabird. "I'm quite surprised. It doesn't seem very organized to me."

"It's a big universe. They're doing their best," said Horizabel. "And on that note, the Great Ones in the Universal Government—UG for short—have just discovered that there might be people on this planet who have been using an illegal Alternative Atlas. Therefore they've sent *other* people to eliminate them."

Horizabel added this last bit in an extra jolly voice, so as not to scare the little humans TOO much. Just enough for them to understand how much trouble they might be in.

"Eliminate them?" said K2, with a gulp.

"That's right." Horizabel nodded. "It's a much nicer word than 'execute.' And, I have to admit, these assassins are GOOD...the universe's finest."

"So, that robot assassin, that's what he's here for?" said Izzabird.

"You've seen him, haven't you?" said Horizabel cheerfully. "Big guy, head like a skull? He's known as THE EXCORIATOR. He's a real hero of mine, always gets his mark. Absolutely terrifying, totally invulnerable...I'd avoid HIM. He's completely ruthless. He'll destroy without asking any questions."

Both K2 and Izzabird thought back with horror to the terrifying robot in the rain that morning.

"So...are *you* one of these assassins, Horizabel?" asked K2.

"Oh, no," said Horizabel hurriedly. "I'm just a bounty hunter, and we bounty hunters only do *necessary* violence. I'm trying to put someone who calls himself 'Cyril Sidewinder' behind bars."

Ah, well, *that* made sense. Cyril Sidewinder definitely should be in prison.

"What exactly *is* an Alternative Atlas, anyway?" asked Izzabird. Something told her that she shouldn't let on that they already had an idea of what an Alternative Atlas was.

"This is a *legal* Alternative Atlas," Horizabel explained. Out of her pocket she produced a tablet device. "You have to be a Universal Government-approved 'Atlas Carrier' to use one of these."

Horizabel showed them the little tablet. "The Alternative Atlas is a guide made up of maps of all the other worlds in the universe where there is life," Horizabel explained, swiping through the pages very, very quickly.

Izzabird's jaw dropped open. "But there are so many of them!" she exclaimed. "People have been wondering about life on other planets for the whole of human existence, and we haven't yet found any!"

"That's because they're very far away," Horizabel explained. "We're talking gazillions and gazillions of miles, numbers too big to even have a name in your language. And you're a bit backward here in this world, so you haven't found them yet."

Wow. K2 and Izzabird tried to absorb this.

"But this is the *truly* clever thing about the Alternative Atlas," said Horizabel. "There is another way to move between the worlds, a much, much quicker way than space travel (which is just crude, like bonking people on the head with a poker)."

"Wormholes?" suggested Izzabird.

"Kind of," Horizabel said. "The worlds are much closer than they may look to the human eye. And there are places on all these worlds, called 'Which Ways,' where the barriers between them are so thin that you can actually break through. The Alternative Atlas marks where those Which Ways are. The Crossing places shift slightly, all the time, because the worlds are constantly moving. The Alternative Atlas absorbs and updates these changes."

Izzabird caught K2's eye and they shared a meaningful look. That explained the moving crosses on K2's maps, then.

Horizabel swiped through an astonishing number of maps. "Let me show you what I mean…"

She clicked into one called BRABANTUA to display an introduction to the planet, then a more detailed map of one of the continents; then she zoomed in to focus on the landscape and its gigantic evolution of inhabitants, terrifying Behegommoth Gargolyles and gentle Longstepper High-Walkers who ambled through waist-high forests alongside the sweeter type of Megaliffic Cyclopes.

Other maps showed planets entirely taken over by robots, and most of these, such as Cadaria, had huge notices that flashed up on their pages reading: "NO ANIMAL OR PLANT LIFE WELCOME," or "WARNING: THE NEXT OXYGEN STOP IS ELEVEN TRILLION LIGHT-YEARS AWAY"…Some planets had two moons, and some had five…There was even one with over *six hundred* moons.

It was bewildering how many planets and places there were.

"Wooooowwwww!" breathed Izzabird as Horizabel expanded a text box with a diagram. "Look, there's a troll! And a minotaur! Does that mean they're not just in fairy tales or myths; they're actually REAL?"

"Of course they're real!" sniffed Horizabel huffily. "Up until now the Universal Government thought that human beings had wiped out all the Magical things on your own planet. You don't have a great reputation for cohabiting with other species."

Horizabel pulled up a page titled PLANET EARTH. There was a big flashing box at the top, saying: "IGNORANT. ALL MAGIC HAS DISAPPEARED FROM THIS PLANET. *Suspected reason: persecuted by local population.*"

"Is that really what happened?" said K2 in horror.

"Perhaps not...," said Horizabel. "Maybe the magical creatures and peoples who were on Earth migrated to kinder reaches of the universe where Magic is welcomed."

"Oh, how *wonderful*!" said Izzabird, enchanted by this idea.

"But why didn't our family go too?" asked K2.

K2 was thinking of his mother and father, both from Magic families, keeping their Magic secret from those in the world who would harm them.

"Good question, K2," said Horizabel. She swiped to a world called ILLYRIA and tapped on the screen.

"This is the map of the place where *I* have come from," she explained.

Illyria was a strange world indeed, full of weird pointed mountainsides with blackened tips and valleys that dug deep into the earth. It was particularly "Witch-y" in feel, with an extraordinary variety of Warlocks and Werecats and Wizards and Grimalkins, and owls with seven eyes and treacherous talking birds, because peoples or creatures who are migrating often head for places where there are already life-forms like themselves.

"A tricky place to grow up," admitted Horizabel, "but excellent training for a Grimm bounty hunter. You have to be smart to survive on Illyria. Now, let me show you how I got here."

She pointed to a spot on this map marked with an "X," on top of one of the pointed hills, in the middle of a small ring of stones.

"If I press on the 'X' marking where the Which Way is at the moment," said Horizabel as she moved

Treacherous Birds of Illyria

Mockingbirds and Liarsqwawks

The birds of Illyria are known for their inventive, lying storytelling, mimicry, and mischievous natures. If you bury a Liarsquawk feather underground in the right soil it can grow into a Witch.

the cursor and pressed down, "it takes me straight to THIS map *here...*"

On the screen there was now a detailed map of their own house and garden and, as they watched, the image zoomed inward on the upstairs bathroom, where the washing machine was marked clearly with an "X."

"See!" Horizabel said. "It's taken me to that exact place where I can push through into YOUR world. Clever, isn't it? We call this star crossing! Saves a lot of time and money on space travel...

"And I've never bothered to look this closely at Earth before, but can you see something odd about this map of your house?"

"It's covered in 'X's...," said Izzabird slowly. When Horizabel scrolled out, there were numerous "X"s scattered all over the map.

"Someone deliberately built this house on a Crossing of the Ways, somewhere where many worlds collide," Horizabel explained.

Our father's family, thought K2 and Izzabird.

"So, what I'm wondering *now* is whether pirates have been operating from this house for many, many centuries?" Horizabel said.

"Pirates—like Cyril?" said K2, thinking of Cyril's tattoo.

"Exactly like Cyril. Anyone using an illegal Alternative Atlas is known as a 'pirate,'" said Horizabel, more good-humoredly than ever. "And it's a good thing if we imprison anyone using one, because if the pirates really have been operating from Earth, the Universal Government will eliminate the entire planet."

"What do you mean?" gasped K2.

"I mean *BOOM!*" said Horizabel, with a snap of her twiglike fingers. "Just like that, no Planet Earth, gone in a heartbeat. They explode planets and stars like that all the time. I'm afraid the Universal Government is completely ruthless where piracy is concerned."

"But that's not fair!" said Izzabird. "Think of all the innocent humans and pigs and beautiful flowers and numberless little insects who would be destroyed at the same time! *They're* not using any illegal Alternative Atlases!"

"I know," said Horizabel, "but the Universal Government sees things from a 'big picture' perspective, and pirates can wreak havoc, particularly if they don't know what they're doing."

K2 and Izzabird were both struggling to take all this in.

"Travel by Atlas is very strictly controlled by the UG," continued Horizabel. "Only *twenty-four* of these legal, computerized Atlases were ever made, on the instructions of the original Atlas-Maker, thousands and thousands of years ago. The Atlases are like gold dust for they give the Universal Government a huge advantage when dealing with rebellious planets. You can lead armies by Atlas far quicker than you can travel by spacecraft."[*]

Horizabel stroked the beautiful shining sides of the computerized Alternative Atlas as if she were polishing an astonishingly rare jewel.

The Atlas purred back at her like a cat.

"Twelve of the legal Atlases are owned by the twelve members of the High Council of the Universal Government... and the other twelve are owned

---

[*]Also helpful with trade. Anyone without access to an Alternative Atlas is faced with staying home, or taking a slow ship somewhere and all the hideous paperwork that entails...

by twelve of the finest bounty hunters that the skies can provide. The youngest and the cleverest being... *me*," said Horizabel proudly.

Horizabel reached out a finger and pressed an "X" on the map on a spot in their garden beside a big holly hedge.

The screen changed...

...to a map of EXCELSIAR.

The exact same map, with the spotted lakes and the jungle creatures and the twisting skyscrapers, that K2 had drawn earlier that evening!

"So," Horizabel said, turning off the screen, "just after the legal Atlases were made, the original Atlas-Maker disappeared in highly suspicious circumstances, along with his original homemade Atlas. High and low the Universal Government searched, across the many misty miles of the dusty distant galaxies, but he and his family seemed to have vanished into thin air. But what I am wondering *now*, is...

"...was the original Atlas-Maker an ancestor of YOURS?"

K2 and Izzabird stiffened.

"Has *your* family been using an Alternative Atlas to travel between the worlds for many centuries? Have they made copies of the Atlas over the years, used them themselves, given them to Magical creatures to help them emigrate, lent copies for pirates to use? Because these illegal Atlases have been coming from *somewhere*, and it has been the job of the bounty hunters to track the Atlases down and destroy them. But there is something even better than a copy of an illegal Atlas." Horizabel paused and looked at K2 and Izzabird carefully. "Is there any one of you who might have ... *the Atlas Gift*?"

"What is the Atlas Gift?" said Izzabird, pretending not to understand her.

"The ability to create a complete and accurate Atlas out of your own head," said Horizabel. "The Universal Government has been looking for the family of the original Atlas-Maker for centuries because Gifts, however rare, tend to run in families.

"Could there be someone in your family who has this Atlas Gift?"

Suddenly Izzabird was a little concerned that maybe they had already told Horizabel too much ...

She looked the bounty hunter straight in the eye. "Not that I know of." She shrugged. "Do you know, K2?"

K2 shook his head.

"Hmmm...," said Horizabel thoughtfully. She bent down and picked up something from the floor.

It was the remains of the map that K2 had drawn in the geography lesson, now very soggy and falling to pieces. But you could still see the faint outline of a shakily drawn "X" on it.

"So...who drew *this*?" Horizabel asked, trying to sound casual.

There was no good answer to that question.

Luckily, at that moment, they were interrupted by Theo barging into the bathroom, followed by Mabel.

Horizabel and Blinkers and the other little robots moved so quickly to hide behind the door that the blast of their movement blew K2's hair back.

"What are you creeps doing?" whispered Theo. "You've woken us up! And if you wake up Annipeck, you're going to be in BIG TROUBLE."

It seemed like there was indeed going to be BIG TROUBLE.

For all four children stiffened as a Very Loud Noise Indeed came from downstairs.

KNOCK! KNOCK! KNOCK!

Something was knocking on the big front door.

And it was a much louder knock than the knock on the washing-machine door.

KNOCK, KNOCK, KNOCK!

Chapter 15 SERIOUSLY, DON'T OPEN THE DOOR! How many times do you have to be told?

Izzabird and K2 and Theo and Mabel looked at one another.

They immediately thought of THE EXCORIATOR.

"Don't open the door to anyone...," whispered Izzabird as they crept out of the bathroom toward the stairs. "Don't open the door..."

But Daniel, who had woken up and jumped out of his armchair down in the hall, was already slamming open the thick, heavy bolts of the front door, whispering "SHHHH!," desperate for the noise not to wake the baby and hoping beyond hope that this was Freya.

Behind Daniel's back, all four children were frozen stock-still up on the landing.

Don't open the door!

TOO LATE.

They watched as Daniel grabbed an umbrella out of the umbrella stand and wrenched open the door, just enough so that he could see through the crack.

There was a small pause. Daniel opened the door a little wider.

AND...

...to the children's surprise—they could just see over Daniel's shoulder—standing on the doorstep in the rain, was an extremely wet professor.

The wet professor gave an ingratiating smile that showed WAY too many teeth. In the background, there were great crashes of thunder and lightning.

"My name is Professor Cyril Sidewinder," he said politely. "I am teaching geography at Soggy-Bottom-Marsh-Place School. I think I may have the honor of teaching your children? Are you the father of"—the professor checked some names he had written in pen on his arm—"Izzabird and K2 O'Hero?"

A small pause, as if Daniel were unable to take in what he was seeing or hearing.

"I'm their *stepfather*," he managed eventually. "And I know who YOU are, Professor, because I am the *head teacher* of

Soggy-Bottom-Marsh-Place School, and I appointed you myself only this afternoon!"

"We substitute geography teachers offer a twenty-four-hour service," said the professor, still smiling. "So I popped around to suggest that your children may need extra support. They are falling behind in their geography and I wanted to offer them the benefit of some one-to-one tutoring."

A HERO KNOWS NO LIMITS

"What... *NOW?*" said Daniel.

"If it's convenient," said the professor, his smile so fixed it looked frozen. As he spoke, he wedged his toe in the crack of the door.

"I'm afraid this isn't a very good moment," snapped Daniel. "We will discuss this in the teachers' lounge on Monday morning."

Daniel tried to shut the door, but Cyril's foot was in the way. His eyes had narrowed to flinty pebbles, his smile had disappeared, and now his tone had an edge of switchblade menace. "Some people might say that it isn't very friendly to not even offer a visitor *a cup of tea* on a stormy night..."

"Oh, for goodness' sake!" spluttered Daniel. "IT'S THE *MIDDLE* OF THE NIGHT! But I suppose you'd better come in for a bit and shelter from this stor—!"

At that, Cyril pushed back the door and barged in, sending Daniel catapulting backward.

The little robot that Izzabird and K2 had seen in the classroom earlier zoomed in behind Cyril, beeping twice. The telephone in the hall made a strange fizzing noise, and smoke came out of the end of it.

Theo reached for his mobile, but Izzabird had broken it, of course.

"We're in the right place!" snarled Cyril, looking around at the many portraits and photographs of an amused Everest smiling down at him. "*BUZZ OFF AND FIND THE ALTERNATIVE ATLAS!*"

"I'm buzzing!" said Puck hastily.

The little robot flew through the hall and up toward the landing. The four children shuffled on their knees away from the banisters, but they didn't have time to hide and he spotted them immediately.

"Oh, *hello* and how do you *PHEW*?" said the little robot, transforming himself into a friendly little balloon and tipping his head at them by way of hello. He seemed pleased to see them. "My name is Puck! Delighted to make your sequaintance... We're looking for the Alternative Atlas! *But don'ts tell Plant Foodie and the Bear...*"

My name is Puck!
Delighted to make
your sequaintance.

Who were Plant Foodie and the Bear?

But Puck had already flown off, down the corridor on the first floor, toward the children's bedrooms.

Izzabird and K2 and Theo and Mabel peered over the banisters in horror.

Down below, Daniel had got to his feet and was brandishing the umbrella at Cyril in a threatening manner.

My cricket bat is RIGHT THERE, Dad..., thought Theo in frustration. *Wouldn't that make a better weapon than an umbrella?*

"STAY WHERE YOU ARE," Daniel said in his calmest, most commanding voice.

"Or what?" said Cyril Sidewinder, drawing some sort of stick out of its scabbard and pointing it at Daniel.

Daniel halted.

Daniel had an umbrella. Cyril had a—well, Daniel wasn't quite sure what it was, but it looked dangerous.

"You should have offered me a cup of tea," said Cyril, with a truly sinister smile. "Now, tell me, or I will kill you. *Where is the Alternative Atlas?*"

"I have no idea what you are talking about!" said Daniel.

Puck flew anxiously back down the upstairs corridor, squealing: "Remumber, Cyril, no unnessequary violence!"

Theo stood up. "Don't point that thing at my father! I know where the Atlas is—it's underneath the mattress in the baby's crib!"

"I *knew* it was *you* who moved it!" hissed Izzabird.

"There," said Cyril soothingly, "I thought someone would see sense."

Somewhere in the distance, Annipeck had woken up and begun to cry.

"*I'll* get the Atlas for you!" insisted Theo, suddenly realizing that in trying to save his father he might have put Annipeck in danger.

"Stay still, boy," said the pirate-professor. "I'll collect it myself."

"Don't you go near Annipeck!" shouted Daniel, charging at Cyril.

Cyril pointed the stick at Daniel, and small bolts of forked, luminous light shot out of the end of it.

Daniel dropped the umbrella with a cry of pain and collapsed to the floor.

"Daddy!" screamed Mabel in horror.

Theo and Mabel tried to run down the stairs to get to Daniel, but Cyril was already halfway *up* the stairs, his Spelling Stick pointed toward them. Just as Cyril was about to shoot another blast, Theo pushed the others around the landing corner, from where they watched helplessly as Cyril roared at Puck to follow him.

Annipeck..., thought K2, petrified. *He's going to go after the baby!*

"Stop him!" shouted Theo as he and Mabel ran downstairs to help their father.

"Horizabell!" yelled Izzabird. "Help us! *Horizabell!*"

Chapter 16 BAD THINGS IN ANNIPECK's ROOM

orizabel was in Annipeck's room already. She had put on her star cowl so she was invisible.

Close up, Annipeck looked like a perfectly normal baby: cross at being woken, standing up in her crib, wailing.

But the baby had stopped crying as soon as Horizabel walked in, even though it ought to have been impossible to see her.

Interesting, thought Horizabel.

Horizabel sent Clueless running out of the room and noted the plastic toothbrushes, who were on high alert, the electric one making growling noises.

Even more interesting, Horizabel thought.

And then she leaned on the edge of the crib, just next to where Annipeck's nose was peering over the edge, to wait patiently for Cyril.

Cyril ran in, followed by Puck. He slammed the door and locked it. Izzabird and K2 were hammering on the other side within seconds, Izzabird still shouting for Horizabel to help them.

Annipeck stiffened.

Her eyes grew wide as she took in Puck, flying this way and that.

She liked the robot.

Cyril strode straight over to the crib, pushed Annipeck out of the way, and lifted up the mattress.

Oh, how that man's face lit up when he saw the book hidden underneath! A greedy look of pure joy.

"At last *the Alternative Atlas*!" crowed Cyril Sidewinder, hugging the book to his chest, hopping from foot to foot in glee like a malevolent, tweed-suited scarecrow. "Where is Everest in this Atlas, Puck?"

"The planet of Excelsiar. See! I rembembered!"

Cyril flicked through the Atlas to see if it had what he needed. "Aha, got it!" He stopped at the pages marked EXCELSIAR.

"I lefts Everest on the edge of No Man's Land in the Forest of the Abhorrorghast...right...*there*," said Puck, pointing with his little robot arms to a spot on the map. "But..." The little robot's limbs drooped and his voice trembled. "I thunks he mights be dead by now. I's never seed him in so much trouble before..."

"Oh, that's very sad," said Cyril, licking his lips with satisfaction. "But on the bright side, you said you knew where he buried the treasure...Every cloud has a silver lining! Now, where do I go to travel to Excelsiar?"

The pirate located the "X" on the map that marked the Which Way to Planet Earth, and then turned the page to find the cross on the other side. It was in the garden of the O'Heros' house at Soggy-Bottom-Marsh-Place.

"FINALLY I can get out of this godforsaken hole of a pestilential planet!" gloated Cyril. "I can dance again across the dusty galaxies, free as a bird, not staring down at my boots in this infernal mud-pit of a world..."

Poetic, for a pirate, thought Horizabel.

And then he came down to earth, and there was murder in his eyes. Horizabel saw it.

He looked at the baby. He caressed his Spelling Stick.

"There must be no witnesses," said Cyril.

Now, I really do hope that Horizabel would have intervened to help the baby, rather than stood back and waited to see if the baby had powers to save herself.

But luckily Horizabel did not have time to make that difficult call.

For Puck panicked and blurted out: "Don't hurt the baby; *the baby is the Creator of the Alternative Atlas!*"

Cyril paused.

If this *baby* was the one with the astonishingly rare Atlas Gift, well, that made her even more valuable than the Atlas itself.

However... Cyril looked at the baby. He didn't know very much about babies, but surely this child was too small to create such an Atlas?

"Looksee how the baby is doing Cunning Work on the toothscrubbers!" whispered Puck. "And... *the toothscrubbers are made out of plastic!*"

The valiant little toothbrushes were currently attacking Cyril with all their might and main, jumping up and down on the professor's shoulder, and the baby one had tried to insert itself up Cyril's nostril.

Okay, so the baby was Gifted.

If the baby could work that Gift on plastic toothbrushes, it could work it on pencils.

Cyril reached toward Annipeck.

She bit him on the finger.

Horizabel had to put her hands over her mouth to stop herself from laughing out loud.

Cyril let out an exclamation of horror. He reached out to grab the baby again. She bit him on the other finger.

"*NAH!*" said Annipeck furiously.

Cyril's hand itched toward his Spelling Stick. Gifted baby or no gifted baby, this was too much.

"Money!" squealed Puck desperately. "This baby will get you lots and lots of *money*!"

"*Mommy!*" said Annipeck in surprise, mishearing Puck. Her eyes filled with tears. "MOMMY!"

"Your mommy is fine, baby," said Puck soothingly. "Your mommy will be back soon I am sure..."

Annipeck fixed them both with her clear gaze, and it was disconcertingly as if her baby eyes were looking straight into their internal workings, human and robotic.

"Worra MOMMY," said Annipeck with decision, holding her two arms up in the air in a regal fashion.

Cyril picked up the baby and ran toward the door. (But not before Horizabel had grabbed some diapers from the chest of drawers, shoved them in his backpack—he was going to need those—and sprayed him with one of her special cleansing sprays. She had a strong feeling that the pirate was intending to do some intergalactic travel without applying Steri-gas first.)

Cyril opened the door so violently that Izzabird and K2 fell to the floor. He was holding Annipeck and the toothbrushes in one arm and the Alternative Atlas and his Spelling Stick in the other.

He was followed by the still-invisible Horizabel, wrapped in her star cowl.

Cyril's Spelling Stick was now pointed at the baby. Annipeck's vulnerable little baby face was crumpled from crying. Her hair was sticking up.

K2 and Izzabird stood still on the landing while Theo and Mabel looked up from downstairs. Daniel was thankfully still breathing but seemed to be in a very deep sleep.

"Or wah nah ya *MOMMY*," Annipeck explained chattily, waving cheerily at her siblings as she passed.

Oh no, oh no, oh no, thought K2. *Please don't let anything happen to Annipeck.*

"Nobody move or the baby gets it," said Cyril Sidewinder.

He walked down the stairs.

K2 and Izzabird followed him, carefully, moving like little shadows down the staircase to stand with Theo and Mabel.

"Now, Professor Sidewinder," said Theo desperately, "you have what you want...this Atlas thing-y...You can leave our sister here..."

"But I need the baby...This is a very special baby," said Cyril.

Surely Cyril didn't think Annipeck had drawn the Atlas? thought K2, before disjointedly blurting out, "*Hang on!* Take *me*! *I'm* the one who—"

"SHUDDUP all of you!" roared Cyril. "Another word and I kill the baby anyway! Back off, you *worms*!"

K2 shut his mouth and the three children stood

very still, scared to even *move* in case he hurt Annipeck.

Cyril walked to the door. "Okay, Puck, you useless piece of flying mechanical junk," he said. "I order you to kill all these witnesses so that they cannot follow us."

"The master would not want that...," bleated tender-hearted little Puck.

"You're a robot! You're not supposed to think for yourself!" screamed Cyril. "And if you are disobedient *one more time*, I will personally hunt you down and dismantle you screw by screw with my very own hands! After you've killed the witnesses, come after me and the baby."

Cyril opened the door.

BAM! roared the thunder, and there, on the threshold, was a gigantic seven-and-a-half-foot-tall cloaked figure on springs, standing quiet and ready.

It was THE EXCORIATOR.

Chapter 17 NOW THAT IS WHAT I CALL A PROPER ROBOT ASSASSIN...

I t was a pretty impressive vision, I have to admit, specifically designed to be darkly beautiful so as to strike both awe and terror into human hearts.

The wind blew back the hood of THE EXCORIATOR's cloak, revealing the star-stamped skull, the sleek plastic sheen on the terrifying weaponry, the jaw agape in a great wind of a shriek, screeching at just such a pitch that it set every nerve in K2's body a-jangling in horror.

"Wow...," muttered Horizabel in admiration, staring down into the hall from the landing above, because this was the first time she'd seen THE EXCORIATOR up close. "He really is magnificent..."

THE EXCORIATOR took a step forward.

Smothering a small scream, Cyril flung the door shut, slamming the bolts across. Which would gain him some time at least.

Remember, in a house like this one, you have to be invited in.

Cyril leaped up the staircase two steps at a time, still holding Annipeck. "Destroy the staircase after I've climbed it, Puck!" he shouted. "Kill the witnesses and then follow me!"

Puck flew upward. Two metallic, hollow tubes came out of the side of his shoulders, and once Cyril reached the top of the stairs the little robot shot out two bright green lasers.

ZAP!

K2 blinked in astonishment as the ancient staircase, which had been standing there since 1859, was reduced to wood dust in one stroke. Pillows of smoke billowed through the hallway, making the children's eyes water.

Meanwhile, the handle on the front door turned once, twice. The bolts shook a little as if someone on the other side of the door was testing them.

"*COME IN!*" shouted Izzabird.

"*Why are you inviting him in?*" said K2.

"Have you lost your *mind*?" said Theo.

"He's an assassin!" shrieked Izzabird, waving her arms around. "He's probably after Cyril...Have *you* got any better ideas?"

BOOOOOOOOM! The door exploded off its hinges, the bolts ricocheting to the ceiling, and the terrifying EXCORIATOR bounded into the house.

He paused, swiveled around, his searchlight beams revolving.

The children froze in horror.

The robot assassin sprang forward and vaulted high in the air, *gloriously* high, grasped the edge of the landing with two seven-fingered robotic hands, and propelled himself over the edge in a graceful somersault, landing on his springs again.

He stopped beside the stock-still figure of Horizabel who was, most unusually for her, also frozen into immobility by this starstruck moment.

Strictly speaking, THE EXCORIATOR shouldn't have been able to see, smell, or hear her, for Horizabel had the very latest in anti-robotic shielding built into that star cowl...but apparently THE EXCORIATOR had the very latest in *anti*-anti-robotic shielding...for he turned and looked straight at

Horizabel with those extraordinary, moody, strangely human-but-not-human eyes.

"Oh, wow again...," breathed Horizabel. "He is *dreamy*!"

THE EXCORIATOR leaned forward and gently plucked the Universal-Government-Authorized Alternative Atlas out of her motionless fingers.

Horizabel was so taken by surprise that she did absolutely nothing.

THE EXCORIATOR carried on bounding down the corridor after Cyril and Annipeck.

Horizabel just stood there, saying, "WOW, wow, wow..."

"Now THAT is a proper grown-up robot assassin..." Puck sighed jealously. "Unlike me..." Then the little robot flew around and around in circles, beeping wildly and lurching from left to right in the air with indecision, pointing in four directions at once like a tiny dizzy flight attendant, before finally concluding: "Oh dear, oh dear... I can'ts KILLS you, whatever Cyril says... Toodle-oo!"

"Wait! Puck!" shouted K2. *"Where is Cyril taking Annipeck?"*

"Excelsiar," said Puck. "Must dash!"

"*Excelsiar! I knew it!*" said Izzabird triumphantly.

"Excelsiar? Where is Excelsiar?" said Theo in bewilderment.

Puck buzzed out of the broken front door.

"The garden!" shouted Izzabird over her shoulder as she ran out of the front door after Puck. She was followed by Theo and K2. Mabel stayed with Daniel, holding his hand.

"Don't worry, Annipeck! We're coming!" shouted Theo, even though Annipeck couldn't possibly hear him.

"K2, that 'X' you drew in the Atlas yesterday...," panted Izzabird as they ran across the lawn to the side of the house. "Can you remember exactly where it was?"

"In that muddy bit by the holly tree in front of the bottom hedge...," said K2.

Meanwhile, Cyril Sidewinder had run back into Annipeck's room and was now climbing out the window and down the drainpipe, along the side of the back porch, still holding on to the baby.

Where is that ridiculous little Puck drone? thought Cyril. *I'm going to need him in Excelsiar…*

On the porch stood Annipeck's stroller, a large old-fashioned, secondhand one. Transportation for the baby would be useful. Cyril grabbed the stroller by the handles and dragged it after him across the lawn.

"WET," said Annipeck disapprovingly.

"Yes, of course it's *wet*, baby," snapped Cyril as he fled. "It's *raining*. Rain is always wet."

He checked the Atlas again.

Where is the Which Way?

Finally, he spotted what he was looking for hovering quietly in a muddy bit by a holly tree in front of the back hedge.

A small shimmering piece of air that formed a slight darkening of the atmosphere at that one precise spot, like a round, old-fashioned looking glass. Perhaps you might not have noticed it at all if it hadn't been raining and some of the raindrops weren't dashing against and slowly dripping down it, as if it were a solid object instead of airy nothing.

Cyril breathed on it, and it misted up a bit. "Found it!"

Cyril drew his Air Stick.[*] He made two bright cuts in the air. For a moment, they hung there, two distinct clear white marks in that darkened atmosphere, like he had drawn an "X" in the air with a sparkler...

...and then the "X" blew open, the two parts flying apart as if they were flaps in a tent, and a blast

---

[*]An Air Stick is different than a Spelling Stick. You'll see how...

of hot air and smoke came belching out of the dark opening in the air in front of him.

"Oh my goodness . . . ," breathed the pirate, in horrified excitement. "It's been so long . . ."

He was about to step into another world.

"Hurry up, Puck!" he muttered impatiently, looking over his shoulder.

THE EXCORIATOR exploded out of Annipeck's window, crumbling the surrounding brickwork, sending glass shards everywhere, and landing gracefully on the soaking wet lawn.

Cyril couldn't wait for Puck.

He plunged through the black hole without him.

K2 and Izzabird and Theo pounded through Aunt Trudie's vegetable garden, skirted the edge of Aunt Violet's surprisingly well-kept maze, and ran up the edge of the back garden, following Puck.

They arrived on the scene just in time to see Cyril make the sword cuts . . . a shining "X" in the air . . . and Cyril and Annipeck disappearing.

THE EXCORIATOR bounded athletically after the pirate, covering the lawn in one gigantic leap.

THE EXCORIATOR didn't bother with an Air Stick. *BOOOM!* A laser-guided projectile bomb shot out of his hands and blasted the "X" wide open, and then he LEAPED right through.

One minute he was there, and the next he wasn't.

There was just a lawn, and rain, and wind.

But you could still see the huge broken "X" in the air, though it was growing fainter, a bright, clear scar, steaming in the rain.

Theo and K2 and Izzabird ran toward it and stood on the edge of the known world, staring into the unknown.

K2 touched the ragged edge. "Surely this isn't possible?"

How could there be a tear in the actual *air*?

But they had seen Annipeck go through it, and they knew she was somewhere on the other side.

They tried to push through after her, but the air was healing quickly, and it was already like putting your hand into some rather unpleasant gooey, marshy mud.

"Annipeck!" said K2 in considerable distress. "That robot is going to KILL her!"

They tore hopelessly at the unyielding now-
mixed-with-mud air.

Too late.

Even Horizabel, standing invisible behind them,
could not follow Annipeck now.

"This Which Way has closed up," said Puck
sadly, the driving rain bouncing off his rotary blades,
making him look like a tiny flying garden sprinkler.

"What do you mean 'closed up'?
What's a 'Which Way'?" panted
Theo.

"The worlds shifted,
and it's healed,"
explained Puck.

"But…how is that possible?" said Theo. *"Where is Annipeck?"*

"Annipeck is now…" Puck checked his memory systems. "Ooh…roughly…TWENTY gazillion miles away on the gorgetastic planet of Excelsiar. Three moons, abundimasses of plentiful plant life, human beings extinct but some closely related humanoid species still clinging on in there…And they've taken the Atlas with them, so there's absolutely no way of following.

"Unless you have one of those sooper-dooper fancy new rockets with the hyper-trajectory drive. Do you happen to have one of those?"

The children looked at him blankly.

"No, I thought not," said Puck wistfully. "And even then it would take about three thousand years. I'm imagining you human beings don't live much longer than—"

"—ninety or a hundred years, if we're lucky," said K2 hollowly.

Yes.

Twenty gazillion miles.

That IS a long way.

CHAPTER 18 A SHOT FROM ANOTHER WORLD

e need Horizabel! She'll know what to do...," said Izzabird, running back to the house.

"Who's Horizabel?" yelled Theo. "WHAT ON EARTH IS GOING ON?"

"She's somebody from another planet...she came out of our washing machine...she has her own Alternative Atlas...," Izzabird replied.

Now, to do Theo and Mabel justice, they took this on board without even blinking. Once your blow-dryer has come to life, and your baby sister has been kidnapped, and someone like THE EXCORIATOR has blown up whole sections of your house, outlandish explanations like this one don't seem so unbelievable after all.

"Horizabel!" yelled Izzabird as they piled back through the door. "Come quick! We need you!"

Horizabel was standing unseeable in the shadows, but at Izzabird's call she took off her star cowl and both she and her flying robots materialized in front of them.

"Who's *she*?" said Theo.

"I just said. That's Horizabel. She's the alien I was talking about," explained Izzabird.

"Mind your language!" Horizabel snapped. "Not an alien, an Otherworlder!"

"Can you help our father?" Mabel pointed at Daniel, lying prone in the hallway.

Mabel and Theo held Daniel up, while Horizabel listened to his heart.

"Will he be all right?" whispered Mabel.

Horizabel needed these children to focus so she could get on with her mission, so she put on her best doctorish-soothing-face and placed one of her twig-fingers lightly on Daniel's chest. There was a hiss like a chemistry experiment. "He's going to be *fine*!" said Horizabel breezily. "He just needs a long rest, and then he'll be right as a robot."

Daniel *did* look like he was sleeping very peacefully, so the children were reassured.

The enormity of what had happened was sinking in.

The thought of dear little Annipeck, all alone in some frightening Alternative World in the clutches of that horrible pirate-posing-as-a-geography-teacher, and being followed by that completely terrifying robot called THE EXCORIATOR, made K2 feel physically sick.

This is all my fault..., he thought to himself miserably. *That should be* me*, not Annipeck.*

The stepsiblings looked at each other with wide eyes.

What were they going to tell Freya and the aunts? "Um, you went away for *one* night and the house got destroyed, Daniel got shot, and the baby has been stolen..."

That didn't sound

My fault good.

"But WHY did Cyril take Annipeck?" asked Mabel.

"It's a bit of a misquanderstanding," explained Puck, in a tizzy. "We've been stuck on Excelsiar for three years, you see, and Cyril's an old pirate friend of his, and he asked me to fetch Cyril but I THUNKS I may have got my wires crossed, and—"

"Who has been stuck there for three years?" interrupted Izzabird. *"Who asked you to fetch Cyril?"*

Puck looked very surprised that she had to ask that question. *"Your father,"* said Puck, as if that was obvious.

Even in the terror of the moment, K2's and Izza's hearts lifted and flip-flopped in joy.

"I *knew* it!" said Izzabird triumphantly, eyes shining. "What did I tell you, K2? HE'S ALIVE!"

"Well," said Puck sadly, because robots cannot lie, "I didn't say he was alive NOW did I? Axiquentally I think he may NOW be DEAD because I saids I woulds come back immediately but I couldn'ts remember the name of the house or—"

"I knew it too!" stormed Theo. "This is all the fault of you O'Heros and your weird Witch-y powers!"

"OUR fault?" said Izzabird, immediately equally furious, and squaring up to Theo so they were nose to nose. "What a joke! This is all YOUR fault for stealing the Alternative Atlas and putting it in Annipeck's crib!"

"Arguing between yourselves isn't going to help," said Horizabel. "Do you do this Completely Unhelpful Blaming of each other a lot?"

"All the time," said K2. "What should we DO, Horizabel?"

"Don't ask *me*," said Horizabel, admiring her reflection in the mirror across the hall. "This is your problem, not mine."

Playing it cool.

"It's perfectly simple," said Izzabird stoutly. "We just go into the Alternative World and get Annipeck and our father back."

"On our own?" said Mabel, with round eyes. "But we're *children*!"

"Ands everyones on that planet REALLY hates human beings...," Puck warned them.

"Who cares?" cried Izzabird. "AN O'HERO KNOWS NO LIMITS! THE SKY IS JUST THE

BEGINNING!" She punched the air. "NO RIVERS
CAN STOP US! NO MOUNTAINS CAN STAND IN
OUR WAY!"

"Very Heroic," approved Horizabel. "A couple of
small points to bear in mind, though. The Which Way
they used has healed, the worlds have moved, you
will need an Alternative Atlas to find the new Which
Way, and you have no Atlas."

"What IS an Alternative Atlas, anyway, and why is
it so important?" asked Theo.

Extremely condescendingly, Izzabird explained
how it worked, and filled Theo and Mabel in on
everything else, as if she'd known all this for years,
rather than only finding out herself in the last half
hour.

"Horizabel, we're going to need to borrow your
Atlas," she finished.

"Please," K2 added.

"I have absolutely no idea why you think I might
help you," said Horizabel, her eyes turning very
cold and her smile as quick as a light-switch. "We've
only just met, and us bounty hunters normally work
alone. And under ordinary circumstances, the idea

that I might lend you my Alternative Atlas is, quite frankly, laughable. But I may make an exception in this case because I do admittedly need YOUR help right now."

It seemed very unlikely that Horizabel might need their help.

"Why?" asked Izzabird suspiciously.

"THE EXCORIATOR took my Alternative Atlas," admitted Horizabel. "Just took it off me! What a guy!" She shook her head in admiration. "That's why he's the best assassin in all the universe. He wants to get Cyril himself, so he takes *me* out of the equation, in one brilliant move! With the least violence necessary! You've got to admire him for it…"

The children weren't in the mood to admire THE EXCORIATOR.

This was terrible.

Even Izzabird's heart sank into the depths of gloom at this news. "But how can we travel to the other end of the universe to find our sister and dad without an Atlas?" said Izzabird.

"Puck just said he thought our father was DEAD, Izza!" warned K2.

Horizabel's eyes narrowed. "One of *you* has the Atlas Gift. You're not telling me that *the little baby* has it! She may have a very unusual Gift of her own, that baby. I've never seen Magic-That-Works-On-Plastic before, not until I saw those toothbrushes."

Yes, they all missed that Gift.

"OH!" K2 exclaimed as he realized that that explained a lot about his sister.

"But only someone as clueless as Cyril would believe that a baby that young could draw an Alternative Atlas," said Horizabel. "One of you other children has the Atlas Gift, so you do have an Atlas, it's just not drawn yet..."

"Of course!" said Izzabird.

"So I'll show you how to use the Atlas," said Horizabel, "if YOU work TOGETHER to help us get to Excelsiar...Do we have a bargain?"

"All right, I promise we'll work together to get the baby back," said Izzabird.

"I promise too," said Theo.

Mabel and K2 exchanged a disbelieving look.

"Okay!" said Horizabel buoyantly. "Let's get ready!"

They grabbed their school bags and began

stuffing them with supplies. Izzabird was obsessed with survival programs so she knew they needed one of Aunt Violet's barbecue lighters to light campfires. A rope or two always comes in handy. Her father's crampons.

Izzabird had her stolen keys to their aunts' secret workshops, so they could take some proper Magical equipment too.

Aunt Trudie's workshop was a riot of Bunsen burners and bubbling spells and plants growing everywhere, up the walls and out the windows and through the floor.

"We're traveling light," warned Horizabel. "So we can't take everything..."

She took a whole raft of Aunt Trudie's Cures, though, from the "Loshuns and Poshuns" cupboard, and Izzabird sneaked a few for herself too, including some more Animation Potion.

Freya's workshop consisted of an entirely empty room with one armchair in the middle of it.

"So BARE...," sniffed Izzabird scornfully.

"It's bare so she can think without being distracted. Sometimes things are going on that you can't see, Izza," said Horizabel, collecting some of the air from Freya's workshop into a bottle.

Aunt Violet's workshop was like the lair of Dr. Frankenstein.

"Whoaaaa...," breathed Theo, peering around at the gigantic sleeping robots in various stages of construction.

"Hmm...," said Horizabel. "Construction of robots to this Gifted level needs a Universal License. Would you say Aunt Violet was sufficiently ethically advanced to be involved in such construction?"

"I would say, definitely *not*," said Theo.

There were gigantic tanklike creatures and more humanoid constructions, all with a distinctly homemade, Aunt Violet spin to them, being made out of recycled equipment, old bits of car, and suchlike.

Izzabird argued that they might need some of the more militaristic inventions, but Horizabel said they wouldn't be necessary.

"Going into Excelsiar in one of those tanks would really draw attention to yourself. But a tiny little Flymaster Superb-O flying very low over the territory? *That*—mostly—goes undetected." Horizabel brought out something from her backpack that looked like a cross between a skateboard and a snowboard with a hole in it. She took out a beautiful orb, stamped with stars, and fitted it into the hole. The Flymaster immediately hummed into life, hovering at elbow height above the ground as soon as she let it go. Horizabel caught and stroked it affectionately. It was covered in battle scars: The edges were burned off in places, and there was a great bite out of it on one side, after a nasty encounter with a Dust-dragon on the edges of a black hole a couple of years ago.

"Anyway, we have Blinkers to protect us," said Horizabel.

Theo looked dubiously at the robot.

"Blinkers!" ordered Horizabel. "Bulk Mode!"

The children watched open-mouthed as Blinkers transformed from an adorable little buzzing balloon into a seven-foot goliath, made out of the latest and most advanced technology that Horizabel had been able to get hold of, complete with shining robotic muscles and impressive rocket-launcher back legs.

Not quite as terrifying as THE EXCORIATOR, but still a robot that commanded respect.

"You'll need thinking caps to concentrate your thought powers...any old headgear will do," said Horizabel next. "Pencils and paper for your finger powers...eyeglasses for your looking powers...And some-things-that-you-love for luck and protection."

Theo had a baseball hat, Mabel had a hat with a feather, K2 had an old woolly hat with a pom-pom, and Izzabird had a sombrero with a big wide brim. Pencils and paper were easy, eyeglasses were a bit trickier...K2 was fine, of course, but they could only find one pair of sunglasses, and so Theo fetched Mabel some binoculars and Izzabird made do with a pair of Aunt Trudie's reading glasses.

Izzabird took her scallop shell, K2 his drawing equipment, Mabel

Flymasters

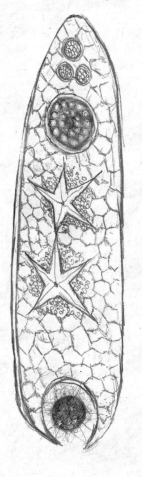

Flymasters are hoverboards that are very light and portable and can operate in whatever territory you wish: snow, desert, air, even underwater, if you have the correct breathing equipment. They are powered by an orb, which is placed in the hole at the tail-end of the board.

The Silver Starwalker, pictured here, is a particularly swift and rare Flymaster, which can reach extraordinary speeds, and should only be used by a professional Fly-rider with a great deal of experience.

her favorite book. Theo had his skateboard, and he ran up the backstairs to fetch the blow-dryer from the drawer in Annipeck's room.

"Oh, for goodness' sake," said Izzabird. "This really isn't the time to start doing your hair, Theo..."

"I'm not bringing it for my hair," said Theo. He switched the blow-dryer to On.

The blow-dryer woke up, and it seemed to be straining to go out into the garden.

"Horizabel said Annipeck has Magic-That-Works-On-Plastic," said Theo. "I thought I'd brought the blow-dryer to life with one of Aunt Trudie's potions, but it must have been Annipeck, like the toothbrushes, so maybe it can help us track her in the Alternative World. Look, it's already trying to follow where she went..."

Curses! Izzabird tried not to look too impressed. That beastly boy Theo! He'd only learned about all this stuff two minutes ago, and he was already deducing things she hadn't worked out herself.

"We have to take Dad," said Mabel, pointing at Daniel. "We can't leave him here on his own."

Horizabel shrugged her shoulders. "Suit

yourselves. I'd have thought he'd get in the way, but... Blinkers! Could you carry him, please?"

"Certainly," said Blinkers. Her squeaky voice didn't really match her new Bulk Mode.

She brought out winches from her nether regions, and gripped Daniel under the arms.

"Let me make him comfy," said Mabel, adjusting her father's head.

Blinkers lifted off, Daniel suspended underneath her, legs dangling about a foot above the floor.

Clueless didn't want to leave the ghosts in the house, who were her friends. Mabel left out large bowls of dog biscuits and set up Aunt Violet's automatic dog feeder.

"All right then!" said Horizabel. "We're ready!"

She made sure her eyes were *not* lighting up with greedy excitement.

"All we need now," she said, trying to keep it casual, "is the one with the Atlas Gift to draw the map that shows the new Which Ways between here and Excelsiar..."

"You told us not to trust *anybody*, even you, Horizabel," said Izzabird.

"Good plan," agreed Horizabel.

There was a pause.

"Unless, of course, you have no choice," Horizabel added.

Izzabird sighed.

Theo and Mabel waited for Izzabird to step forward.

Izzabird gave K2 a shove. "Go on!"

K2 pushed his glasses more firmly onto his nose, sat down at the kitchen table, and took out his pencils and one of his school exercise books.

"K2?" said Theo, in astonishment. "You're not telling me that *K2* has this Atlas Gift? Wow, that's funny...Izza, you must be so cross that it isn't *you*..."

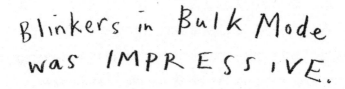

Blinkers in Bulk Mode was IMPRESSIVE.

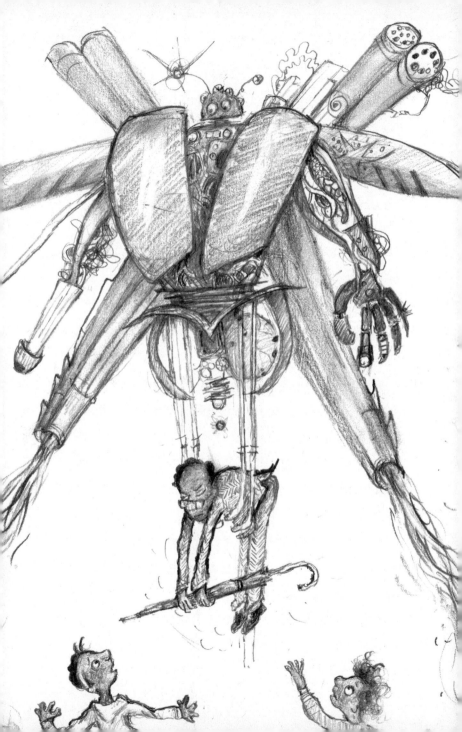

"I'm fine with it!" said Izzabird, red in the face.

"It does seem unlikely," said Horizabel dubiously. "I can generally tell from the color of people's auras how Gifted they are. Izzabird, now, you have an aura so red it's almost scarlet...that's a sign of great Giftedness, so I assumed it would be you."

Izzabird beamed with relieved satisfaction.

"What color is *my* aura?" asked Mabel curiously.

"Green," said Horizabel.

"But... *I* can't be Gifted, can I?" said Mabel. "Because I'm just an ordinary person, not like K2 and Izza..."

Horizabel didn't answer—she was watching K2. "His aura is so quiet and pale blue it is almost gray. How can it possibly be him?"

"I can't do it with all of you doubting me!" said K2, throwing down his pencil in exasperation.

"Outside!" said Izzabird fiercely, shepherding her brother out of the kitchen. It was raining hard, so K2 had to stay undercover on the porch, while the others waited some distance away; all except for Mabel, who Izzabird decided might be helpful for K2's confidence.

"Take your time, K2!" shouted Izzabird, hopping from foot to foot to keep warm.

"Just relax," whispered Mabel, sitting by K2's side. "*I* think you're brilliant."

That was helpful, but still the pencil was clumsy however much he started, over and over again.

"This is ridiculous," shivered Theo as the rain bounced off his jacket. "We can't rely on K2, he's hopeless. And this is very bad science."

"Are you saying *I* am Bad Science?" said Horizabel, offended.

"No, no, of course not," said Theo hurriedly.

"Humph. Bad Science, indeed," sniffed Horizabel. She tossed her hair, which seemed mysteriously unaffected by the rain, and then permitted herself a small smile, secretly quite pleased with the description.

Horizabel Delft: Very Bad Science. It suited her.

K2 wrote in big capitals: *EXCELSIAR*.

And then half an hour passed, with K2 getting more and more frustrated, and Izzabird shouting out every so often: "You have all the time in the world!," and Mabel whispering, "Don't worry, K2, none of this matters!"

And then it happened.

Mabel hummed something to distract K2, and he was so busy wondering what she was humming that he forgot to get in the way of what he was doing for a second, and the pencil took off, drawing the maps of the great world of Excelsiar. The sizzling deserts, the twisting skyscrapers on the floating cities, and then finally the living, breathing, tangle-thick jungle. And then he was IN there, in that trancelike state, and he forgot the porch of the House of the O'Heros at the Crossing of the Ways in Soggy-Bottom-Marsh-Place, the rain, the wind, the desperate emergency they were all in, and everyone waiting for him to finish.

He was flipping the pages, this way, that way, and the next thing he knew, Mabel was gently stopping his hand.

He came to and looked down with a start at the paper in front of him, covered in intricate maps, quivering with life, warm with the smells of a faraway world.

The others had crept closer and had been watching him for some time in a quiet semicircle as the rain poured down. Theo and Mabel were looking at him with a kind of awe.

"Thank you, K2," said Horizabel gravely. "We can go now."

She took the papers out of his hand.

The worlds seemed to have shifted quite a bit, for K2 had drawn the new Which Ways between this world and Excelsiar in a completely different spot in the garden. They had to traipse some distance through what once had been a lawn and was now a very wet meadow, past Aunt Violet's maze, to the aunts' garden shed.

The door of the shed was vibrating, just a smidgen.

As Horizabel opened the door, she took out the same sticklike weapon they had seen Cyril use. She made two quick slashes in the air, and the air itself fell apart into the Great Cross of a portal between worlds.

"So, Mr. Clever-Clogs Theo," said Horizabel, "are you going to call this 'Bad Science,' or are you going to believe the evidence of your very own eyes?"

"Impossible," breathed Theo, staring in

astonishment again as the flaps blew open and a blast of much warmer air from the other world came steaming out in a great rush, hissing into billowing clouds that made their eyes water as soon as it hit the cold rain of Soggy-Bottom-Marsh-Place.

Horizabel sheathed her Air Stick. She activated Stealth Mode and sprayed them all with Steri-gas.

"Step through very quickly. Ignore the improbability of it all," Horizabel advised.

And they pushed into the void.

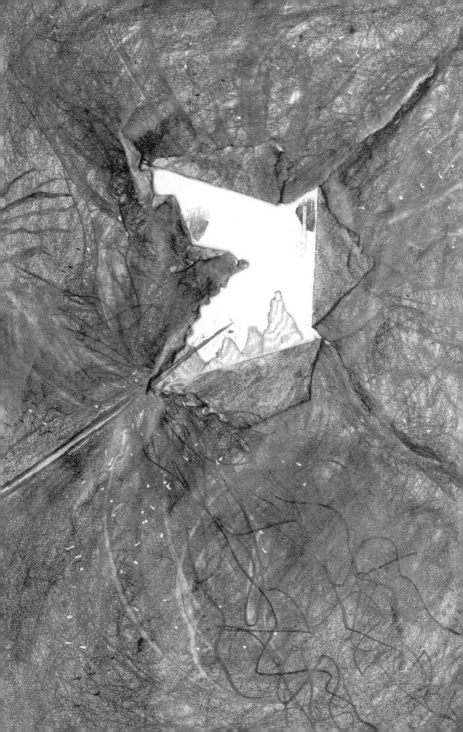

ORDINARY MOMENTS

You don't really appreciate the ordinary moments until the *extra*-ordinary things happen.

When death or illness or robot assassins come to your house...

Well, *that's* when you long for an ordinary moment.

A peaceful day. Rain on your roses.

A delicious sandwich, one of the really good ones.

Lovely, quiet, *ordinary* moments.

Take a big deep breath and enjoy the ordinary moments, people.

They're more wonderful than you think.

Part
Two

Reader, take a breath.

Have a cup of tea or a glass of orange juice.
Collect yourself before you follow.
Maybe wear some glasses, like K2.
And a stout pair of walking shoes because the
terrain could be tricky here.
Are you wearing a hat to help you dream and
imagine?
If you haven't got a thinking cap,
perhaps you should make your own...
You're going to need your wits
about you when you enter this world.
And these children need you.
They need your advice and your goodwill
and your love. You can help them if you wish to.
So. Adjust your thinking caps. Cling tight to the
thing you love the most.
Make brave your heart, wise your thoughts,
clever your fingers.

WE'RE GOING IN.

Chapter 19
GROWING A LITTLE GUMPTION

ntering Excelsiar through the "X" made by Horizabel's Air Stick was not a matter of stepping from one side to another with no resistance.

They had to PUSH their way through, and it was terrifying, thrusting through something that was more solid than air. For a second, K2 thought he was going to suffocate, but once he was halfway through he couldn't go back. He opened his mouth, tried to scream, and something choking filled his lungs...

Theo hauled on one of his arms and pulled him to the other side, coughing. Izzabird was already there, and Mabel, and Blinkers holding Daniel. All of them were on their hands and knees. Only Horizabel was upright, looking about her, very alert, Air Stick drawn, Puck and the other little robots flying above her head.

K2 gasped, breathing in the hot, unfamiliar air.

He was exhausted to the bone.

He had a headache. And he felt sick. K2 always got motion sickness, but this was far, far worse.

There was such a jumbled assault of unfamiliar sensations on his senses that it was difficult to sort out from the strange, high-pitched howling of the wind, the clamor of rich and pungent smells, the burning brightness of the colors all around, what *exactly* was going on.

All around them was a great flat desert, stretching away forever like the drifting sands of the Sahara, but it was a most extraordinary multitude of colors, some of which K2 had literally never seen before. (Try to imagine *that*.)

And his limbs seemed to move through the atmosphere in a slightly different way. No wonder Theo was taking a step and falling over. It was as if they were babies again, learning to adjust to slightly different distances and circumstances and forces than those they were used to.

But they had to adapt *fast*.

Because no sooner had they got there than

Horizabel said, casually, "Okay, Blinkers and I will be off for a bit. See you."

"Where are you *going*?" gasped Theo.

"You can't leave us here!" said Izzabird. "We have no idea what we're doing!"

"And Mabel is only nine years old!" said Theo, horrified. "We could be in DANGER . . . Didn't Puck say that everybody on this planet hates human beings?"

"Oh, for goodness' sake," snapped Horizabel. "I am not your mother. I am a bounty hunter from out of this world, and I genuinely do not care if you live or die. Because I am not only Bad Science, as you so helpfully pointed out, I am also a *very* Bad Babysitter. Are human beings always this helpless?"

"Yes," said Puck simply.

"*I* have been fending for myself since I was three and a half," said Horizabel smugly. "Time for you to grow a little gumption and begin looking out for yourselves. I have given you all the information you need, so start using it."

She smiled, that brief light-switch smile of hers, and tossed her hair. "I have alarming and possibly bloody business with THE EXCORIATOR, and I need to move fast. I have to get my Atlas back or I will be in big trouble with the Universal Government, and that is far more important than *your* piddly little difficulties. We may meet again, however, because we are both on the trail of Cyril. Your bravery may not be enough to save your baby sister!"

Izzabird stamped her foot. "We WILL be able to save her!"

"Oh, I'm sure *you* know best, Izza," said Horizabel, looking amused and shrugging her shoulders. "*I'm* only making an educated guess, after all. Trying to give you a hint, so you're not disappointed later on."

She paused a second.

The wind howled over the ghastly reaches of the endless desert.

"Well?" snapped Horizabel, tapping her foot. "I'm waiting—?"

What on earth was she waiting for?

"Um...*thank you*?" said Mabel.

"At last!" huffed Horizabel. "A little gratitude! I mean really, I give you all this helpful intelligence, both local and intergalactic, and a few hours of my precious time, so a thank-you or two should be the least I can expect…"

And grumbling, she disappeared, snuffed out into thin air in that disconcerting way of hers. As did Blinkers, still in Bulk Mode, cooing: "Bye, everyone! Nice to have met you!" and dumping Daniel on the ground as she did so. Leaving them standing all alone on an alien planet, looking rather ridiculous in their thinking caps, as the endless sands stretched out around them.

Horizabel briefly materialized again, making them jump. "Oh, and a final piece of advice, just because Mabel said 'thank you.' Head for the forest, and DON'T BE AFRAID. Remember, there are things in that jungle that hunt by the smell of fear, so if you are frightened they will track you down in seconds."

And then she was gone again.

And this time she didn't come back.

The wind screamed with such violence over the endless dusty wasteland that they could barely stand up, stinging them with sand grains like they were being bitten by millions of hungry flies. In the

distance were strange striped mountains in garish colors so vividly bright and wild that they might have been painted by a child in a hurry, around which yelled a storm of such screeching, deafening fury that it made the stormy weather back on Planet Earth look like a gently breezy day in comparison.

"She tricked us into helping her get here and then she abandons us!" shouted Izzabird. "I mean, quite apart from anything else, Blinkers was supposed to be carrying the Stepfather. Can *you* do that, Puck?"

"Off course! Naturalistically! No problemo, *amigos*!" said Puck.

"Do you have a Bulk Mode?" asked K2 hopefully.

"Well, not *as such*," admitted Puck. "But I do have... *these*!" With an air of a conjuror, a couple of teeny can openers popped out of two of his armholes.

"Those are useful when you want baked beans, Puck, but not for carrying fathers," said Theo.

"Oops! Sorry…I meant…*Squeeze!*" With a whirr, Puck went through the various implements contained in his abdomen: "Knitting needles…*no*…spoons…*no*…screwdriver …*no*…nose-hair clippers…*no*…funny little hook-type things…Yes!" Two miniature winches scrolled down from his undercarriage, hooked beneath the arms of Daniel, and launched him enthusiastically into the air.

"OOF…he's…heavy…" The Stepfather's legs remained dragging in the sand. "Easy-peasy, lemon-squeezy…," said Puck.

The four children looked dubiously up at the little robot, being blown this way and that way in the furious warrior-winds.

"That's absolutely the last time I trust a double-crossing trickster of a Grimm bounty hunter from another world, HOWEVER cool she is…," fumed Izzabird. *"This way!"*

They roped themselves together and staggered through the glowing blur of the multicolored sand.

• • •

An hour later they had made it to a tiny grove
of trees, blown so violently that they were
permanently pointing sideways, like the mean
crook of a Witch's fingers.

They rested a moment in the shelter of one great
blasted giant of a tree, somehow comforting in its
familiarity, although larger and considerably more
green than any tree that you might find on Planet
Earth.

They looked at each other.

K2 could ALREADY feel himself getting
scared, but he squashed the emotion before it got
dangerous.

Izzabird adjusted her thinking cap determinedly,
and got out her Plan Book. "Okay, we need to decide
what we're going to do next."

"Hang on a second, who made YOU leader?"
demanded Theo.

"I'm the smartest," said Izzabird.

"You are *not* the smartest! You're the most
conceited!" said Theo. "*I* should be the leader

because I'm the captain of both the football and cricket teams, so I have lots of experience."

But they weren't back at school now.

K2 and Mabel looked at each other. Horizabel had said they should work together, and here they were only an hour in, and they'd already started arguments again.

"We can't waste time arguing. I vote *Mabel* as the leader," said K2.

Mabel's and Izzabird's and Theo's mouths dropped open. "*Mabel* can't be the leader!" objected Theo. "She's too little."

"I second Mabel as leader," said Izzabird unexpectedly. Anything to stop Theo. "Which means you're outvoted, Theo. Okay, Mabel, what do we do?"

"Mabel won't have a clue what to do!" argued Theo. "She's only nine and she can't even tie her own shoelaces!"

"That's because *you* always tie her shoelaces for her, Theo . . . ," said Izzabird.

Mabel was at first astonished. But Izzabird was right: Theo always did everything for Mabel, so in her gentle unsure-of-herself way she had got out of the habit of thinking for herself. But the swagger of her thinking cap—a rather magnificent one of Aunt Violet's, with a great sweeping swirl of a pheasant feather in it—had given her confidence. So she found herself tipping that hat at an even jauntier angle, as if it were the hat of a swaggering Grimm bounty hunter, and she surprised everyone, even herself, by saying, "Actually, I *do* know what to do. K2, you didn't draw much of this 'Forever Desert,' so you need to add to your map and put in as much detail as you can..."

K2 sat down in a crook of the tree, pulled his woolly hat down low over his head, and began to draw.

As soon as he put his pencil to paper it took on a life of its own, filling in place names and labels on the seemingly endless Forever Desert, which took up most of the largest and most central continent in Excelsiar, and then the incredibly frightening No Man's Land in the heart of the Forest of the Abhorrorghast.

"I last saw Everest *here*...," said Puck, gesturing to the edge of the forest.

"Our dad!" said Izzabird, eyes shining.

"But when I left him, he was on his way *here*..."
Puck pointed to No Man's Land, which K2 had
focused on with increasingly frenzied scribbling
pencil marks, writing *BEWARE* and *DO NOT
ENTER* alongside drawings of rivers smoking and
gigantic serpents and even more gigantic plants that
appeared to have actual *fangs*. "And the precious
treasure of Everest is buried HERE," said Puck,
pointing to a spot at the corner of this scary territory.

"So we don't know exactly where Cyril and
Annipeck arrived in Excelsiar as they took a different
Which Way than us, but we do know that they will be
headed in that direction," said Izzabird.

There seemed to be a huge amount of desert to
get through before they reached the forest.

"We could use this Flying Gas?" suggested Theo,
taking out Aunt Trudie's old scent bottle, which had a
rather volatile mustard-colored gas inside it.

"The wind is too strong here, and we should
keep that stuff for when we really need it. We haven't
got very much," said Izzabird.

And so the little party of humans adjusted

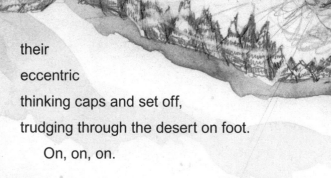

their
eccentric
thinking caps and set off,
trudging through the desert on foot.

On, on, on.

Flying way above, Horizabel looked down and saw
the pathetic insect tracks of the little human beings
and the tiny broken robot dragging the unconscious
Daniel through the huge endless swathes of desert.

They haven't got a hope, thought Horizabel.
*They'll die of thirst in the Forever Desert. And they'll
be hunted down by Flytraps if by some miracle they
ever get to No Man's Land. The story will deal with
them and then I won't have to. I mean, no WONDER
they haven't been very successful intergalactically.*

It was her first close-up experience of human
beings, and she was discovering what many had
found before her. They were

ridiculous, pathetic, but in their dogged hopeless determination, also kind of...

...sweet.

She shivered, as if she had licked a slug.

And accelerated so she wouldn't have time to think about it.

The weather in the desert was extreme.

Puck spotted an incoming sandstorm on the horizon and shrieked, "Take cover!"

"Where?" cried Theo, for all around them was just a blur of sand.

"Dig a tunnel!" yelled Izza, on her hands and knees already. The others joined her, furiously scooping out the sand with their hands.

Puck dropped Daniel, thrust pincer-spades through his armholes, and got to work. He dug the fastest, spraying sand around like a gigantic beetle. By the time the gale hit them they had dug a hollow sufficiently deep to crawl into to take cover, although when they dragged the unconscious Daniel down after them, his feet stuck out of the tunnel opening as he was too long to fit.

The storm raged, the rainbow sand above turning sharp as needles, so wildly was it blown by the winds.

And when the storm died and they emerged, blinking like little moles, into the glittering Excelsiar sunlight, they had to trudge on. Every now and then the clouds cleared and K2 caught his breath as they got an astonishing glimpse of one of the immense floating cities drifting on the clouds far away on the horizon, or a plume of smoke and an explosion that must be coming from the diamont mines to the north. But other than that it was just sand, sand as far as the eye could see, and the howling of the wind.

After six hours of trudging, they were a pathetic sight indeed. Theo was carrying the newly elected leader, Mabel, on his back, so tired she was nearly asleep.

Izzabird got K2 to check where they were on the map.

"But we've barely moved!" said Izzabird in horror as K2 pointed with an exhausted finger to somewhere that seemed to be exactly the same place they had been in six hours earlier. "How are we ever going to cross this desert?"

And then K2 could feel his stomach dropping with horror as the ground around them seemed to rumble, and...

...*BRRRMMM*...

...the sand shook and rippled as though it were a sea.

BRRRMMM...

"What's that?" whispered Theo, eyes round, arms around a shaking Mabel. "Is it an earthquake?"

They sheltered behind a sandbank, trembling.

BRRRMMM BRMMM...

The shaking grew louder, louder. And on the horizon they could see them. Great moving *things*, traveling through the desert in unbelievable numbers.

"What are they, Mabel?" whispered Izza through white lips.

"They look like...*trees*...," said Mabel, passing her binoculars to Izzabird, because she couldn't believe her eyes. "But they can't be! They're WALKING. And SINGING."

Walking, singing trees?

Impossible, unimaginable, inconceivable.

But they were indeed trees.

Thousands upon thousands of trees migrating in dreadful desperation, for many miles to the west, the lovely, life-giving sludge of the ground underneath them had dried up.

In terrible thirst, the trees had slowly, painfully, pulled out their roots from the desert underneath and began moving purposefully eastward, dragging their poor skeleton branches behind them, in search of a forest where they could plant their roots and grow their leaves and drink again once more.

And as they walked, the trees were singing the slow, sad song of The Traveler, familiar to all those who have had to leave beloved homelands in search of more welcoming climes.

Izzabird handed back the binoculars to Mabel. "I have a Plan," she said. "They're going in the direction of the forest, aren't they? Let's hitch a lift."

"But they're too big! They'll crush us!" objected K2. "Mabel, what should we do?"

"Izzabird is right," said Mabel, lifting her weary head. "Quick! Before they move past us!"

Theo didn't like doing anything that was Izzabird's idea. But he was exhausted too.

So Theo set Mabel on her feet and took her by the hand, and the four children ran toward the great trees.

K2 thought his heart would burst with the effort of trying to catch and keep up with the Great Singing Trees.

Theo leaped first, onto a flailing root, dragging Mabel up after him.

Luckily the tree didn't seem to mind, too involved in the misery of its relocation to pay much attention to its human burden.

Izzabird was next. K2 tried to get there, stumbled, missed, and fell flat in the sand. He forced himself up, ignored his burning legs, while everyone shouted, "Come *ON,* K2!" And then he leaped again and this time landed safely, clinging onto the comforting bark. He slowly dragged himself up the tree, hand over hand, scratching his face but not even caring, until he was sitting next to Izzabird and Mabel and Theo on a thick branch.

Puck was last, dragging the dead weight of

Daniel behind him, and they had to haul him up together, balancing him on a fork in one of the branches, his arms and legs swinging limply on either side.

They peered out through the branches of the tree as it walked in huge purposeful strides toward the distant smudge of the Forest of the Abhorrorghast.

Finally, they were on their way to find Annipeck.

How would poor, little, defenseless baby Annipeck be coping in this terrifying world?

Chapter 20 HOW IS POOR LITTLE DEFENSELESS BABY ANNIPECK COPING?

As it happens, I am a little concerned about how poor little defenseless baby Annipeck is coping myself, so I am going to take you to a quite different part of Excelsiar to find out.

Cyril and Annipeck had come through a Which Way a little farther to the east, already in the forest.

"Everest buried my treasure in somewhere called 'No Man's Land.' We'll have to travel fast, little baby, in case that large, scary robot is following us." Cyril checked K2's Alternative Atlas and noted all K2's warnings about not getting frightened, so he drank a swig of Calming Potion to take away any feelings of alarm.

Annipeck wasn't scared at all, but looking around at this new environment with excitement and fascination.

Cyril put Annipeck's stroller on a little swing attached to a small carrier drone that he always had ready in his backpack, and kept a sharp eye out for any of the nastier life-forms that might be interested in attacking them.

But that first day, Cyril and Annipeck went through the jungle unchallenged.

The vegetation was tangled and impenetrable on the jungle floor, and covered by a smothering blanket of cress. The cress grew over everything, up trees and around thorns and vines in a thick carpet, making it hard to see what was going on underneath.

Cyril used Stilt Boots to carry himself over the difficult terrain and Annipeck was so interested in the swing, and Cyril's boots, and in where she was, that she spent most of the time wondering and pointing at all the extraordinary jungle creatures, like the great green tiger-griffs with their saber teeth and pointed wings padding carefully along the tree branches, and snakes every color of the rainbow curled among the cress. But eventually she said: "Worra YOW ARGH."

"*What?*" said Cyril, fiddling with the handy translation device he had in his ear[*] (the same one that Horizabel was wearing, as it happened). But although the device worked on every possible language you could think of—Elf, Werewolf, Tree . . .

---

[*]This is a bit more convenient and less yucky than a fish in your ear (see Douglas Adams).

I do mean *everything*—unfortunately it did not speak Annipeck's own private language.

Cyril was going to have to work this out on his own.

"What are you talking about?" he barked. "Why don't you speak proper English, you silly little baby? I don't understand."

Annipeck spoke some English for Cyril because he was clearly struggling to keep up, poor man. "FOOD!" she said patiently, but also loudly and firmly. "FOOD *NOW!*"

Cyril still hadn't quite recovered from the horror of his first diaper-changing experience, which had happened half an hour earlier, so he wasn't in a good mood.

"We can't stop for food; we're in a hurry...," he snapped.

Annipeck began to wail.

Cyril's eyes opened wide in horror. "No!" he hissed. "Be quiet! You're going to draw the attention of the jungle that is currently ignoring us! There are BAD THINGS out here in this jungle..."

Annipeck wailed even louder.

"Okay, okay!" he said hurriedly, coming to a halt

Omni-babel-o-phone

This enables you to speak and understand any language: Elf, Werewolf, Tree. It will eventually attune itself even to Annipeck's private language.

For example:

← translation device

Speakers

mouthpiece

Annipeck: Worra worra aw ma yow car car coo?
Translation: Can we go and say hello to that leopardshark?

Annipeck: Sooarah, war urgle me o oar roawoit.
Translation: I am so sorry, my Lego needed to sleep in your socks.

Annipeck: Lor war co poo poo yow.
Translation: My diaper needs changing.

and letting down his Stilt Boots. "We'll stop here for the night, and have some tea! Lots of lovely food for you . . . ," he cooed, and then muttered under his breath, ". . . you horrible little brat."

Cyril hadn't traveled in a while, but he knew enough about jungles on alien planets to set up camp halfway up a tree, with branches so vast they were like the floors of a house.

Cyril had brought plenty of supplies with him. "There you are, baby: a PB&J sandwich for you, and hummus and pickle for me . . ."

"AR way," said Annipeck, pointing at the hummus and pickle sandwich.

"Surely you don't want MY sandwich?" wheedled Cyril through gritted teeth. "Nobody but me likes hummus and pickle. You're a baby . . . babies LOVE PB&J!"

Annipeck gave a little warning scream, wriggled her fingers, and one of her toothbrushes stood to attention, covered itself with toothpaste, and smeared it over Cyril's sandwich.

Cyril gave her the rest of his hummus and pickle sandwiches.

After Annipeck had polished off all Cyril's sandwiches, she toddled over to Cyril's sleeping bag and lay down in the middle of it.

"That's MY bed, baby," said Cyril firmly, removing the sleeping bag from underneath Annipeck, and getting into it.

Annipeck just laughed, held out her two little arms, and made grabbing motions with her fingers, and the sleeping bag unzipped itself, tipping Cyril out on the tree branch.

Cyril sat up in astonishment.

He zipped himself up in the sleeping bag again. And found himself unwrapped, rather more roughly this time, rolling over and over before he sat up, to see the sleeping bag wriggling across the branch as if it were a live creature and snuggling itself around Annipeck.

Cyril's heart sank.

This baby's Weird Magical Powers were going to make the whole kidnapping operation rather more taxing than he had hoped.

He put on his most beseeching singsong voice. "You can have the baby blanket, because you're a baby!"

A steely look came into Annipeck's eye. "Wor arra whoa YER oway," said Annipeck.

The electric toothbrush turned on its motor. "Ggrrr...," it whirred warningly.

Cyril was beginning to speak Annipeck's language.

Glumly he settled down on the tree branch and pulled the baby blanket over his shivering knees.

Annipeck gave Cyril a bright, approving smile.

She made grabbing motions with her hands again. The toothbrushes brushed Annipeck's teeth, kissed her good night, and hopped into the lovely, warm, snuggly sleeping bag beside her while her Lego bricks built themselves into a tiny Lego teddy bear.

"Grandpa, SING!" commanded Annipeck. "Worra, worra, ickle STAR!"

"I'm not your grandpa and I really can't sing," begged Cyril.

But the glint in Annipeck's eye told him otherwise.

With a sigh, he submitted to the voice of authority.

There, in that alien jungle glade, halfway up a tree smothered in cress, heady with the scent of exotic flowers, and the leopardsharks and dolteeth no doubt sleeping not far by, came the familiar little tune of "Twinkle, Twinkle, Little Star," sung in the grating voice of the pirate, every word out of tune and spat out like a threat.

> *"Twinkle, twinkle, little star*
> *Heading to Ex-cel-si-ar*
> *Way beyond the distant Poles*
> *Watching out for great black holes*
> *Wander, wander, little star*
> *Heading to Ex-cel-si-ar."*

After a while, to Cyril's relief, Annipeck gave a big yawn.

She looked around at the darkness of the strange forest.

She was not frightened, no, for she was going to find and rescue her mommy, who was in trouble.

But she *did* put on her dinosaur hat.

"*REOORR...*," growled Annipeck fiercely at the forest. *"REOOORR!"*

And then she fell asleep.

Yes, I think that although she is still in dreadful danger, it does seem that Annipeck is quite capable of dealing with Professor Cyril Sidewinder.

In fact before too long he may even feel that *he* is the one in need of being rescued.

But there were far darker things than sleeping leopardsharks listening to the baby and the pirate, watching and waiting in the shadows. No, not THE EXCORIATOR, he's still miles away, though closing fast.

There was the Beast, way in the background.

And some things without faces, only jaws.

Some things that looked like a whole load of jungle vines twisted around each other. But vines that *moved*, this way, that way, like the slow weaving of a gigantic boa constrictor.

In one of the Something's jaws was an entire leopardshark, slowly being digested.

For although this Something was made out of plant material, it was not a herbivore itself.

These dreadful plant Somethings were carnivores.

They ate leopardsharks.

They ate poglets.

And they ate human beings.

Chapter 21 PUCK'S NOT VERY RELAXING BEDTIME STORY

he trees were still walking in the desert to the east, with K2 and Mabel and Theo and Izzabird and the unconscious Daniel perched up in their branches.

On they went, till the sun went down over the desert and K2's arms were trembling with the effort of continuing to cling to the Walking Tree.

"Okay!" said Theo. "We need to get some sleep."

"We're going to sleep *here*? In a Walking Tree?" said Mabel.

"Well, we haven't reached the edge of the desert yet, and we still have a long way to go," said K2, checking the map.

Theo had the bright idea that they should roll themselves up in the big leaves of the tree, as if they were settling down in hammocks.

"Let me tells you a relaxing bedtime story," said Puck as they ate their packed food, and Mabel gave her sleeping father some water, and three moons

rose above the miles of long and
lonely desert. "I'm not sure if this
is a ghost story, or *his*-tory...,"
said Puck. "And I's not sure if it's
true or not...

"But...

"...*I has been here before*," whispered Puck.

There was such a something of horror in the
robot's tone that the hairs on the back of K2's neck
prickled to hear him.

"Well, of course you have, Puck," said Izzabird.
"You came here with my dad. Can't you tell us about
that?"

"Don't remumber, is too reece-quent," said Puck.
"I is better with a long-time-ago. The heart of me is
old, you see. People *adds* to me, and they *tinkers*
with me," said Puck,
"but...the heart of me
is old."

Tick-tock, tick-tock
went the beat of his little
alarm clock of a heart as
Puck began his story.

The Tale
of
the Beast

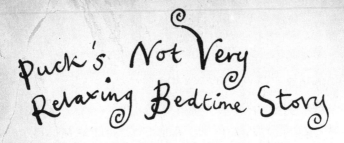

Puck's Not Very Relaxing Bedtime Story

"I has come here, ooh, many more than one squndred years before, with a Mr. Bernard-the-Dane O'Hare, Esquire, who was an an-questor of yours," said Puck.

"Hang on a second," said Izzabird, "shouldn't he have been called O'*Hero*?"

"Shhh," said Theo.

"Bernard-the-Dane was a desquendant, just like you, Izza and K2, and your father, of the very FIRST Atlas-Maker," Puck continued, "the only one befores K2 here to have the Atlas Gift…"

K2 blushed.

"The FIRST Atlas-Maker was way back in the mists of time," said Puck. "As soon as he creates that Atlas, he knows he is in trouble, and the UG will want to kill him, for it gives him too much power. So he flees through all the star-speckled galaxies, until he and his family finds a safe hiding place right on the edges of the universe on little old Planet Earth.

"And for a long time the family stays mouse-quiet so nobody knows they are there.

"But this is a family with itchy feet...

"*They* starts using that Atlas to help the Magic things escape from Planet Earth, to go adventuring, and to go adventuring themselves.

"Bernard-the-Dane now, *he* was a jolly gentleman-burglar, if you like and, O, what a time it was...," said Puck. "When we *first* comes here to this yumptious land, 'twas none of this endless desert, none of this sand that gets in the creaks and the wheels of a body. Not a thing there were but miles and miles of Silk Trees, blowing mild and milken in the endless breeze, leaves softer than a honey kiss, far as the eye could seek-um. And you could not move for butterflies."

Puck gave a sigh at the memory.

"The perfect place for a picnic, which is exactly what he had—a very deliciousness one—herring-and-cress sang-wiches, strawberries 'n' cream, all washed down with great gulpings of mead. But when we next comes *back*...." Puck's voice got deeper.

"Why, I thought Mr. Bernard-the-Dane O'Hare's blood-ticker would break in two, I did. He hadn't used the Steri-gas, you see, and a single strand of cress he had brought with him in his sang-wich had brought a plague upon this land, which made my eyes of metal weep such tears of loss to see it… The trees were dead, the sprites were starved to matchsticks, and the butterflies fled to the last remaining forest.

"And worser still were the *other* pirates that came after, many using pages of the Atlas given to them carelessly by Bernard-the-Dane O'Hare. Crooked of heart and mean of claw, *Warlocks*, nasty things." Puck gave a shiver. "The dying of the silk trees had exposed a precious mineral called diamont. The Warlocks came through the Which Ways, with their diggers and their robots, to mine the diamonts and rip the soul from the peaceful land while the trees they were a-dying all around…"

K2 remembered diamont mines on the edge of his maps, the belching smoke they'd seen on the horizon earlier in the day.

"Now, Bernard-the-Dane he was a bad'un, but he was a bad'un with a *heart*," said Puck. "So that's when Mr. Bernard-the-Dane O'Hare, Esquire, made the solemn swear." Puck put one of his little robot arms up in the air to replicate the long-dead ancestor of the O'Heros making his vow. "That he woulds make amends and bring a Cure for the Plague of the Silk Trees to this land of ghost-leaves, and conjure it back to life!"

"Oh, well done him!" cried Mabel.

"Quite right," said K2.

"But what *happened*?" said Izzabird, eyes round as moons. "Did he do it?"

"Well, you can see he didn't," said Theo sadly.

"It weren't for want of *trying*, though," said Puck. "He tried to find that cure all his life, poor star-soul, mortal thief-of-leaf, human earfling, *oh* how he tried, his window bright with light, late into the watches of the night in the House of the O'Heros, making his messes and his noises and his chemical reactions, but an earfling life is as quick and short as a moth's, and he died without ever finding it."

There was a short pause.

"Well, *that* isn't a very cheerful bedtime story, Puck," said Izzabird.

"It hasn't comes to the scary bit yet," said Puck, in a very small voice. "You sees the Beast they call 'The Abhorrorghast,' why *he* was a young'un when that happened. He only had the three tusks then, and his poison not come in yet. And his beastly heart, it broke in two to see his yumptious trees all fallen. So he makes his OWN swear...

"He swears by all the fish in the sea...

"He swears by all the stars of the sky...

"He swears by all the galaxies in the universe...

"He will not rest...

"Until he has KILLED every single human being on the entire planet of Excelsiar.

"Starting with his Curse on the family of Bernard-the-Dane O'Hare...

"...and *every single one of his desquendants, especially anyone with the Atlas Gift.*"

"And by desquendants he means...?" asked Izzabird.

297

"*Us*, Izza," said K2 nervously. "By 'descendants' he means *us*. And me in particular."

"That's right," said Puck. "Desquendants means Mr. O'Hare's family, his grandchildren and his great-grandchildren, and his great-great-grandchildren, going right back down 'unto the end of time,' I thinks he said. He was quite specifiwhatsit about that. And he's indeed killed ALL the human beings on the planet since then, and turned his anger on the elves and the centaurs in the cities. That was the dying of a great dream of harmony, that was..."

Puck shook his little robot head.

"And now the cities becomes all FLOATY," said Puck. "They used to be peacefully down on the ground, with elves and centaurs and Cunning People and Wild Things all living happylike together, in harmony, with silk trees in the streets, the buildings and the jungle all growing around each other. But the Beast found out the citizens of those cities were in league with his miner enemies. He started attacking them so angrily that the cities cut loose the rocks that bound them to the ground, and went flyings up, up to the safety and freedom of the sky on a bed of gas, where they wander across the continents and the oceans, forever hoping for a time when it might become safe to land once more.

"And the Warlocks and the robot diamont miners is still tearing out the soul of this planet and putting it out of balance, poisonings the air and creating the warrior-winds and making the Forest of the Abhorrorghast smaller and smaller and smaller. If the Abhorrorghast doesn't win the war against THEM, and the cress, this whole WORLD will turn to desert."

This *wasn't* a very happy story.

"But at least Mr. Bernard-the-Dane O'Hare was all right!" said Puck, trying to cheer himself up. "He skedaddled right back to the safety of Planet Earth to seek his cure, where the Beast could not get him, and changed his name to O'Hero."

"Because no one would break *that* code," said Theo sarcastically.

"And so . . . the O'Hero family lived happily ever after!" finished Puck.

Can a Tale with such a Beast in it have a happy ending?

The joyful ending seemed rather hastily joined on to the rest of the tale, so nobody was very happy about it.

The wild wind yearned over the great bleak reaches of the desert. K2 felt sick.

"Puck," said Mabel at last. "Was Bernard-the-Dane O'Hero a man with a Viking helmet and a long gray beard and a walking stick?"

"Yes!" said Puck eagerly. "That's him, the poor misguided young earfling! Did you know him?"

"I think I may have met him once," said Mabel, thinking back to the lean gray ghost she had once seen curled up in the linen closet, trying to get warm, in the House of the O'Heros.

"But here is what has been worrying me," said Puck longingly. "Can a tale with such a Beast in it have a happy ending?"

"Of course it can!" said Izzabird optimistically.

"You just need a plan," said Theo.

"A really, really imaginative one," said K2.

"Poor Beast," said Mabel.

"Oh, that has made me feel better," said Puck with an admiring shake of a head. "I'd forgotten how great

the young

humans are."

Hmmm.

They were

entering the

territory of a

Beast that had not

only wiped out every single human

being on the planet but also had a personal

vendetta against the entire O'Hero family, and K2 in

particular.

They didn't fall asleep for quite a while after that.
The desert was alive with eyes, and the noise of who
knows what battles and creatures having their nighttime adventures. But they knew that Puck, ticking
comfortingly in the background, would sound the
alarm if any real danger approached them; so they
all fell asleep eventually. Being wrapped up in the
big warm furry leaves swaying in the breeze was like
sleeping in the lull of a hammock on a ship, riding the
waves that were taking them across the wild desert
of the seas into uncharted waters.

302

They slept as peacefully as could be expected, given they were worrying so much about Annipeck and trying not to think about what Horizabel said about them being orphans. And perhaps they would not have slept at all if they could have seen what was following them...

THE EXCORIATOR.

The minute or so later that THE EXCORIATOR had come through the Which Ways after Cyril and Annipeck had been enough time for the worlds to shift, so that he arrived in a rather different place in Excelsiar than they had.

He too had been making his way through vast reaches of the desert.

And now he had picked up their scent, and he was following them at a distance.

For they would lead him to whatever he was looking for.

Chapter 22 NOBODY SAID THIS ADVENTURE WAS GOING TO BE EASY

Cyril and Annipeck were still some way ahead of K2's party.

And as time wore on, the two unlikely traveling companions got used to each other's little ways. There was the odd temper tantrum from Annipeck because Cyril wouldn't let her use the Stilt Boots, but apart from that they settled down into quite a cozy rhythm, with Annipeck still happy that they were traveling toward her mommy, and Cyril still happy that with every day that passed they were traveling closer to where Everest's treasure was buried. Their happiness hid them from the jungle.

To the west, the Singing Trees were still walking, and the children perched up in their branches passed the time in their own way.

This was a time for thinking, Izzabird said, and they might not get that later.

So they pulled their thinking caps extra firmly on their heads.

K2 drew map after map of Excelsiar, searching for a Which Way back to Earth that was closer to the Forest of the Abhorrorghast than the one they'd come through. "We may have to make a quick getaway when we find Annipeck," he explained to Mabel.

Inspired by watching the aunts on the back of their Hoovers, Theo was obsessed with creating flying apparatuses to travel across difficult terrain. So he experimented with tiny mixtures of Flying Gas and Animation Potion on his skateboard and on broken branches of the Singing Tree, drawing designs and adding bits and taking them away again.

"Waste of time," said Izzabird with a sniff. "You haven't got enough equipment and you're not even a Cunning Person, and you're never going to make that old skateboard of yours look anything like Horizabel's Flymaster Superb-O."

But secretly she was just as thrilled by the idea of flying as Theo was. Gradually, she edged closer to look over his shoulder at what he was doing. And after a while she said, "It's hard enough balancing on a skateboard on the *ground*, Theo, but if you fall off midair you could die. Riding a tree branch would be better..."

"Nobody asked *your* opinion, Izza!" snapped Theo. And Izzabird withdrew again, in a huff, until her fascination overcame her sulking, and she moved back to his side.

This time she had a more positive suggestion for an improvement.

"I brought a Sticking Potion," said Izzabird. "You COULD borrow some of it and stick your shoes to the skateboard, a bit like ski boots..."

"*That*," said K2, in a heartfelt sort of way, "is a completely ridiculous idea."

But Theo *liked* this ridiculous idea.

So although he pretended not to hear it, he shifted just a smidgen on his tree branch, making room for Izzabird to sit beside him.

From then on, Theo and Izzabird worked together.

And from then on Theo and Izzabird worked together, Theo's thinking-cap baseball hat bumping against Izzabird's thinking-cap sombrero, mixing potions and pulling their glasses over their eyes, and taking turns to draw prototypes that they christened "Flymaster Homemade-Os" in Izzabird's Plan Book.

Before long, Izzabird was secretly wishing *she* had brought a skateboard so she could make her *own* Flymaster Homemade-O, but Theo generously said she could borrow his sometimes, and they would make a really cool tree branch flying-thing for her.

"They're both completely reckless. But at least they're not arguing," said K2 to Mabel.

Izzabird got Puck to tell them lots of stories about Everest, because Puck had been Everest's traveling companion ever since he was a little boy, and Puck had a much better memory about things that happened in the past than things that happened only yesterday.

Mabel sat with K2, helping plan their journey on his more and more detailed maps. "There's a river we can pick up here, in the forest, that leads right into and through No Man's Land," Mabel pointed out.

And, throughout all this, Daniel still lay in the branches, sleeping. Mabel sang to him in the hope that it might wake him up.

Typical of my father, thought Theo, raising his eyebrows exasperatedly. *Here we are in danger on an alien planet, and he's unconscious.*

They finally reached the end of the desert and the edge of the Forest of the Abhorrorghast.

"It doesn't feel like the trees are going to stop anytime soon," said K2, checking the map, "and we're heading toward those pointed mountains in the north. If we're going to find that river, I think we need to get off now!"

They climbed down the tree and jumped off one of the roots, waving goodbye and shouting a "thank you for the lift,"

although the tree was so intent on
its journey that it did not respond.
And then there was a hair-raising
half hour in which they had to dodge all the other
migrating trees to get out of the walking wood.

"Shouldn't we try flying now?" suggested Theo.
He and Izzabird were dying to test their creations.
He was pretty sure they'd got the quantities of
gas and potion just right, and they were looking
beautiful. They had drawn dragons on Theo's
Flymaster Homemade-O and flames on Izzabird's
tree branch—in red to match her aura—and they
had even made tree branches for K2 and Mabel, with
birds and dogs on them.

But to Theo's and Izzabird's surprise, K2 put his
foot down. "I don't care *how* many dragons or birds
are on them. They look incredibly dangerous," he
said. "It's still too windy. And we need to save
the Flying Gas for an emergency.
In any case, Mabel and I
have a plan."

"We need to find the river," Mabel insisted. "It will take us right into the heart of No Man's Land. We shouldn't be doing things just because you want to try out your inventions anyway. It's not going to help Annipeck if we kill ourselves falling out of the sky."

It was the longest speech K2 had ever heard Mabel make, and he thought it was very sensible.

It didn't please Theo at all. "That's the last time I carry you on my back, Mabel Smith," he grumbled.

But the distance they'd run, trying to get out from underfoot of the Walking Trees, meant they'd overshot their original route. So they headed into the forest on foot, hoping they'd pick up the river later nonetheless.

On, on, on.

Many hours more, avoiding creatures that looked like they might hurt them, tripping over vegetation, too weary to marvel at the sights, a wakeful, uncomfortable night up a tree, another meal of biscuits and bread, and then hours again the next day. Getting dirtier and tired-er, and trying not to get more scared.

Nobody said this adventure was going to be easy.

Chapter 23 CYRIL GETS A
LOVELY SURPRISE AND A DREADFUL
SURPRISE ALL IN ONE AFTERNOON

B y the next day, Cyril and Annipeck had
traveled across the border into No Man's
Land. Cyril had begun to think K2's Atlas
must be wrong about this supposedly-scary Forest
of the Abhorrorghast. Nothing bad had happened.
The moonflowers did seem to be turning their heads
in their direction, clouds of wandering butterflies
were following them as they walked, but they did not
appear to bear the pirate or the baby any ill intent.
There was no sign of any predators.

And then, to Cyril's joyous, hungry excitement,
he found the spot where it said that the treasure was
buried.

Down dug the greedy pirate, heart trembling.
Down, down and, two feet under, he found a
promisingly heavy little box covered in dirt and muck.

His eyes lit up with glee, and he danced a jig of
joy right there with Annipeck clapping along beside

"I'm going to be RICH!" him and the toothbrushes and her Lego bricks jumping up and down too, for Cyril's elation was infectious.

"I'm going to be RICH!" gloated Cyril.

It took him two minutes to break open the lock of that box with the edge of his Air Stick. But when he opened it up, no winking jewels and gold of astonishing value greeted his hungry eyes.

Only a key.

And a note.

What a blow!

Cyril threw the box to the ground and bit the key in temper.

But maybe the note would say where the treasure was hidden?

With unsteady, frustrated fingers, Cyril opened it.

All it said in large, fancy, loopy handwriting, was "DO NOT BE AFRAID."

What did *that* mean?

312

Cyril looked around the clearing. Nothing there. He'd been tricked.

But as he looked, his disappointment, his fury, turned to a tiny *itch* of disquiet.

For as soon as someone tells you NOT to do something, suddenly that is *exactly* the thing you want to do most.

DO NOT BE AFRAID...

Cyril felt the stir of fear in his pirate innards.

And as fear turned to little beads of sweat on his forehead, the tempting, delicious smell of anxiety wafted off Cyril's skin and out into the forest all around him.

What was that?

Cyril turned his head sharply.

A rustle in the edges of the dell. A lick-spit of concern. And then a coil of vine crept into that clearing all of its own accord.

A sick lurching in Cyril's stomach, and the coil of vine grew faster, unfurling like beautiful, menacing fingers. And as the lithe ringlets of racing creepers gathered pace, pushing into the cress, even the massive Propiandibur trees were hauling out their roots, shaking off the clogging earth and vegetation, and staggering out of their path.

UH-oH...

For these were vines you did not want to stand in the way of.

One large tree did not move its roots fast enough, and six of the vines wound themselves around it, strangling it, until it melted into sap with the violence of their poison.

Puck could have told them that these vines were carnivore plants known as Mortifer Flytraps, and the heads of the Flytraps, as they entered the clearing after their reaching tendrils, were larger than tigers and bristling with thorn-sharp teeth as deadly as daggers…

In a blink of an eye, twenty of the Mortifer Flytrap heads were now in the clearing, their faces turned toward the human beings in the center.

Annipeck's eyes opened wide as the horrified, faithful toothbrushes tried to brush off the first lick of Flytrap tendril touching her cheek.

And then one Flytrap whirled a thicker tendril around and around its head like a lasso, before shooting it out. The tendril caught one of Annipeck's plump little legs, grasped it firmly, drew her back across the forest floor, and held her upside down in front of the Flytrap's expressionless skull of a head. Juice dropped from its open jaws.

Annipeck tried not to be frightened.

She peered out fiercely from her dinosaur hat and shouted:

"REEOOOWWWRR!"

For a moment, it looked like the Flytrap was going to swallow her in one gulp, but then it changed its mind, pulling her out of the clearing instead.

Two more Mortifer Flytraps wound themselves around Cyril, disarming him, and dragged him roughly in pursuit.

"Annipeck!" screamed Cyril. "Get us out of this!"

But Annipeck's powers did not work on flowers.

Her Gift only worked on *human-made* things.

It's going to be fine, thought Annipeck to herself, *because they're taking me to my mommy*...

I'm afraid I'm not as sure as Annipeck that it *is* going to be fine.

For the Mortifer Flytraps were carrying the baby and the pirate deeper and deeper into No Man's Land, where the story becomes a truly terrible place for humans to be.

IT'S GOING TO BE FINE, THOUGHT ANNIPECK.

THEY'RE TAKING ME TO MY MOMMY.

Chapter 24 THE CAPTURE
oF ANNIPECK

he snaking, ravenous plants dragged the baby and the pirate to a part of the forest where the winding plants were so thick and heavy that the Mortifer Flytraps had to bite their way through.

They dropped Cyril and Annipeck in a clearing shrouded in deep fog, drawing back to surround them in a ring, their heads moving from side to side like charmed snakes. Through the fog, Cyril could hear the rushing of a river nearby, and just make out the trunk of a huge tree, as broad as a house.

Cyril cautiously tried to get to his feet.

One of the Mortifer Flytraps went for him, teeth bared.

Cyril got back down on his hands and knees again.

On a frequency that was too high for the humans to hear, the trees, the vegetation, the animals were chattering and humming, and sending scent waves to one another.

Is this the Child-with-the-Atlas-Gift? they were asking.

CRASH! A great noise from deep in the forest.

Cyril's eyes went wide with horror as Something Vast approached.

The Abhorrorghast was a creature of the deepest jungle. It had the body of a tiger, but it was as large as an elephant, its stripes over-scored with the scars of ancient battle; a matted mane of serpents tangled around with vines and fury; a thick and mighty tail from which there grew great long harpoons, each loaded with deadly venom, one pinch of which could snuff a human out in a winking. In peace time, the harpoons dropped naturally to the ground, like shedding hair, and where they fell, no flowers grew. In war, there were 160 of the things hidden inside that tail, and the Beast could shoot them with a swift rattle like a submachine gun at its enemies, and by the time it had shot the last of them, it would have already grown more.

It was never peace time in Excelsiar now, only war.

The Abhorrorghast had been fighting the Warlock

miners that had invaded its territories for so many centuries, and had lost so many companions in the fight, that the creature had lost his heart.

And it had a human face.

The Beast opened its dreadful jaws in a terrible roar that made Cyril's and Annipeck's ears tremble.

"EEOORRAWWWWWWWWWW!"

Annipeck had done very well so far. But this was too much for her. She *was* only seventeen months old.

She burst into tears.

As did Cyril.

He wished he had never come to this beastly, dangerous world. *If I ever get out of this alive, I will never travel again*, Cyril swore to himself. *I won't even go on a BUS…*

They looked at the Beast blankly through their tears. Annipeck threw her arms around Cyril's knees and held on really tight.

All around, the jungle creatures had quenched their chatter.

The Abhorrorghast looked down at them like a Beast carved out of stone. A little blue monkey sitting on the Beast's shoulder fixed them with its watchful eye. Juices dripped from the dreadful jaws of the Mortifer Flytraps.

"Greetings," said Cyril at last, just to break the terrible silence. "The baby and I seem to have lost our way."

Still that silence.

Cyril tried again.

"The baby and I are from... *Out-of-Town*... never mind where, and we went for a stroll, and we got a little lost. We're no one special..." Cyril gave an unhappy little laugh. "We're not pirat—"

Cyril stopped himself. *Won't that be a bit of a giveaway that I actually* am *a pirate?* he thought.

"We're not piemen," he corrected himself. Then, realizing that a pieman wasn't really a *thing* on Excelsiar, "I mean—we're not pilots... oh dear..."

The Beast twitched an eyebrow, one tiny tremor.

The horrible little monkey creature that had been sitting on the Beast now hopped onto Cyril's shoulder.

Cyril froze.

He tried to shout: "*Eeearghhh! Stop it!*"

But the monkey's stare made every muscle in his body stiffen and freeze. He couldn't so much as tremble.

The monkey put his finger into Cyril's ear.

Cyril felt a horrible churning, nauseous feeling as if his mind was being turned upside down.

Don't think about being a pirate ... or Alternative Atlases ... or anything that might get me killed ... Think about ANYTHING else ... Liarsquawks! Moontime in Celestia! thought Cyril desperately. *Great-Aunt Murderus! Queen's Cross Space Station! Lollipops and ice beans! I mean, shouldn't there be such a thing as a pieman even if there isn't one already? I really could do with a pie right now ... Alternative Atlas ... Oh goodness gracious ...*

The monkey took his finger out of Cyril's ear.

Thank goodness I did that Advanced Course on Mindreading Prevention, thought Cyril. *I knew that would come in useful one day.*

Yes, I'm not sure that Cyril had done as good a job of stopping his mind being read as he thought.

The monkey took the backpack off Cyril's back and undid it.

He shook out the contents.

And out fell...

...a mixture of candy wrappers and apple cores and half-empty bottles of potion and whatever else Cyril thought was essential for a transgalactic-and-universal journey...

...and K2's *Alternative Atlas*.

"Good gracious!" said Cyril, feigning surprise. "Who put *that* in there?"

Cyril picked up the Atlas.

WHHIRRRRRR! A harpoon came sizzling out of the Beast's great tail and pierced through the Atlas, whisking it out of Cyril's hands. On and on it continued until it landed twenty feet behind him, pinning the Atlas to the trunk of a great tree. The tree let out a terrible scream and shed all its leaves, now poisoned by the spike.

Cyril gulped. That could have been *him*. "Now, Great Beast," he said, trying to stop his voice from shaking, "I was hoping we could come to an agreement."

The Abhorrorghast said nothing.

And then, to Cyril's absolute horror, a long, lean

shadow of a *something* slipped out of the darkness and tangle of the Beast's hair as if it were a deep drip of blood coming out of his brain.

The *something* landed on the forest floor, and Cyril found himself staring down into an elegant, if extremely unsettling, face. "Greetings...," managed Cyril, bowing low. "Whom do I have the honor of addressing?"

"To *you*, I am just His Excellency," whispered the creature, eyes narrowed in dagger-splinters, "but I, too, am from Out-of-Town. I am an agent of the Universal Government, and the friend

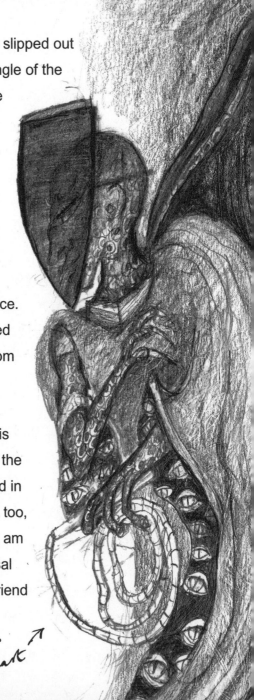

The Rider of the Abhorrorghast

and Rider of the Abhorrorghassssst. I'm here to help."

Only now did Cyril spot the Rider's saddle nestled among the Beast's fur on his broad back and the swinging stirrups that hung from it.

The Rider of the Abhorrorghast's "s"s slipped out of him like the hissing of a snake, and a V-shaped tongue emerged, flickering elegantly out of his mouth a moment before disappearing again. His extra eyelids slipped up and down in a considering tremor.

The monkey hopped onto his shoulder, and His Excellency softly stroked it.

"Righto," stammered poor Cyril, bowing even lower.

"You are lucky to catch me in town, so I can do the talking for the Abhorrorghasssst," purred the Rider. "For the Beast does not speak much. And definitely not to humans." The Rider giggled. "He has ssssssworn, you ssssssee, to kill the entire human race."

The Flytraps leaned forward eagerly.

"I'm only HALF human being," blustered Cyril. "My mother was a Lurkim..."

"I'm not sure this will sssave you," said the Rider thoughtfully. "For the Beast will kill *one* half, and you might need that half to live."

Dear, oh dear, oh dear, oh dear, oh DEAR.

"But as an agent of the UG *you* might perhaps... intervene on my behalf?" floundered Cyril desperately.

"I might," agreed the Rider, still stroking the monkey, who appeared to be terrified of him. "If I felt like it. Tell me who you are."

"My name is Professor Cyril Sidewinder, and I am a poor half-Lurkim Wandering Geography Teacher," said Cyril, trembling. "I am looking for a friend and business associate... who owes me a considerable amount of money."

"And who is this friend and busssiness associate of yours?" asked the Rider.

"Well, when I met him in a pub on my home planet of Celestia he was calling himself 'Dave,'" said Cyril. "But it turns out his *real* name is Everest O'Hero. Quite good-looking, middle-aged... and a double-crossing, treacherous TWISTER of a guy!"

"Ah," said the Rider.

At the mention of the O'Hero name, the Beast had crouched down, shaking his head violently from side to side, making a deep ominous growl that grew louder and louder.

"Oh dear," said Cyril nervously. "Did *Everest...* er...*annoy* His Beastly Majesty in some way?"

The Abhorrorghast seemed to be trying to speak. It was dreadful to see him struggle to form the words, spitting and choking as he tried, eventually giving up and ending on an inarticulate, strangulated ROAR of rage.

"Don't perturb yourself, dear Beasssst," said the Rider, patting the Abhorrorghast's leg. "I shall explain the situation to this ignorant and impertinent stranger."

The Rider turned back to Cyril. "The O'Heros brought the PLAGUE of the sssilk trees here." The Rider sighed.

The Beast gave a roar with a depth of sadness most terrible to hear.

"And when the sssilk trees died, hidden beneath them, the largest deposit of DIAMONTS that this galaxy ever saw was uncovered. *That* brought the Warlock miners and their robots from the farthest reaches of the universe, likely using pages of O'Hero's cursssssed Atlas to get here.

"But now I am here too," said the Rider, putting a hand on his heart and looking ever so virtuous. "Sent in recent years by the Universal Government as a noble Rider of intergalactic law to help this poor Beast in his struggle. I was able to warn him that the treacherous city dwellers, who used to be in harmony with the Wild, are now IN LEAGUE with the miners. O, yes, I ssssaw it with my very own eyes. I had to tell my Beast, for I am hisss only friend."

The Rider stroked the furious Beast reassuringly.

"I cannot be here all the time, unfortunately," the Rider went on. "And he needs to know when there are *traitorsss* in his midst. Especially those acquainted with an O'Hero."

Oh dear. Cyril swallowed hard.

"I'm glad you mentioned Alternative Atlases," said Cyril nervously, changing tack, "because I have managed, at great personal risk to myself, to capture the child who drew the Atlas over there." Cyril pointed to the tree where the Alternative Atlas was harpooned.

A murmur of agitation went around that forest clearing.

"I found her in the House of the O'Heros, and she has the Gift that no one has seen since the original Ancestor O'Hero thousands of years ago...

"...the Gift of creating a living Alternative Atlas that shows in real time where the Which Ways are between the Worlds...yes..." Cyril paused dramatically. "THIS is the Child-with-the-Atlas-Gift."

He pointed at Annipeck.

Annipeck peered around Cyril's leg and smiled at them all politely. "I Annipeck," she said.

But the Abhorrorghast and his Rider were not quite as impressed as Cyril hoped they would be.

The Rider stared fixedly at Annipeck. "Professor Sssidewinder," he said, "I know that the UG will be delighted to hear that you have finally located the O'Hero family they have been seeking for so long...But this is a *baby*! She's barely big enough to hold a pencil, let alone create an entire Alternative Atlas..."

"I'm a p...er...*professor*, not a *babysitter*!" snapped Cyril with some considerable spirit. "I know nothing ABOUT babies, and having spent time with this one, I really do not care if I never see a baby again in my entire life. She is absolutely impossible!

"She needs constant feeding...and singing to...and don't get me STARTED with the *diaper changing* ...I've never met anyone more demanding, and I have worked with some of the most terrifying pirat—*pilots* in the Seventy-seven Inner Galaxies!...I'd rather do hard labor under Chief Aero-ruthless the Skyripper, than spend FIVE MORE MINUTES with that nightmare baby, but one thing I know for sure, is, this baby has ABILITIES... She's definitely capable of creating this Atlas.

"Which is why I was wondering," Cyril took Annipeck's arms from around his leg and pointed at her, "whether you might be interested in a SWAP?"

Suddenly Annipeck was really and truly frightened.

The Mortifer Flytraps moaned in excitement and

drew a little nearer, their dreadful, blank, eyeless
heads moving from side to side.

Annipeck's smudged baby face looked obstinately
and bravely up at the monkey and the Rider and the
Beast.

She pointed into the fog overhead.

"Mommy," said Annipeck.

The Abhorrorghast stared at her.

And Annipeck returned the terrifyingly wild,
Gorgon-like gaze of the Abhorrorghast, unwaveringly.

Oh, what an unbelievably brave baby she was.

"MOMMY!" she said again.

There was another really long, terrifying pause.

But at last Annipeck's little face crumpled,
and slow, silent tears crept down her face. "No
Mommy...," she said hollowly, hugging tightly onto
her toothbrushes and her Lego bricks, which had built
themselves into a small, brave little sword, before
collapsing again in terror.

She looked around her at the jungle and the
hostile creatures.

"*HOME*," said Annipeck.

She tried to put her hand in Cyril's, but he swatted it away.

"Quiet, Annipeck!" he snapped.

And that was the moment Annipeck realized that Cyril wasn't really her grandpa.

She'd just made up that bit to make herself less frightened.

She was entirely alone.

The Abhorrorghast's eyes opened greedily.

"Let me and my Atlas go," said Cyril, pointing to the Atlas harpooned to the tree, "and I will give you in return, this Child-with-the-Atlas-Gift."

The Abhorrorghast licked his lips.

"I'll need MY Atlas," said Cyril. "But the baby can draw you new ones...THINK how you can travel!"

Cyril threw out his arm, painting a picture that he thought the Beast might like.

"So many galaxies, so many worlds...You can dance across the misty deserts, digging out the diamonts with your paws...with a great golden necklace for your mane..."

The Abhorrorghast did not respond. But a single

dribble of saliva was slowly dripping from his mouth, like one dark tear.

"You'll be the richest, most powerful Beast in the entire universe..."

The Rider interrupted this prettily painted picture in a voice that was truly chilling.

"If this is the Child-with-the-Atlas-Gift," he said, "my dear Beassst will kill her."

Chapter 25 RUN, BABY, RUN !!

yril had lost many a moral along the primrose way of the pirate path. And a while ago he had been contemplating something rather similar himself.

But this suddenly seemed extremely, well, *drastic*.

"Um...really? Are y-you quite sure?" stuttered Cyril. "I mean, she IS only a baby; one has to draw the line somewhere. And don't forget, if you kill her, she wouldn't be able to draw you any more Atlases."

"I thought I'd explained," said the Rider of the Abhorrorghast. "My Beasst doesn't WANT more Atlases."

"He's not interested in *travel*, then," whispered Cyril, nervously flicking his eyes around the clearing to look for possible exits. "More of a homebody type? You do have a lovely place here...Nice open-air lifestyle..."

This didn't seem to be cheering the Beast up.

"And that's the great thing about an Atlas, you

see," said Cyril heartily. "You can find yourself a nice *new* planet to live on when your own one is destroyed."

This enraged the Beast even further. Wild eyes rolling, the Beast's howls made Cyril's and Annipeck's eardrums sing with the noise.

The leopardsharks crept nearer; the Flytraps made ominous gulping noises.

And then something extraordinary happened.

Even though Cyril had complained so bitterly about Annipeck, somewhere along the journey he had grown just a *weeny* little bit fond of her. Enough to not want her to die, anyway.

So mean, dreadful Cyril, that appalling villainous fake-professor- and-substitute- geography-teacher,

stepped in front of Annipeck and
looked the Abhorrorghast right in
the eye. "I'm sure we can work this
out to everyone's satisfaction," he
said soothingly. He put his hand into
Annipeck's sticky one, to comfort her.
"I've made a slight mistake. I don't think the baby has
the Atlas Gift after all."

The Rider of the Abhorrorghast's eyes were as
cold as platinum pebbles.

"Cyril Sssidewinder," he hissed. "Kindly move."

"No," said Cyril.

And then he whispered out
of the corner of his mouth:

"Run, baby, run!"

Chapter 26 WHERE IS A HERO
WHEN YOU REALLY, REALLY NEED ONE?

uick as winking, the largest Mortifer Flytrap shot forward, unhinged its great plant jaws, and swallowed Professor Cyril Sidewinder in one big gulp.

"*Grandpa!*" gasped Annipeck.

"I'm fine, little baby." Cyril's voice echoed from inside the mouth of the Flytrap. "Don't you worry about me. *Run!*"

Annipeck gave a sob and began to toddle off as fast as she could on her stout little legs.

But she didn't get far. A nasty lick of a creeping vine snaked around her ankle, tripping her up.

She was dragged back across the forest floor to the Beast.

The Beast opened his jaws wide, pointed that terrible tail with the poisoned harpoons on it at Annipeck...

...and Cyril banged frantically on the walls of the Flytrap. His voice sounded muffled and far away. "I've just remembered! *What's important about the baby's Magic is that it works on plastic!*"

"What?" hissed the Rider, fixing his grim gray eyes on the little toothbrushes, who were now jumping up and down on the Flytrap creeper, trying to get it to let go of Annipeck's ankle.

"HALT!" The Rider tugged on the Abhorrorghast's mane.

Reluctantly, the Beast paused, still snorting and salivating.

The Rider knocked on the Flytrap head, and it spat Cyril out.

"The baby...the toothbrushes...the baby's Magic works on plastic...," gasped Cyril, covered in revolting Flytrap goo.

"In-ter-esssting...," said the Rider thoughtfully.

"I've never seen THAT Gift before...Perhaps we should stay our claws a moment, Beast, my old friend..."

The Abhorrorghast let out a bellow of frustrated fury.

"You are right, dear Beast, to be anxioussss." The Rider's purring, hypnotizing voice seemed to act on the Beast like a soothing tonic. "But think, O Hairy One, how you hate the miners' machinery and robotsss. Many of them are made entirely with plassstic. Maybe this child holds a clue to how we could...unpick that."

On the last two words, the Rider snapped out his switchblade talons and did something unspeakable to an unfortunate nearby forest creature by way of demonstrating the unpicking he had in mind.

The Beast paced restlessly, uncertain.

"Worry not, dear Beast, of courssse we will kill her *eventually*," the Rider continued. "We jussst need to wait a while, to study her powers."

Annipeck got to her feet. She wasn't frightened anymore; she was absolutely beet-red in the face with fury.

She put her fists on her hips.

"BAD MAN," she hissed to the Rider of the Abhorrorghast.

The Rider gave a slow smile. "You are a very brave and powerful baby. But, unfortunately, your powers don't seem to work on my Flytraps. Tell me, Professor, who else was in the O'Hero house when you found her?"

Cyril had used up all the little heroism he had for the day. "Annipeck-has-at-least-two-brothers-and-two-sisters-and-I-think-there-was-a-DOG-and-there-was-definitely-a-man-with-an-umbrella-and-Puck-talked-about-some-Ants-and-a-Bear-but-I-wasn't-really-concentrating-at-the-time-and-they're-all-from-Planet-EARTH!" he babbled.

It was perhaps ill-thought out of Cyril to tell the Beast and Rider all this at once, because now they didn't need *him* anymore.

But luckily for Cyril they were interrupted.

There was a commotion behind them. Then an exhausted doltooth landed in front of the Beast and his Rider. "We saw a GRIMM...," it panted.

"A *GRIMM*?" snapped the Rider. "Not possible..."

Grimms were bad, bad news.

Nobody wants a powerful creature like a Grimm poking their nose in their local affairs.

"Where?"

"In a fight with a giant robot…up by the Sea of Cress…"

This needed investigating immediately.

The Beast's tail thrashed so hard it felled a small tree in one.

"We'll return, Professor," the Rider promised, "after we've dealt with this little problem. In the meantime, please let us offer you and the baby a bed for the night."

The Mortifer Flytraps wound their tendrils and stems around a protesting Cyril and Annipeck so they could not run away.

The Rider leaped onto the Beast's back in one fluid movement, grabbed hold of his snaky mane, and kicked his heels against the Beast's mighty flanks. With a wild, furious, stamping snort, the Beast took off into the night, followed by an angry retinue of dolteeth, leaving only Flytraps and leopardsharks to guard the clearing. Two of the leopardsharks spread

their wings and dragged
Cyril and Annipeck out of the
grip of the Flytraps, and up, up,
into the fog, to who knows where?
But I have a strong feeling that it is going
to be very basic accommodation.

The story has turned very dark now.
WHO is going to rescue Annipeck and Cyril?
Where is a Hero when you really, really need one?

As, according to K2's map, they passed into No Man's Land, K2 and Izzabird and Theo and Mabel got their first real clue that they were on the right track.

To be precise, it was Puck who found it, and Izzabird's sharp eyes that spotted him, dropping Daniel to the ground a moment to swoop down and gobble it up, as if it were a scrumptious little snack.

"Puck! Stop that! *That looks like a piece of Annipeck's Lego!*"

"Whoops!" said Puck, spitting it out. "I'm sorry... I's using up rather a gazigallon of energy carrying this Stepfather so I thoughts I'd keep my strength up... Is this 'Lego' one of our friends?"

"It certainly is," said Izzabird excitedly, taking the little red Lego brick out of Puck's hand and looking closely at it before she put it in her pocket. "I'm sure this belongs to Annipeck! It means we must be getting close...Have you seen any more of these?"*

"Oh, lots!" said Puck. "Blue ones...green ones... the yellow ones are particularly tasty, banana-flavored, but crunchier. I've been eating them for a while...but I won't anymore if they are our friends," he promised.

Well, that put heart into all of them.

"Let's see if the blow-dryer can track Annipeck, now we know we're getting close?" said Theo. He opened his backpack.

The blow-dryer popped out, sniffed the ground excitedly, and passed out.

"It's dead," said Izzabird in disappointment.

Theo turned the switch on the handle of the blow-dryer to On and air roared out so strongly from its mouth that it took flight, backward. Theo only just managed to grab the plug in time. And then it was straining at the cord, as if it were a little aerial backward-facing hovercraft.

• • •

---

*If Annipeck was dropping Lego bricks intentionally, she really was a VERY clever baby, and knowing Annipeck, that is possible.

The blow-dryer was particularly good at finding Lego bricks.

It would suddenly rear up in the air, snorting wildly, then do a graceful Olympic swallow dive into the cress where it would rootle around with such violence that Theo had to hang on hard to the end of the plug to not let go. And when the blow-dryer emerged, it would be balancing another piece of Annipeck's Lego on the top of its head.

Four hours later, Izzabird had quite a collection of building blocks in her upside-down sombrero.

"Here in this howlation is where things get *really* dangerous," said Puck, as if things hadn't been quite perilous enough already. "Breathe calmlike in No Man's Land, and not a blade of grass will stop you.

"But...

"One *hint* of fearful sweat, one *bead* of perspification, and they will catch our scent and track us down and we will never have the chance to save your baby sister."

"What happens if we start feeling frightened?" said K2, who could already feel an uncomfortable fluttering in his stomach.

"Breathe deeply," instructed Theo, "and think of something else. Imagine you're about to ace that math test or score the winning goal in a match...In your head, you must be anywhere but here."

I must not be afraid..., thought K2 to himself, peering ahead at the ominous tangle of fearsome forest.

I must not let everyone down.

I have to follow Annipeck, but I must not be afraid.

And then they came to a clearing with lots of Lego bricks, dropped all around the tree.

They searched the area thoroughly and found some crusts of PB&J sandwiches, but Annipeck had gone.

From there, the blow-dryer led them into the

deepness of the forest and to the "X" where Everest's "treasure" had been buried. They saw the marks of digging.

But no sign of Annipeck.

The blow-dryer was becoming increasingly agitated, hopping in circles around long skid marks on the forest floor, where there were signs of a struggle.

K2's heart dropped. "I think they may have been captured..." The blow-dryer was pointing east, in the same direction as the skid marks. "What's that way?" asked K2.

Mabel looked up from the map. K2 knew the answer before Mabel even said it. "The Prison of the Abhorrorghast...," she whispered.

They looked at each other with stricken faces. The first beginnings of real cold dread for Annipeck crept into all their hearts. The jungle around them smelled their fear, waking up, tendrils reaching out toward them.

And into the silence, the sound of a river.

The river ran through No Man's Land and right past the Beast's terrible prison.

"The forest creatures can't reach you on the river!" said Puck.

But when they reached the river, hearts pounding, desperately hopeful...

"You didn't mention it was a river of FIRE..." said Theo.

It was an extraordinary sight, fire flowing like water.

Flames of orange, yellow, red, and even blue, streaming through the forest with a great steady crackling roar, and the odd explosion of bright jet-green fire off the surface, sending pinwheeling balls of energy bowling down the river. Sparks of every different color burst like fireworks all around, making the wailing noise of rockets as they shot up into the air and erupted in the sky.

Puck had to drop Daniel and put up his umbrella to protect them from the raining pieces of red-hot ashes, and they backed away from the river, coughing as the sulfur smell of the great cloudy billows of smoke itched their noses and burned their faces and made their eyes tear up.

Yes, this presented a problem.

Izzabird ran forward, sombrero over her face, dipped a finger in the river, jumped in pain, and ran back to the others. How were they going to travel on a river this burningly hot?

Mabel was crushed. "I didn't think it meant actual *flames*," she said, in dreadful disappointment. "I'm sorry, everyone, this wasn't such a good plan after all!"

"It's an EX-equellent plan," said Puck stoutly. "Is as I said, the bad things wonts be able to track us on the river...we just has to work out—"

"—how to go down it *without* catching fire, like those trees over there," K2 finished Puck's sentence, pointing at the trees on the riverbanks, many of which had branches trailing in the river. *They* weren't bursting into flames. Every dancing leaf on those trees was dark as midnight, black as coal, and when the fire touched them, it snuffed out with a hiss.

Because here's the thing about nature and evolution, wherever you are in the universe. If trees are going to grow beside a river of fire, well, they'd better be incombustible.

"Good spot, K2!" cried Izzabird.

It took a while to haul a great fallen hollow log, large enough to carry all of them, to the river, even with Puck helping them. But when they finally lugged it in, although it was satisfyingly unaffected by the flames, it was worryingly unstable, flipping over immediately.

"It'll be FINE once we put the Stepfather in the bottom to stabilize it. He's really heavy," said Izzabird optimistically. But the more cautious K2 and Mabel insisted that they haul the whole log out of the river again, and K2 had the bright idea of putting little bits of Sticking Potion on the underside, to make sure it stayed the right way up.

So off they set, sitting inside their great floating incombustible log, now sticking most satisfactorily to the surface of the river, sheltering under a little tent of tree branches they were carrying with them to protect them from stray sparks, with Puck snuffing out any bits of clothing that accidentally caught fire.

There was a constant humming hiss of hatred coming off the vegetation on the riverbanks, and K2 felt a tightening band of tension around his forehead as if his woolly thinking cap was way too small.

Once he caught a brief nightmare glimpse of twisting buildings, apparently abandoned, decaying, and *something* seemed to be *eating* them in revolting, gulping swallows... but who knew what those somethings *were*?

Another time he spotted a gigantic sky-blue leopardshark with wings, watching them from a tree branch, and his heart beat a little quicker, and then he saw a curl of vegetation or vine, suddenly freezing and turning toward them...

Don't get frightened...

Don't get frightened...

Don't get frightened...

Over and over K2 repeated it to himself as he tried to squash the nasty, sick feeling in his flip-flopping stomach.

Hours passed, the sun went down, the three moons began to rise.

K2 and Mabel were next to each other, Mabel holding the unconscious Daniel's hand for reassurance. Theo had his hoodie way over his head, so the others wouldn't see how alarmed he was getting, and underneath the swagger of her

sombrero, even Izzabird's hair was beginning to
creep up with fear.

K2 checked the map in his shaking hand as the
forest quieted, and the river wound past a particular
spooky clearing, and there was a sinister silence,
apart from a

drip

drip

drip of something dropping somewhere
nearby, that might have been tears or might
have been blood. K2's mind panicked and
screamed, *LET'S GET OUT OF HERE!*

But the drawing on his map was moving in front
of his eyes and telling him Annipeck was *here*, the
edges of the paper quivering upward, and the
blow-dryer that Theo was hanging on to
was trembling and seeming to be saying the
same thing.

"Look up...," whispered Mabel, handing K2 the
binoculars.

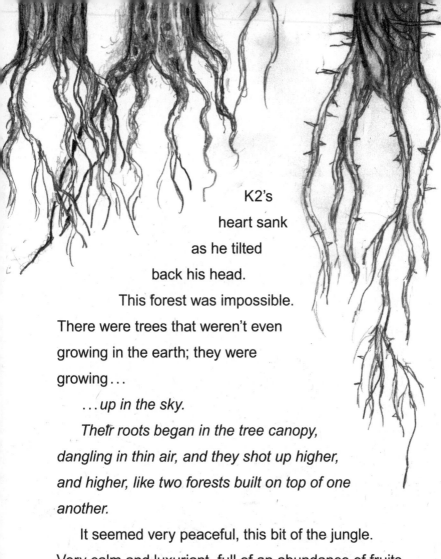

K2's
heart sank
as he tilted
back his head.
This forest was impossible.
There were trees that weren't even
growing in the earth; they were
growing...

...*up in the sky.*

Their roots began in the tree canopy,
dangling in thin air, and they shot up higher,
and higher, like two forests built on top of one
another.

It seemed very peaceful, this bit of the jungle.
Very calm and luxuriant, full of an abundance of fruits
and flowers.

But as K2 looked more closely, he realized
something strange was going on up in the treetops.

Miles and miles of
peculiar hanging pods,
shaped like giant chrysalises,
stretched away from them, as
far as the eye could see. What
on earth were they?

K2 knew what they were,
in his heart. He had already
written the name on this map.

The Prison of the
Abhorrorghast.

Each of those pods was
larger than a human being,
and they enclosed a prisoner
of the Abhorrorghast.

Some of them were
dark and silent, others
were lighter, and you
could see movement
within them and catch
faint sounds of moaning
or calling.

K2 shuddered.

"I thought all the human beings were dead on Excelsiar?" whispered Izzabird.

"Yes, they are," replied Puck. "Up there are captured gergashes, cyclopes, dormindrads, whispering elves from the floating cities...becuzz they is in league with his enemies, the diamont miners. He can'ts quite bear to kills them, so he imprizzes them instead."

"Annipeck is definitely somewhere here," said Theo as the blow-dryer reared this way, that way, snorting and bucking.

"But NO ONE has ever escaped from this prison before," shivered Puck. "It's guarded by the Beast's scariest followers."

"Just because something has never happened before, doesn't mean it can't happen NOW! An O'Hero Knows No Limits! The Sky Is Just the Beginning," whispered Izzabird, punching the air. "No Rivers Can Stop Us. No Mountains Can Stand in Our Way!"

Izzabird and Theo steered the hollow log to the edge of the riverbank and they all quietly clambered out, every nerve jangling.

Where are the human-eating plants? thought K2 as he tried to peer through an odd, dreamy, golden-colored mist that hung heavy in the clearing, mingling with the fog. *They must be somewhere...*

But there was an eerie silence in the ink-night of the forest, apart from that unsettling moaning and whispering from the prison pods above.

Not a fern moved. Not a bird sang.

Something strange was going on, because all four children yawned simultaneously. Suddenly, K2's eyelids were so heavy he could barely keep them open.

They stared drowsily at the impossibly high trees.

"How are we going to get UP there?" whispered Mabel. "The roots are in the air."

"We're going to have to FLY." Theo's eyes shone like stars as he shook off the weird lethargy that was trying to come over him. "Mabel, you were right. It was worth waiting till this moment to bring out the Flymaster Homemade-O. Thank you for making us save it until we really needed it."

Theo untied the Flymaster Homemade-O from his back. Izzabird took off the flying tree branch she had strapped to her backpack. Unmoored, skateboard and tree branch wanted to move upward, but Theo and Izzabird held them down.

They put on their glasses, like two ragged scarecrow scientists, and held the skateboard and branches steady while Theo solemnly sprayed three squirts of the Flying Gas on the skateboard and branches. Finally, Izzabird applied the Sticking Potion to the underside of Theo's shoes and he scrambled up onto his Flymaster Homemade-O, crouching down to a surfing position.

The skateboard and branches lurched excitedly, ready to take off.

"Puck, we're going to need you to come with us to help break open those prison pods," whispered Izzabird.

"You're leading again, Izzabird!" said Theo, but he was too excited to really mind.

"Sorry," replied Izzabird, to K2's surprise. "Mabel, do you think Puck should come with us? And perhaps you should stay here and look after your dad?"

"Okay," agreed Mabel sleepily, thoroughly relieved by any plan that meant she was going to stay on the ground.

"Maybe K2 should stay here too," suggested Theo. "He's looking a bit scared..."

"We're ALL a bit scared, Theo!" whispered Izzabird loyally. "Anyone who isn't a *bit* scared in this situation is completely mad. K2, you can do it, can't you?"

"Of course he can!" said Mabel.

I'm my father's son, aren't I? thought K2. *There's that story about how he traveled three times across the Atlantic in a hot-air balloon without stopping...Goodness* knows *why anyone would want to DO that. I mean, how are we even RELATED? But that isn't the point of the story, which is that HE hadn't been frightened...*

Don't be frightened...

Don't be frightened...

K2 pushed his glasses more firmly onto his nose.

Feeling completely sick, K2 climbed astride the second branch. It lurched forward, and he fell off. Luckily, Izzabird still had hold of it.

K2 pulled his thinking cap down low over his eyes so he wouldn't be able to see the horror of what he was doing and got back on.

"Is easy-peasy, lemon-squeezy when you get up here, K2!" said Puck encouragingly from above.

"Get really steady before you take your feet off the ground," advised Izzabird, and she let go.

UP the branch shot, taking K2 with it, clinging on for dear life.

Izzabird followed, trying to repress a "*WHOOP!*" of excitement as she took flight herself, her hair streaming out behind her.

Theo balanced on the Flymaster Homemade-O and let himself be pulled along by the blow-dryer, who was charging forward like a bloodhound on the scent. Its head was pointing in the direction that it thought Cyril and Annipeck had taken, and it moved so fast it was all Theo could do to hold on to the end of it, water-skiing upward like he was attached to an extremely fast speedboat.

"It's working!" whispered Theo exultantly. "We did it!"

NOT BAD for a first go at making a flying skateboard.

It was the combination of the sheer joy of flying for the first time, and the strange effect of that golden mist, for all three of them forgot to be frightened the instant they hit the air.

I'm going to drown in the night sky, and I don't even care, thought K2 as he swooped toward the starry sky. He was heady, giddy, loop-di-loop with joy and a warm golden feeling deep inside like he had eaten the most delicious chocolate cake in the world, little bubble honeycombs of happiness radiated out from his stomach, tingling all over him, down his legs and his arms, right to the tips of his fingers, as he steered that tree branch lopsidedly upward.

Like riding a bicycle, if K2 tipped slightly to the right, the branch responded instantly, and he had to readjust hastily. The three of them seemed to be the

perfect weight, not too light to shoot up into the air
endlessly, not too heavy to plummet toward the world
laid out beneath them—although they could swim
down if they wanted. Izzabird tried it, moving her arms
in a breast-stroke motion, pushing aside the air, to
help the tree branch along.

Up they soared, past the swinging tree roots,
through the many sinister levels of the Prison of the
Abhorrorghast, until the prison pods were hanging
all around them in such vast numbers that it was
impossible to count them, but as they flew above the
last swirling billows of the golden mist, the euphoria
left them and they remembered their mission once
again.

But the blow-dryer was a bit whoozy and didn't
seem to know which way to go.

"How on earth are we going to find Annipeck?"
whispered Izzabird. "There are so many!"

"I'm sorry to disturb," said K2, stopping at one of
the prison pods, "but do you know where I might find
a baby and a pirate who may have been captured
recently?"

There was a rustle inside and the gruff voice

361

replied: "Not here...but I did hear a rumor from higher up..."

So, on they traveled, navigating their way, with the help of the pod prisoners who directed them with muffled instructions: "Not here," or "Maybe farther on," or "Good luck."

"Sorry...I'm so sorry...," K2 whispered to them as they flew on.

The blow-dryer, still wildly overexcited, wove in and out of the jungle canopy with such violent haste that Theo would have been dragged off the skateboard if Izzabird hadn't used the Sticking Potion on it.

But there was still no sign of Annipeck. It felt like they'd been looking for hours. K2 had forgotten what solid ground beneath his feet even felt like.

And then, at last, suddenly the blow-dryer stopped.

Slowly it turned around, looking back in the direction they had come from. Then it set off at speed, dragging Theo toward two prison pods that were hanging on their own from an extremely tall tree, less visible than the others because of the especially leafy branches surrounding them.

Tickle, tickle, ickle star...

"Listen...," whispered Theo. "What is that?"

A very faint, very sweet sound, drifted out of one of the prison pods as they got closer.

What was it?

"Tickle, tickle, ickle STAR
O oar la ba Er-SER-si-ar
Da reHEhar doohah POOS
Oo woYAwah vo war HOOS
Worra, worra, ickle STAR
LAhow WIRla war Errah..."

It was ANNIPECK.

Chapter 28 AS WE ARE TALKING OF HEROES...

A s we are talking of Heroes, some time earlier, when the Rider and the Abhorrorghast had left to see what was going on in their northern territories, and K2 and Mabel and Theo and Izzabird were still on the log boat on the River of Fire leading into No Man's Land, a *real* Hero had turned up without anyone noticing.

Let me show you the entrance of a *real* Hero...

It was quiet in the air above the nighttime forest of No Man's Land.

No birds called.

But what was this faint *swish, swish, swish* noise, way in the distance?

And *who* was the stylish, elegant person, dressed all in black, the lone surfer skimming expertly across the breaking waves of the topmost leaves of the forest on their Flymaster?

Why, it was *Horizabel*, of course.

Horizabel coming to complete the rest of her mission.

She, too, had heard the sound of "Twinkle, Twinkle, Little Star," though from a couple of miles away, for Horizabel's hearing was far more acute than a human being's.

She stopped on the tree where the singing was coming from, without a sound, the curve of her braking Flymaster making a beautiful line in the leaf waves. She tipped it up with one oh-so-elegant toe and strapped it on her back.

Hanging from the tree were two pods.

The smaller one was shining with a very faint light that lit up the covering of the pod like sunlight behind a leaf, as inside Annipeck sang and the toothbrushes glowed like stars to help keep her spirits up.

Horizabel got out her Air Stick and quietly, gently started to cut through the vine that attached the larger pod to the tree.

Horizabel was not there to rescue Annipeck.

She was there to take Cyril, in his prison pod, back to the Prison of the Evergods, to face stern justice in front of the Universal Government. She would take Cyril away without him even realizing she was there, so smooth would be the transfer from his

365

pod swinging gently from the tree to his pod
swinging gently from underneath Blinkers.

Annipeck would be so unaware, she
wouldn't pause in her singing for a moment, and
no one would be any the wiser.

This was Horizabel's *job*, and it was quiet,
efficient, unappreciated work.

But suddenly Horizabel stiffened.

Something was approaching.

Who could it be?

She looked down.

And for one second was so surprised out
of her normal polar-ice-sharp coolness that
she nearly fell out of the tree.

Three little raggedy figures, two on
ridiculous flying tree branches, one on
an even more eccentric skateboard
with a sort-of-flying blow-dryer pulling
it in two different directions at once,
were flying haphazardly and messily through the
terrifying Prison of the Abhorrorghast!

The little human beings!

Impossible! thought Horizabel in bewilderment.

*How did they
get through
the desert? And
the forest? And how
are they not falling asleep?*
For Horizabel had sent Blinkers
here earlier to spray the entire area
with a honey-colored mist of Tranquo-gas, to
render the guarding Mortifer Flytraps unconscious,
so she could carry out her mission without being
disturbed... It was all part of her brilliant plan.

The little human beings appeared to have grown
rather more gumption than Horizabel had dreamed
they were capable of.

But it was definitely *them*.

Apart from anything else, they were still arguing, if just a tad more amiably than before.

"I'm sure we should be going in that direction," came the clear, carrying whisper of Izzabird, as her flying tree branch swayed erratically from left to right.

"Well, the *blow-dryer* thinks it's this way," Theo was saying back.

"Theo might be right," whispered the one called K2. How could he even see what he was doing when he had his ridiculous pom-pom of a thinking cap pulled right down over his eyes like that? "I think she's up there! Puck, can you see her?"

Horizabel was so frazzled she only just remembered to put up her invisibility star cowl and put Blinkers and crew into Stealth Mode.

K2 tipped his head as far back as he could so he could see out from under his thinking cap, and pointed unnecessarily with one arm upward...

Don't do that! You'll need BOTH hands on that tree branch!

...and he went into a spiraling wobble downward.

Oh, for the stars' sake.

He's going to fall off.

Horizabel shut her eyes. She couldn't look—it was all so...untidy.

But when she opened her eyes again, by some miracle K2 had regained control of his flying contraption, and all three human beings and their broken robot were wobbling upward once again to disturb Horizabel's peaceful and neat covert operation, which had all been going brilliantly to plan right up until that moment.

Inside the prison pod, Annipeck stopped singing.

She was listening.

Horizabel couldn't see her, but she could sense the baby listening inside the prison pod, hear her breathe softly, in-out, in-out, and feel the trembles of the baby's heart, which was not yet daring to hope that what she *thought* she heard was true.

"*K2!*" whispered Annipeck to herself. "*Mabel! Feo! Izza!*"

No one but Horizabel could hear her whisper yet. It would take a heart of stone not to melt at the passionate relief in that baby's voice as she realized she *might* be rescued.

Lucky, then, that Horizabel had that heart of stone.

But shivering stars and blistering black holes! Horizabel was going to have to grow a little more gumption *herself.* Even though she had plenty of gumption in the first place.

A Grimm hates changing her plans.

But sometimes the story requires...a little tweaking.

In order for said Grimm to stay one step ahead.

Chapter 29 STAYING ONE STEP AHEAD, MY HEARTIES

p, up, up, Theo and Izzabird and K2 and Puck flew to where the two prison pods were hanging.

Now they could hear Annipeck calling to them, a little muffled, and the soft banging of her excitable toothbrushes from inside the pod.

Theo landed first, rather messily, grabbing hold of a branch above, the wheels of his skateboard spinning on a branch below, as the blow-dryer threw itself at Annipeck's prison pod in excitement.

"Annipeck?" whispered Theo.

"Hel-lo, Feo!" replied the little voice of Annipeck joyfully from inside.

"Don't worry, Annipeck!" said Izzabird, landing a little more elegantly. "We're going to get you out of there…"

K2 crash-landed beside Izzabird with such violence that the tree branches and the prison pod swayed wildy, nearly shaking all three little human beings out of the tree in one swoop.

"How?" said K2.

It was a good point.

They hadn't really thought this bit through.

"Puck, you'll have something to open this prison pod, won't you?" said Izzabird hopefully.

"Offcourse I squill!" said Puck, running through his little assortment of Swiss-Army-knife attachments again. "Spoon!...*no*...can-openy-thingummy...*no*...fork!...*no*...knitting needle!...*no!*...ooh...I know...*bottle opener*!"

In great excitement, Puck poked at the prison pod repeatedly with his crooked cork-remover, as if that was going to make any impression whatsoever on the strange plant-mixed-with-dark-matter material that those prison pods of the Abhorrorghast were made out of.

Like trying to spear a diamond with a cotton bud, really.

Cyril had been woken up by all this commotion, and now his voice came wheedling out of his own prison pod. "Don't forget about helping your old pal, the professor... No hard feelings, eh? You're going to help *me* escape too, aren't you?"

"Grandpa! Wor heow GRANDPA!" said Annipeck loudly, from inside.

"Who's Grandpa?" asked Izzabird. "Oh, you mean *Cyril*? Nice touch, Annipeck. *You* don't deserve to be rescued, Cyril Sidewinder, you terrible, baby-stealing pirate...," said Izzabird. "Puck, maybe try the hairdresser scissors? I think they could be sharper..."

The little human beings were so intent on their hopeless task, maybe Horizabel could quietly finish the job without them noticing? She was still invisible to them.

Ve-ry softly, Horizabel moved her Air Stick back to sawing through the vine attaching Cyril's prison pod to the tree.

Unfortunately, something sensed Horizabel's gentle movement.

The blow-dryer flipped around, snorting, in her direction.

Horizabel froze.

The children looked around, freezing too.

The blow-dryer moved slowly forward, hot air blowing out of its mouth.

Maybe the wind of that hot air slightly shifted Horizabel's star cowl, making her visible for a second, who knows? But Theo's hand whipped forward and closed on the bounty hunter's invisible arm, the one holding the Air Stick.

"Horizabel!" whispered Theo.

Busted!

Horizabel took off her star cowl and put up her gas mask. She didn't need it if the Tranquo-gas was so faint now it wasn't working on the little human beings. And suddenly there she was, in front of them. Immaculately turned out as ever, not a hair out of place, perfectly balanced on that branch as if she had spent her whole life up a tree.

She gave them a tiny, deliciously executed, half bow that, if they weren't so ignorant, they would have known was a sign of reluctant respect.

"Ill met by moonlight, small human beings," said Horizabel.

"Horizabel, you double-crossing trickster!" gasped Izzabird. "What are YOU doing here?"

"It's unwise to insult a Grimm, especially one who is prepared to help you, Izza," advised Horizabel. "I told you, I have business with Cyril here." She pointed to the larger prison pod.

"Galloping galaxies!" swore the voice of Cyril Sidewinder loudly. "Is that Horizabel, the Grimm bounty hunter?"

"It is indeed," said Horizabel.

Cyril went very quiet.

"I'll offer you a deal," said Horizabel to Izzabird. "*I* will get your baby sister out of that prison pod, if *you* get out of here immediately afterward and go back through the Which Way to Planet Earth, leaving me to conduct my business with Cyril in peace and quiet."

"We accept your deal," said Theo promptly, back.

"Wise choice," sniffed Horizabel, briskly moving her Air Stick toward Annipeck's prison. "Move away from this side of the pod, Annipeck. I'm breaking in."

"We were doing perfectly well on our own!" said Izzabird indignantly.

"You've done a lot better than I expected," admitted Horizabel as the Air Stick buzzed efficiently through the plant-and-dark-matter surrounding Annipeck, "but there are reasons no one has ever busted out of this prison before, and one of them is the stuff these pods are made of."

"Why are you helping us?" asked Theo.

A good question.

Horizabel had timed this to perfection.

She had retrieved her own Alternative Atlas from THE EXCORIATOR (let's not go into how), simultaneously organizing a diversion in the north to get the Abhorrorghast and his Rider out of the way; instructed Blinkers to come ahead and administer a touch of Tranquo-gas around the clearing to knock out any plant and animals left behind, just for an hour or so, to give her enough time to cut free Cyril's prison pod; and leave before anyone realized she was there.

Immaculate planning and execution.

But she had not reckoned on the arrival of the

noisy little human beings. They were in danger of waking the plants on the forest floor, as the effects of the Tranquo-gas were beginning to wear off.

And she didn't have long before the Abhorrorghast and his Rider returned, so the sooner she could get the humans out of the picture and back on their way, the better.

That was her reasoning.

"I'm assuming you ditched the smaller girl and the big adult along the way?" said Horizabel as she carried on working with her Air Stick. "Very sensible of you. They were holding you up."

"No, they're waiting at the bottom of the trees on the ground," said Izzabird.

Horizabel raised an eyebrow but made no comment.

The Air Stick had now cut a large enough hole for Horizabel to reach in and pull Annipeck out. The baby buried her face in Horizabel's hair a moment. Horizabel put her firmly in Izzabird's arms.

Izzabird hugged Annipeck in total bliss, Theo and K2 putting their arms around them both, limp with relief and happiness. Puck perched on Theo's head, wiping the tears away from his eyes with his ice-cream scoop, and the toothbrushes and the Lego bricks jigged around them all in a victory dance of celebration.

They had done it! Against all odds, they had done it!

Horizabel turned back to Cyril's prison pod.

"GRANDPA?" said Annipeck.

"Don't worry, I'll take good care of 'Grandpa,'" said Horizabel grimly. "I won't let him out of my sight."

As her Air Stick cut through the last bit of vine attaching Cyril's pod to the tree, Horizabel clicked her fingers and Blinkers materialized out of nowhere. Horizabel hitched up Cyril's pod to Blinkers's winch, gave it two satisfied pats, and said, "Very neat. I couldn't design a better portable prison myself."

Cyril banged on the inside of the prison pod. "You should know, bounty hunter," he hissed, "that I am a close personal friend of Chief Aero-ruthless the Skyripper and he will exact the most terrible revenges if a single hair on my head is harmed!"

"Well, that IS a coincidence," said Horizabel chattily, "because as it happens, I, too, am a close personal friend of Chief Aero-ruthless the Skyripper. I'll send him your regards the next time I see him. Take him away, Blinkers!"

Blinkers launched into the air, the pod swinging underneath her, disappearing into the night sky, *poof!* just like that, as she turned on her Stealth Mode.

Horizabel turned back to the little human beings. "Goodbye, good luck, and remember our deal," she said briskly. "No noise, back to your own planet, and if you make it, I'll come check and find you later. I can keep a secret if you can."

"Thank you, Horizabel!"

Horizabel noted that they were saying "thank you" this time; even the baby was joining in with "*Thank*-oo!," so at least they'd learned *something*.

She put up the hood of her star cowl and disappeared once more.

DOWN Theo, Izzabird, K2, Annipeck, and Puck flew, their hearts singing with happiness.

"The Flymaster Homemade-O works like a dream!" Theo grinned proudly.

Annipeck squealed with delight as the warm night air blew back her curls.

All four of them were filled with the jubilant joy of an Impossible Task completed.

But as they circled downward, Mabel's little face peering up at them was mixed with delight at seeing Annipeck behind Izzabird on the tree branch and an agitated concern about *something else*. She was jumping up and down and pointing repeatedly.

Izzabird and K2 and Theo looked over their shoulders.

"Mommy!" said Annipeck in delight, her eyes following Mabel's pointing finger.

For there...

...on the other side of the clearing...

...at the bottom of a tall tree...

...all entangled and choked up in a strangle of vegetation...

...were the three vacuum cleaners belonging to Aunt Trudie, Aunt Violet, and Freya!

Chapter 30 WHO IS RESCUING WHO?

hile Izzabird and Theo and K2 were having their flying-and-rescuing-Annipeck adventure, Mabel had a smaller but no less interesting on-the-ground adventure of her own.

She had been left all alone with only her unconscious father, in a terrifying forest, with an overwhelming and unexpected compulsion to go to sleep, so to keep herself awake and unafraid she had made up a ridiculous game of Eye Spy, pretending she was playing it with her father rather than against herself.

It was during this game that she spotted the Hoovers.

She had been saying, in an imitation of her father's deep voice, as she scanned the clearing: "*My* turn, now, Mabel . . . I spy with my little eye . . . something beginning with . . . '*H*'!"

And there they were, on the other side of the clearing, the Hoovers that she had last seen flying

Freya and Aunt Trudie and Aunt Violet out of the garden at Soggy-Bottom-Marsh-Place, a gazillion miles away on dear old Planet Earth.

Mabel had gone to investigate.

Tiptoeing across the clearing, passing the vast trembling heads of creatures with no faces that could be plants or sleeping dragons, stiff with the effort of not feeling fear, walking like a little girl made out of wood.

Why were the "things" not waking, when Mabel's heart was pounding so hard she felt it might burst out of her chest?

She reached the Hoovers, all wound tight in such a wrangled nest of thorns as if the thorns had been growing around them for centuries. Yes, they were definitely the right ones; that was Aunt Violet's scarf wound around the handle of one of them...

But that meant that...

Aunt Trudie and Aunt Violet and Freya were HERE!

Or HAD been at some point.

Just as Mabel was absorbing this information, there was a noise from the other side of the clearing.

Her head whipped around. The floppy figure of her father crumpled on the forest floor was jerking a little and making confused noises of "Wossat? Werrami? Wossgoingon?"

He was waking up, at last!

As Mabel tiptoed back, she was sure she could see, at the edges of her eyesight, those sleeping no-faced things stirring, as if they too were coming back to life.

By the time she got back to her father, he had collapsed into unconsciousness again; and that was when she saw the others flying down with Annipeck.

Theo and Izzabird and K2 and Annipeck and Puck flew-wobbled over to the tree where the Hoovers were parked at the bottom. When they realized what this meant, they nearly fell off their flying machines with astonishment.

"They're HERE...," whispered K2, with round eyes.

"But how are we going to find them, when there are so many pods up there?" Izzabird whispered back.

Theo's mind was whirring: figuring out what was going on was like trying to work out the next move in a fiendishly complicated chess game, while balancing on a wobbly flying skateboard, and blocking out the noise of the stirring Flytraps.

"Maybe Horizabel will help us one last time," said Theo. "If we're quick, we might catch her before she leaves."

"But Horizabel will be invisible," said K2, staring up at the numberless pods, framed by the numberless stars of the night sky. "How will we know where *she* is?"

"Oh, *I* can find Horizabel," said Izzabird unexpectedly. "I sneaked a piece of Annipeck's Lego into her pocket just in case we needed to keep an eye on that trickster of a bounty hunter."

Theo looked at Izzabird with real respect.

"Blow-dryer!" he said. "Lead the way!"

Chapter 31 WHAT HORIZABEL DID

Horizabel had not yet left the forest.

She had been carrying on with the rest of her own mission: silently, invisibly, she was working away with her Air Stick at detaching another pod from a cluster of prison pods hanging a little distance away from where Cyril and Annipeck had been found.

Then to her astonishment, she saw the little humans approaching AGAIN from below. They were calling, as loudly as they dared: "Mom! Aunt Trudie! Aunt Violet!"

I told them to go HOME! thought Horizabel furiously.

She went on sawing with her Air Stick, picking up the pace a bit.

Inside three of those prison pods were, you guessed it, *Aunt Trudie, Aunt Violet, and Freya.*

"Was that the children's voices? How are *they* here?" exclaimed Aunt Trudie in astonishment.

"They're wearing *thinking caps!*" said Freya, pressing herself against the side of her pod so she could get a better view through the chinks in the vines. "Who told them about thinking caps? But nobody's wearing a winter coat..."

"Black holes to the winter coats!" said Aunt Violet. "They're Heroes, every last one of them, coming here to rescue us! Whoever would have thought it?"

"They need to get out of here quick though," said Aunt Trudie. "Before the Abhorrorghast, and that devil, his Rider, return and catch them."

"No, children, no!" cried Aunt Violet. "Don't try to rescue us! You haven't got time!"

The two aunts and Freya were waving their arms inside their prison pods and shouting, "Go away! Leave us! We'll be fine! Save yourselves!"

But the children could not hear.

Up they flew, Theo being pulled by the blow-dryer that could smell the Lego in Horizabel's pocket, until Freya could see clearly the faces of the children that she loved more than anything in the world.

This is the thing about children.

You give away your heart to them, and then your heart is flying around the world, out of your control.

O be careful, heart. Fly gently. Fly safely.

Put on your winter coat.

"Horizabel!" called Izzabird from below. "We know you're up there! Where is our mother? Where are the aunts? We're not leaving until we've rescued EVERYONE!"

Horizabel?

Horizabel! thought Freya and Aunt Trudie and Aunt Violet all at once.

HORIZABEL is here?

Oh, they knew that tricky Horizabel, those Heroes, for they had been about the worlds a bit.

Horizabel put back her cowl, stepping out into visibility. Standing above the children, she looked older, grimmer, very stern.

"You broke our deal, little human beings. I told you to LEAVE," said Horizabel. "You don't have time to rescue anyone else, and K2 has the most dangerous Gift in the universe. You have your sister. You have your lives.

"GO HOME."

And she snarled like a cat.

The children looked up at her in shock.

And then there was the most appalling, world-shaking, ear-drumming noise from below and...

Chapter 32 THE MOST DANGEROUS GIFT IN THE UNIVERSE

The Beast ERUPTED into the clearing.

The most dangerous Gift in the universe, thought K2.

I have THE MOST DANGEROUS GIFT IN THE UNIVERSE…

This is all my fault. It's all my fault that we're here. And all my fault that the Beast is after us.

What would my FATHER do in this situation?

Something brave, something reckless. Something HEROIC.

With a white face, K2 turned to the others: "I'm the one putting everyone in danger. I'm the one everyone really wants. *You* all get away while they are running after me."

And before he could change his mind, because he was really very frightened, he turned his tree branch downward and headed to the forest floor.

"Puck!" cried Izzabird. *"Go after him! Save him!"*

"Absquo-lootely!" said Puck, zooming after K2 in blurry haste.

The first part of K2's descent was really extremely impressive. His O'Hero forefathers would have been very proud of him. Crouched down over the raggedy tree branch, wind screeching about his ears, mouth grim with O'Hero determination.

But K2 had to do things K2's way.

So the *second* part of K2's descent went a little differently.

The roaring from the Beast suddenly increased in violence, and it startled K2, who was already struggling with holding on to the tree branch at speed.

He wobbled violently... tried to regain control... his woolly thinking cap fell over his eyes... he put up a hand to push it upward... lost his balance and flipped over... went into a tailspin... and when he was still about forty feet above the ground...

He fell off.

Down,

down,

down,

K2 plunged toward the ground.

Horizabel shut her eyes, but *this time* when she opened them again, K2 was still falling.

"K2!" the other children cried with such desperation, it was as if they could turn their loving words into fingers and catch him as he fell.

Puck reached him too late, only managing to grab his thinking cap when he was a few feet from the ground while the rest of K2 carried on downward.

Luckily, K2 hit the ground on a sweet spot below the trees, where the carpet of cress that had invaded Excelsiar was as thick as a feather mattress.

This broke K2's fall, but he still knocked himself out for a moment.

When K2 opened his eyes again and sat up, he wasn't sure where he was.

He had forgotten he had to tell himself not to be frightened.

His heart panicked, beating *quick-quick* with the fast pulse of terror, and sweat poured out of him, reeking of the strong smell of fear.

All around the forest, the Flytraps smelled it. Their terrible eyeless, faceless heads turned toward him. The leopardsharks were waking too, as the Tranquo-gas had worn off, and they turned as well.

And, roaring behind him, twice as terrible as K2 had ever thought, was...

The Beast.

K2 was lost in the jungle, and the jungle was alive and waking up. The Beast was hunting him, and bounding nearer and nearer.

He had woken straight into his recurring dream, the one that had made him close the Atlas he was drawing in so many times in the past.

AT LAST, we have reached where we started in chapter 1.

It's taken a while as, if I'm honest, I didn't *really* want to get here.

Because K2 was in terrible trouble now. *This time* it wasn't a dream at all.

K2 stumbled to his feet and tried to run.

He could feel his shirt sticking to his back with sweat. He was so terrified that when the branches on the trees began to uncurl their twigs and claw at him, and the whispering, hissing, spitting glow of nettles reached up from below to sting his ankles, he hardly felt them.

WHEEOOOOOOOOOWWWWWW!

One of the Beast's harpoons ripped through the air, missing K2's head by inches, and struck a tree.

"I's *sorry* too, K2!" wailed Puck. "I's got nuffink helpful!"

"Don't worry, Puck, that's not your fault. You've done your best...," said K2. "You hide in my backpack. They hate robots nearly as much as human beings. Go in there and keep quiet and maybe they won't find you. That's an order, Puck!"

The other children were flying in pursuit.

And in the treetops above, Freya and the aunts were going crazy. "LET US OUT, HORIZABEL, LET

US OUT!" they yelled. "K2 is going to get caught by the Beast!"

Horizabel had been entirely shaken out of her normal coolness and was madly hacking away again at the same vine as before.

"Well, of *course* he's going to get caught by the Beast," said the bounty hunter furiously. "The boy has just offered himself up like an afternoon snack..."

She didn't know why she was so cross, and that made her even crosser.

"Your children have been VERY BADLY BROUGHT UP!" Horizabel went on. "You wouldn't get this sort of unreasonable behavior in Illyria, I'm telling you... I've done all that I could... offered them plenty of extremely helpful advice that they have totally ignored..."

Horizabel started hacking the vine again. "Oh, by the circling moons of the Exploding Planet of Agrippa... if I never meet a human being ever again, I'm going to be a very happy Grimm... I can't look at what is going to happen next..."

For we ALL know what is going to happen next, don't we?

I already told you in chapter 1.

A Flytrap tendril wrapped around the ankle of K2. And he was dragged to face the Beast.

STAMP! STAMP! Two final earthquakes of the ground underneath him and then K2 was staring up at that great ruined face. The smell was overpowering. But the *look* was worse. It was the stare of hatred of the human, and that was there in every animal eye that was now encircling him: the beautiful leopardsharks with their mighty spotted backs, the birds of paradise with their jewel-prick eyes and gleaming feathers, and the astonishing red lions. They *hated* him and, like all emotions on Excelsiar, that hatred was a smellable, touchable, visible thing.

K2 half sat up, the vines holding him tight.

Over the Abhorrorghast's head, out of its stirruped saddle, jumped something, a thin, elegant figure with alarming yellow eyes who crouched down on all fours in front of K2 and hissed: "Who are you?"

"I'm K2 O'Hero," said K2.

He swallowed. "And I am the Child-with-the-Atlas-Gift."

K2 shut his eyes, ready for
the Abhorrorghast to strike.

"The Child-with-the-Atlas-
Gift!" hissed the Rider in
triumph and exultation. He
sniffed K2 expectantly. "Finally, the
O'Hero line really HAS produced

another person who has the Gift.
Are you sssure, though?"

This didn't look like one of the O'Heros.

"Quite sure," said K2, his voice stronger.

"END IT, MY DEAR BEAST!" cried the Rider
of the Abhorrorghast.

The Abhorrorghast roared the most dreadful,
world-shaking roar of all and turned to
aim his tail, with its scorpion-sharp
harpoons, straight at K2's
heart.

Chapter 33 THE VERY BITTER END

But *just* as the Abhorrorghast was about to strike, his eye was distracted by the little figure of Mabel running across the clearing, as small as a mite or tick bite contrasted to his immenseness.

What in the Great Galaxy of Dielzibub does that little human being think she can do in this situation? thought Horizabel, staring down.

The Mortifer Flytraps, the lions, the leopardsharks paused. All of them thinking probably the same as Horizabel.

And then down ALL the other ones flew toward Mabel: Theo and Izzabird and Annipeck too, but now they were within reach of the

Flytrap tentacles that had sprung back into action, stretching up to catch them, flipping them over, so their Flymaster Homemade-O and tree branches crashed down into the clearing.

Mabel reached the talon of the Beast; she put her hand down to touch it.

"Stop, Beast, stop!" pleaded shy, scared little Mabel, looking up at his great Sphinx face. "Please do not do this!"

I *did* say, didn't I, that adventures bring out sides of people that they never knew they had?

Who would have thought that Mabel would be the one to speak out at such a momentous moment? The little girl whom Horizabel thought they really should have ditched a long time ago because she and the big adult were holding everyone up?

I am the one with the Atlas Gift !

"You're making a mistake!" said Mabel. "If you are looking for the Child-with-the-Atlas-Gift, *I* am the one who has it."

The Abhorrorghast paused in surprise, staring down at the little girl.

For

one

vital

moment.

Then both Izzabird and Theo staggered toward Mabel, leaping over the grasping vines, Annipeck holding on to Izzabird's hand.

"No," said Theo, panting. "The Child-With-The-Gift is ME."

"They're all lying," said Izzabird. "*I* am the One-With-The-Gift!"

"ME 'OO!" said Annipeck, and her toothbrushes nodded along emphatically.

Horizabel was experiencing a stirring in her mid-section that she hadn't really felt before.

Could it be indigestion?

Or could it be...

Galaxies of ghastliness! It couldn't possibly be *sadness*, could it?

Horizabel pulled herself together.

What a ridiculous plan of that silly little Mabel's, thought Horizabel sternly to herself. *So ridiculous that you can't even call it a plan at all, and it's never going to work, of course...*

But then...

"STOP!" cried another human voice from out of nowhere.

And, stumbling into the clearing, came the broken, disheveled figure of Daniel.

His clothes were in rags about him, sand-laden, grass-stained and half-burnt, and still smoking slightly from the fiery river. And he was listing very heavily to the left, for his entire right-hand side was still frozen by Cyril's Magic.

"Dad!" said Mabel happily. "You're awake!"

Annipeck toddled up to Daniel and he hugged her, so tight.

"Daddy!" said Annipeck delightedly, as if she had been expecting him all along.

Daniel smiled at her reassuringly, gently releasing her so he could face the Beast with his umbrella.

Not that Annipeck needed any reassuring. As far as she was concerned, as long as her father was here, everything was going to be all right.

"I beg you to stop!" repeated Daniel. "Do not harm these children..." He straightened his back. "*I* am the one in charge here. Kill *me* instead."

Wow, thought Izzabird, Daniel going up in her estimation.

Theo was staring at his father with his mouth open in surprise.

As we know, Theo had always wished his father was a bit more, well...NOT the kind of father who came last in all the Father's Day races.

But once you've seen your dad in rags, half-frozen, half-burnt, yet calmly confronting a great Beast and his Rider, all on another planet, as coolly as if he were standing in his very own classroom, well, you never really view him in the same way again.

"*You?*" sneered the Rider. "*You're* not even one of the Cunning Ones. I can sssniff that from here. Why would *you* offer yourself up to save the boy's life? Who *are* you, anyway? You are not the boy's father."

"But I married the boy's mother," said Daniel, putting his hand on K2's shoulder. "So although I am not his biological father, I will have to do. And I am doing what any father would do. For love. This is what family *means*."

Izzabird and Theo and Mabel and K2 and Annipeck looked at each other, and without even intending to, they held hands.

What was it with humans and their "love" and their "families"?

"In short, if you try to lay *one finger* on any of these children," cried Daniel, umbrella held determinedly in front of him, "you'll have to deal with ME first!"

Courageous words.

"Well, well, well," purred the Rider. "How charming. It appears that we now have all of you here in front of us. How many did that old rascal of a pirate, Cyril, say there were?"

The Rider ticked them off on his fingers. "Two brothers, *check*; two sisters, *check*; one baby,

This is what
family means!

check; man with umbrella, *check*...yes, all seem to be present and correct...How clever of us to keep the baby and those others alive as a lure for you all to come here!" gloated the Rider. "It's very thoughtful of you to come all this way. It saves me the trouble of going to this 'Planet Earth' of yours, which sounds like a total backwater. Because now would be a good moment to point out that, some centuries ago, the Abhorrorghast swore to DESTROY THE ENTIRE O'HERO FAMILY. And here you all are!"

Yes, that was predictable, thought Horizabel sadly.

Blistering black holes! There it was again! *Sadness.*

This would never do.

This is the moment, thought Horizabel, *for the Smiths to save their own lives by pointing out that they aren't actually from the O'Hero family at all.*

But no, in the contrary way that Horizabel was discovering was a bit of a hallmark of human beings, having argued almost constantly for the last two and a half years, the Smiths and the O'Heros had chosen this particular moment to decide that they *were* all one family after all.

"We're very, very sorry!" shouted Mabel. "For what happened with the sandwiches and everything after that."

"Sssorry?" hissed the Rider furiously, fanning the flames of the Beast's anger. *"Sorry?"*

In two frighteningly athletic bounds, the Rider leaped up and onto the Abhorrorghast's back to rile him with his argument. Knees digging into the furious Beast's shoulders, the Rider poured the poison of his words into the great creature's ears, choosing the exact speech that would whip the Abhorrorghast up to outrage, so he would make the final, fatal strike.

"YOU did this, YOU!" he raged from his vantage point, pointing down at Mabel, as if poor little Mabel herself had been out in Excelsiar for hundreds of years, personally killing silk trees and gouging out diamonts.

The Abhorrorghast was whirling on the spot now, fuming and raging, his wounded flanks steaming with fever, letting out roars and howls of fury at the desecration of his world.

"Because of YOU the golden sssilk trees, mile on mile in the endless breeze, are gone, all gone...And my poor dear Beast," said the Rider tragically, "fading away, a shadow of his former ssself. You should have seen him in his glory..."

You had to hand it to the Rider. It was a virtuoso performance.

"AND LOOK!" said the Rider, almost spitting now with triumph and horror, as he spotted what he knew would be the last straw: the little robot, Puck, peering out of K2's backpack.

"They have one of *THEM! A MECHANOID ABOMINATION!* I bet he has more digger functions than you can count on all your paws, oh Great Beast!"

The Beast gave a horrified intake of breath.

"I is only a very little one...," trembled poor Puck. "And I isss not really here...I is..." Puck searched his robot brain for where he could logically be. "I'sss...surfing the lava streams of Perigon in the second Galaxy on the left..."

But the Abhorrorghast could see the little robot perfectly well, and the sight of him was like putting a match to a bonfire.

The little human family, who had already linked hands, now joined in a circle.

If they were going to die, at least they would die *together.*

As the Great Beast inhaled, such was the strength of his fury, they were physically dragged toward him, still in their circle, like a little band of parachute jumpers.

It's all over..., thought K2 as they were pulled inexorably toward the great jaws in front of them; so close now, they could see the ghastly death-white of the Abhorrorghast's pin-sharp teeth, smell the rot of his hungry breath.

Up above, the aunts and Freya could bear it no longer.

"LET US OUT OF HERE!" they yelled as one.

"*Why?*" hissed Horizabel. "If anyone finds out I've interfered, I could be in Big Trouble with the High

Council of the Universal Government. What could you possibly do to stop the Beast now?"

"Make amends!" shouted Aunt Violet.

"We were bringing the Cure for the Plague of the Silk Trees," added Aunt Trudie. "But that foolish Beast and his hideous Rider bundled us up in here before we could get a word in edgeways!"

Horizabel stopped hacking at the prison pod she had been working on, the one so deeply entangled with vines and vegetation that she had been making very slow progress. "Well, that IS a possible bargaining chip."

Now what . . . ?

She changed course, using her Air Stick to slice open Aunt Trudie's prison pod instead. It fell open immediately, like a broken chestnut shell.

"What are you doing?" cried Blinkers, materializing above Horizabel, the prison pod of Cyril swaying dangerously underneath her.

"Change of plan, Blinkers. We're going to help rescue them after all!" said Horizabel.

"Um, I really wouldn't adviseth that, Mistress!" said Blinkers.

"We're only supposed to *not* interfere if they have No Chance of Survival," said Horizabel. "Now they've produced a bargaining chip that the Abhorrorghast might actually be interested in, I've just upgraded their prospects to Slim Chance."

"But the odds are still overwhelmingly against us!" objected Blinkers, rapidly doing calculations.

Horizabel ignored her, setting to work on Freya's prison pod.

Aunt Trudie was the first to descend down into the forest clearing.

The children watched with open mouths as Aunt Trudie shinned down a forest vine with truly remarkable speed considering she would never see seventy-five again.

Oh my goodness gracious, she thought. *I really don't have the knees for this anymore...*

"STOP!" she cried as she dropped to the forest floor. "We have the Cure for the Plague of the Silk Trees—and if we give it to you, you have to let the children go!"

"The trees will grow again, we swear it!" growled Aunt

Violet, using her impressive upper body strength to drop from branch to branch, landing beside Aunt Trudie moments later.

"Aunt Trudie's spent twenty years creating that Spell," shouted Freya, swinging right down after her.

"Freya!" exclaimed Daniel, eagerly and rather lopsidedly embracing her.

"*Mommy!*" cried Annipeck, K2, and Izzabird as she leaned in to hug them too.

"Freya! Aunt Trudie! Aunt Violet!" cried Mabel and Theo, bundling into the same hug.

The Rider and the Abhorrorghast couldn't believe their eyes. Here was a mother and two retirees busting out of their legendarily impossible-to-escape-from-prison, like it was some kind of treetop *hotel*.

What on Excelsiar was going on?

"So where is this supposedly world-saving Cure of yours, then?" said the Rider through gritted teeth, the Abhorrorghast snorting with hopeful excitement beneath him.

Aunt Trudie rummaged around in her coat. "Now, I know the Cure is in here *somewhere*. I'm absolutely certain I put it in one of my pockets...Ah, here it is!" she said at last with relief, feeling the outline of the two bottles in her zipped-up inside pocket. "I remember now, I put it in there to be safe with that Animation Potion..."

She took out the two little bottles.

There was a nasty pause.

Because I know you will remember, you sharp-eyed readers, that back on Planet Earth...Theo had switched the bottles.

"Oh dear, oh dear, oh DEAR!" said Aunt Trudie, and it was dreadful to hear the despair in her voice. "I appear to have accidentally brought a bottle of nutmeg and a bottle of vanilla instead of the Cure. How did *that* happen?"

"*Scatterbrain*," growled Aunt Violet.

"I'm afraid so," said Aunt Trudie sadly.

"Oh, for the stars' sake!" said Horizabel, looking down from the tree branch above and putting her face in her hands.

"HA!" crowed the Rider, exultant. "What did I tell you, Beast? These O'Heros are all liars and tricksters! END IT *NOW*!"

413

The Beast was only further enraged by this latest disappointment.

With a bellow, he readied to make the final strike.

It's too late to save us now, thought K2.

But you see, K2 wasn't quite right about that: It is very rarely TOO LATE.

Never give up.

Keep fighting, keep thinking, keep hoping, keep dreaming, until the

very...

bitter...

end.

Even in the very last seconds, half a minute to midnight, it is always worth using all the Gifts you have at your disposal to try and find a Plan.

For Theo now remembered something.

The aunts were talking about a "Cure" back when I was listening through the kitchen door, what felt like a lifetime ago, umpty gazillion miles away, back on Planet Earth...

It was just before he had stolen two bottles from Aunt Trudie's coat and switched them with vanilla and nutmeg. One bottle was the Animation Potion. The other bottle . . .

C.4.P.S.T.

Now he knew what those initials stood for.

Cure 4 Plague Silk Trees.

But Theo didn't have the bottle anymore either, he thought with a sinking heart.

Because . . .

Dad confiscated it, when I magicked the blow-dryer.

Theo looked across at Daniel.

His dad was still in the ragged remains of the suit he had been wearing that evening.

What if he still has the Cure for the Plague of the Silk Trees on him?

What if we've been carrying it with us the whole entire time of the journey without realizing?

These were the quick-blink thoughts of Theo in the nick and flick of time.

"Wait! Wait!" cried Theo and, panting, broke away from the circle.

To Daniel's bewilderment, Theo started rifling through his dad's pockets . . . *Oh, please let it still be in there . . .*

Daniel's clothes were in rags about him...maybe the Cure had fallen out?

But at last Theo's hands landed on a small, smooth, round something.

And there it was.

Theo brought out the little bottle, and the letters written on the label in Aunt Trudie's messy handwriting were very faint now, nearly burned away by the River of Fire.

But the initials were the ones that Theo had remembered.

C.4.P.S.T.

Theo turned and shouted at the top of his voice into the wind of the Beast's furiously inhaling mouth,

"YOU CAN'T KILL US BECAUSE WE REALLY HAVE BROUGHT YOU...

"THE CURE FOR THE PLAGUE OF THE SILK TREES!"

Chapter 34 BARGAINING WITH A BEAST

Sensation in the forest clearing.

The Abhorrorghast had brought the little human beings to the brink of his jaws, the only question now being whether he was going to strike first with his teeth or his terrible harpoon of a tail...

But at Theo's words, and the sight of the little bottle in his hand, the wind of the Beast's fury died abruptly.

The Abhorrorghast stood stock-still, head down like a bull about to charge, snorting great bellows of incensed steam from his nostrils, staring at Theo with a wild hope beyond hope.

The Cure for the Plague of the Silk Trees...

The Beast sighed yearningly.

All around the forest clearing, a longing, leafy whisper went from root to plant, from animal muzzle to curling antennae: "The Cure for the Plague of the Silk Trees..."

Aunt Trudie gave a sigh of satisfaction.

417

Fifty years she had spent looking for that Cure. Maybe it had not all been for nothing.

"Look!" said Theo as he held out the Cure in his shaking hand. "See, it *is* the Cure, we promise!"

The Beast roared with indecision, while the Rider on his back shrieked into his ear, "Not true! Do not believe it! The humans lie again and again and again!"

Theo took out the stopper of the bottle.

"Release us!" he shouted. "Or I will pour the Cure upon the ground, and you will never know if it works or not!"

Ah, he drove a hard bargain, that boy.

And you have to, when you are bargaining with a Beast.

Particularly when he is being ridden into the ground by a Rider such as that one.

"Let us live," said Theo to the Abhorrorghast, holding up the little bottle enticingly, "and your trees will grow again."

The Beast prowled this way and that way, howling and shaking his head with confusion.

"It won't be a *real* Cure!" spat the Rider savagely, incandescent now.

"*I* can vouch for the Cure! It most definitely works!" cried Aunt Trudie. "My grandfather told me stories of this forest. Stories his grandfather told him...He told me of the golden leaves of the silk trees that stretched for mile after endless mile."

"They were the glory of the universe," said Freya. "And they will grow again, Abhorrorghast, trust us, they will."

At these words, the blink of the Abhorrorghast's eye took him back to the achingly longing gold of the past. In that moment he was young again, running wild and free, in a wood that never ended.

Another blink, and he was back in the present.

He paced backward and forward.

What should he do?

Hundreds of years of war, and it's hard to turn in an instant, give up revenge for a grasp at a glimpse of hope.

"They're *lying*!" shrieked the Rider. "And if you let the Child-with-the-Atlas-Gift go, more pirates may come...This is your chance to destroy the ENTIRE O'Hero family, the aunts and Freya and—"

"WATCH OUT BELOW!" came the sharp cry of

Horizabel from above. Her
Air Stick had finally detached
the encrusted pod she had been
working on.

WATCH OUT BELOW!

And she'd been intending to
attach it to Blinkers beside Cyril's,
but the pod was so heavy with vines
that it slipped through Blinkers's
waiting arms and plunged downward.

"LOOK OUT!" cried Freya in alarm,
shoving the children out of harm's way as...

...*BOOOOOOMMM!*

The prison pod landed *BAM!* on the clearing floor
with such force that some of the vines and vegetation
encasing it exploded off in all directions.

And a very faint voice from deep inside the prison
pod cried: "*OW!*"

Muffled though it was, Izzabird and K2 would
have recognized that voice anywhere.

It was the voice of Everest O'Hero.

Chapter 35
WELL, THAT'S A SURPRISE

Well, well, well...

Izzabird and K2 stood as if turned to stone.

They had hoped beyond hope that this might happen one day, but never dared truly believe it.

Sometimes you do not fully realize the meaning of the adventure you are going on until you reach the end of it.

The children had found their father a long, long, long—*so* many longs—way from home, in an alien landscape, in another galaxy, but here he was!

Eyes shining like stars, Izzabird ran to the prison pod, threw her arms around it and said in a choked, passionate voice, "*Dad!*"

And then K2 limped up, more uncertain of his welcome, but still pink

Dad!

with pleasure, and amazed and adoring. "We have missed you so very much!"

"Everest? Everest?" hummed Puck excitedly from K2's backpack. "Everest is ALIVE!"

"Yes!" cried a weak voice from inside the prison pod. "It is I, Everest O'Hero! Surely that is not...*my children*?" Inside the prison pod, so wound around with choking vines and thorns, you could just see the shadowy outline of Everest eagerly pressing his hands against the outlines of his children's hands, separated only by the green prison walls.

"My goodness, how you've grown! I'd barely have recognized you!"

"You're *not* a pirate, are you, Dad?" said Izzabird, red with emotion. "It just *looks* like you could be...but you're not, you're not, you're not!"

There was a little pause inside the prison pod.

"Well..."

Where to start with the explanations?

How to begin with the histories, the inheritances, the regrets, and the attempts to make redress?

And no time, anyway.

So Everest changed the subject. "Freya, is that you? It's so wonderful to see you!"

"Yes, Everest, and I'm delighted that you're still alive, of course," fumed Freya, shooting furious looks at Aunts Trudie and Violet, "but I might have *known* you would be behind all this. This is absolutely typical!"

"I shall get us all out of here, Freya, never fear! I'm just in the process of formulating a foolproof plan," said Everest, trying to sound as impressive and noble as possible, but it was difficult to see what exactly he could *do* from such cramped and uncomfortable conditions.

"*Everest?*" stammered Daniel, finding this all rather difficult to take in. "This is your *ex-husband* Everest?"

"That's right," admitted Freya.

"Who IS this ill-dressed scarecrow who is holding your hand?" asked Everest.

"My husband," said Freya firmly. "And this is our daughter, Annipeck."

There was a rather crestfallen pause.

"Well, HE doesn't look like much of a hero," sniffed Everest. "Where's his mustache?"

"Silence! This is not some kind of O'Hero *family reunion*!" raged the Rider, struggling to regain control of the Abhorrorghast. "You'll never get thisssss chance again, you silly creature, I mean"—hurriedly correcting himself—"dear Beassssst, to wipe out the entire O'Hero family in one go! You cannot let them slip through your talons, particularly when ONE among them has the cursed Atlas Gift, with all the damage that can do."

But the poisonous words weren't making the impression on the poor bewildered Beast that the Rider wanted.

Now he was twisting, turning, and finally the Abhorrorghast reared up, and it really looked for the first time as if he were trying to get AWAY from his Rider.

And dropping out of nowhere, the elegant figure of Horizabel the Grimm landed on the forest floor as lightly as a cat.

She put her fists upon her hips, and cried out: "GREAT BEAST, *I* WILL VOUCH FOR THE O'HEROS! IF YOU LET THEM GO FREE *I* WILL

424

PLEDGE TO MAKE SURE THEY WILL NEVER LEAVE PLANET EARTH AGAIN! Besides, you know it's not them that's lying to you—it's *him*!" And she pointed dramatically at the Rider.

Well.

It was quite the heroic moment.

Horizabel had never done such a thing before.

And it made a big impression.

Even here on Excelsiar, they knew a Grimm when they saw one.

For a second, the feeling of doing the right thing and making a big heroic gesture was really quite delicious.

But then Horizabel got a good look at the Rider.

It was the first time she had seen him close up. If looks could kill, the one that the Rider was now giving Horizabel would have done just that in seconds.

"*Horizzzzabel the Grimm...*," hissed the Rider of the Beast.

"Uh-oh...," said Horizabel. *"Vorcxix the Vile..."*

Horizabel *may* have made a teensy mistake.

You may have, up until now, thought that Cyril or

THE EXCORIATOR or the Beast were the villains of this story.

But *this* was a bad'un who put even Cyril's villainy, the Beast's rage, and THE EXCORIATOR's murderous vibes in perspective.

This was a Being whose sheer wickedness and greed made Cyril by comparison look like an angelic little kitten.

The Rider of the Beast wasn't just an "agent" of the Universal Government.

He was one of the twelve all-powerful members of the High Council.

And he was the most formidable.

Awed throughout the universe, Vorcxix was a Were-dread Enraptor of the Imperial line who Horizabel called "Vorcxix the Vile" behind his back. Which is pronounced "Vork-zicks," and sounds, very appropriately, a little like a mixture of a devilishly pointy fork and someone throwing up with fear.

And Horizabel had just broken so many Rules in front of him that could get her into trouble with the Council, it was hard to know where to begin thinking about it. Still in for a penny, in for a pound...

Vorcxix
(the Vile)

"Vorcxix here has been lying to you all along," smiled Horizabel. "He has never been here to help you, Beast. He wants to get the O'Heros, and he has only made the situation on Excelsiar worse. Look, see how your rage against the humans and the floating cities has turned you against the things you love!"

She pointed at the poor stricken tree that the Abhorrorghast had poisoned with his harpoon when he was striking K2's Atlas.

"Yes," said K2, catching on."Those poor, kind, trapped beings in the pods, the ones from the cities, I don't believe any of them are in alliance with the miners. He must be lying about that…"

And as if things couldn't get any more complicated…there was a violent sound of tearing greenery…

…and THE EXCORIATOR bounded into the clearing.

Chapter 36
Enter THE EXCORIATOR

HE EXCORIATOR vaulted in a great leap,
arms turned into machetes and its skeleton
jaw open in a mind-bending shriek. The
digger fixings he had used to plow and chomp
through the cress-choked jungle, biting, slashing, and
devouring, turned into springs in midair, just in time
for him to make a perfect landing, right in the center
of the clearing, his cloak swirling.

In a wild, metallic, robotic roar he shouted:
"WHERE IS THE CHILD-WITH-
THE-ATLAS-GIFT?"

Annipeck let out a wail
of horror, throwing her
arms around Theo's
legs.

The Abhorrorghast
was already in a bucking,
roaring, infuriated mood, with
no idea what to believe or what
to do next.

And now the Ultimate Machine-to-End-All-Machines had violated his plant kingdom and was standing arrogantly in the heart-core of his forest, bellowing.

"GIVE ME THE CHILD-WITH-THE-ATLAS-GIFT!" screamed THE EXCORIATOR, turning one of his arms into a chainsaw and the other into one that had frightening-looking laser-blaster fingers.

The Abhorrorghast's eyes narrowed. His scorpion tail swished dangerously from side to side, the point dripping with death. His leopardsharks and Flytrap minions awaited his next move.

"Patienccccce now, Beasst…Let's not do anything rassssh…," Vorcxix the Rider hissed, plucking the delicate hairs above the Beast's eyes to make him change course, but…

"ROOOOOOOARRRRRRRRRR!"

The Abhorrorghast let out the loudest roar of all, his supremacy in his own jungle made clear.

THE EXCORIATOR started in surprise. His eyes swiveled in their sockets.

"THE CHILD-WITH-THE-ATLAS-GIFT MUST

BE DESTROYED!" screamed THE EXCORIATOR even louder, his tone at a spine-tingling, toe-curling screech of a pitch that furled the ends of the Flytraps' tendrils like they'd just had lemon and salt dripped on them.

Theo was shielding Mabel and Annipeck, Daniel was standing in front of Theo, Freya was in front of Izzabird and K2, while Aunts Trudie and Violet were balanced and ready to avert attack.

But while THE EXCORIATOR screamed, Izzabird's sharp little eyes had noticed three things.

One was that Vorcxix the Vile seemed to be trying to stop the Abhorrorghast from advancing on the robot.

Two was that the robot was rather blingily adorned with an exceptional number of DIAMONT stars, almost as if it had ready access to such rare stones—for example, as if it knew someone who had a secret alliance with diamont miners.

Three was that the swirling cloak of THE EXCORIATOR had blown back to reveal something rather strange swinging from either side of his neck and ringing against his high-gloss shoulders.

*A pair
of stirrups. For
someone to ride him.
Who would ride THE
EXCORIATOR?*

Izzabird made a guess.

"EXCORIATOR!" she yelled. "WHY DON'T
YOU ASK YOUR *MASTER* WHETHER YOU
SHOULD ATTACK?"

Obediently, the great robot swiveled his

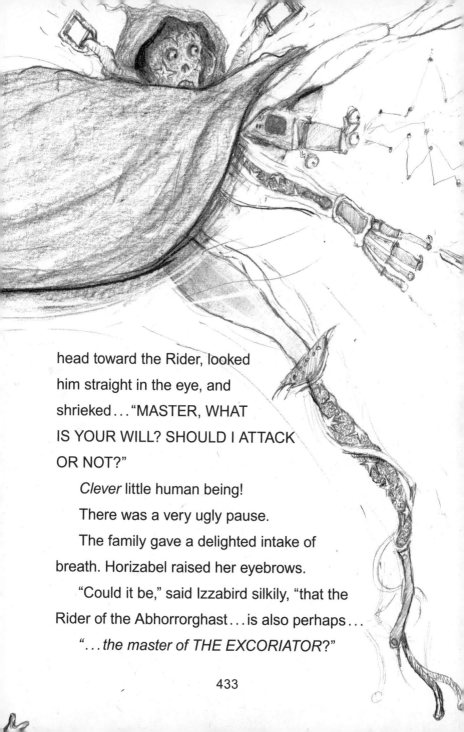

head toward the Rider, looked him straight in the eye, and shrieked... "MASTER, WHAT IS YOUR WILL? SHOULD I ATTACK OR NOT?"

Clever little human being!

There was a very ugly pause.

The family gave a delighted intake of breath. Horizabel raised her eyebrows.

"Could it be," said Izzabird silkily, "that the Rider of the Abhorrorghast...is also perhaps...

"...*the master of THE EXCORIATOR?*"

433

"*NO!*" shrieked Vorcxix, trying to retrieve the situation one last time, giving THE EXCORIATOR a meaningful look. "I LOATHE robots, especially ones with digger attachments, and I've never seen this particular robot before in my life!"

"My mistake, Master," said THE EXCORIATOR, realizing his blunder. "You are not my master, Master."

Oh dear. Robots really are *very* bad at lying.

The damage was done.

Vorcxix had been riding the Beast hard over the years, and the Beast had grown weary of being ridden.

And it was most definitely not happy to find that his supposed-friend and Rider might have secret alliances with enemy robots and had been lying to him all along.

With a bellow of rage, the Abhorrorghast bucked Vorcxix off his back with such violence that Vorcxix sailed right over his head and skidded twenty feet across the clearing.

Vorcxix realized the game was up. And with a scream of anger, he got to his feet and leaped onto the shoulders of THE EXCORIATOR, fitting his feet into the two specially made stirrups with ease.

For Vorcxix had indeed ridden THE EXCORIATOR many times before.

Well, well, well.

It looked like the smart little humans may have caught out a member of the High Council of the Universal Government doing a little illegal plotting on the side.

Using one of the Council's robot assassins!

Robot assassins are meant to be answerable to the Universal Government and not to particular members of the High Council. This is to stop them from using the robot assassins for their own private ends.

Which meant that Horizabel now had some information that Vorcxix would like kept secret as well.

"Excellent!" said Horizabel, rubbing her hands together.

Desperately, Vorcxix kicked THE EXCORIATOR into a charge toward K2, but as he did so, with a great and terrifying roar of pure animal fury, the

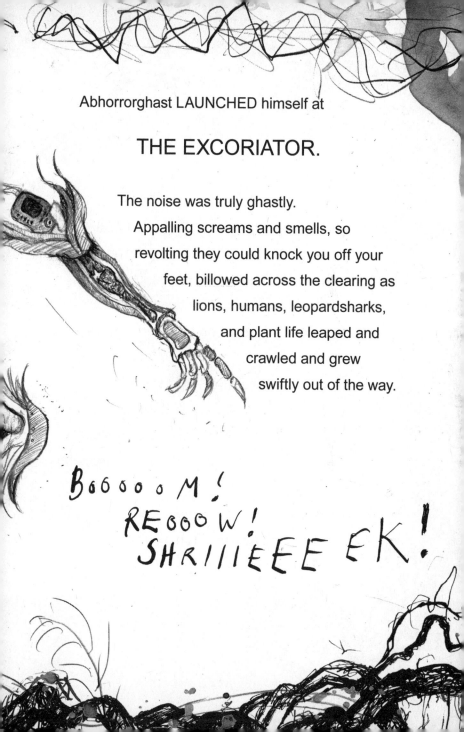

Abhorrorghast LAUNCHED himself at

THE EXCORIATOR.

The noise was truly ghastly.
Appalling screams and smells, so
revolting they could knock you off your
feet, billowed across the clearing as
lions, humans, leopardsharks,
and plant life leaped and
crawled and grew
swiftly out of the way.

BOOOOOM!
REOOOW!
SHRIIIEEEEK!

"*LET'S GET OUT OF HERE!*" roared Horizabel as she and Freya and Aunt Violet herded the children and Daniel toward Aunt Trudie, who had leaped toward the vacuum cleaners, disentangling the vegetation that bound them to the tree trunk with her glowing green fingers.

"Trudie, Freya—the Power of All Three!" Aunt Trudie pulled out her Spelling Stick and motioned it above her in a circle. The other two pulled out theirs and then three lightning blasts buzzed above, combining to create a fizzing, protective Spell Dome of Magic over them, as Aunt Trudie undid the last fiddly bits of vine with her free hand.

438

Wreeooooow! ZinnnnG! sang the Spell Dome as stray laser bolts and Beastly harpoons bounced harmlessly off it, the family sheltering underneath.

But Puck was peering out from K2's backpack and at this extremely unhelpful moment he squealed, "Ooh, look, K2, your Atlas!" and pointed one of his little robot arms at the Atlas that Cyril had stolen, still harpooned to a tree trunk on the other side of the clearing.

K2 couldn't abandon it there in this forest.

"Wait a second!" he cried, scrambling underneath the bottom of the Spell Dome and running out into the chaos of the battle.

"Nooooo!" Freya shouted, unable to move, because if she went after K2 the Spell Dome would collapse. "Horizabel, stop him!"

Unfortunately, Horizabel was momentarily distracted, trying to catch Everest, who also wasn't being very helpful, rolling as he was around the clearing in his prison pod in valiant but violent and nausea-inducing rolls, bowling the leopardsharks over like ninepins, with a very faint muffled yelling coming from within: "AN O'HERO KNOWS NO LIMITS! THE SKY IS JUST THE BEGINNING! NO RIVERS CAN STOP US! NO MOUNTAINS CAN STAND IN OUR WAY!"

Luckily, most of the plants and creatures of the forest who weren't attacking THE EXCORIATOR were attacking the Spell Dome, so K2 made it across the clearing alive, dodging the poison harpoons and whistling bombs.

With trembling fingers, K2 removed the Atlas from where it was pinned and ran back across the clearing, flushed with triumph.

But even mid-fight to the death, THE EXCORIATOR had spotted K2 running out of the corner of his eye.

440

Those terrible robot-assassin eyes closed in on K2 like gunsights. "*THE CHILD-WITH-THE-ATLAS-GIFT!*" he roared.

"Kill him!" hissed Vorcxix from his vantage point on the shoulders of THE EXCORIATOR.

"*Horizabel!*" shouted K2 as he ran. "HELP ME!"

"HORIZABEL!" yelled the rest of the family, helpless underneath the Spell Dome, surrounded by attacking leopardsharks and Flytraps and dolteeth.

But Horizabel didn't hear them. She had *finally* caught up with Everest and was in the middle of the tricky task of attaching Everest's prison pod next to Cyril's on one of the winches hanging from the underside of the hovering Blinkers.

THE EXCORIATOR lifted a hand and pointed his laser-blaster finger at K2, running across the middle of the clearing, clutching his maps to his chest as if they were going to save him.

Chapter 37
MAGIC-THAT-WORKS-ON-PLASTIC

Who knows what would have happened next?

But underneath the safety of the Spell Dome, Annipeck was watching her beloved brother.

She knew he was in deadly danger, and now she knew where *from*.

"BAD man!" said a furious Annipeck, looking at Vorcxix.

She blinked twice and wiggled her fingers a little, and a fizzing of pure, clear Magic, bright

and white as an icicle, came out of those dear little baby palms and *shot* toward THE EXCORIATOR.

It hit the robot's pointing laser-blaster finger. Like most robots, THE EXCORIATOR's shining aluminium silver and diamond body was made out of a considerable amount of metal, but for ultimate protection he was covered entirely in a thin film of plastic.

Because Magic doesn't work on plastic.

Unless, of course, it belongs to baby Annipeck.

THE EXCORIATOR shot up two feet in the air and his entire body lit up with such a fierce shock of Magic that it was as if he had put that finger in an electric socket.

"Wow...," breathed the family as THE EXCORIATOR landed back on the ground, about three feet from where he started.

"WOW...," breathed Horizabel, finally turning around, having attached Everest's pod successfully.

Now she knew the potential of Annipeck's Magic. Now everyone did.

THE EXCORIATOR lay on the ground, still in one piece... until one of the tough little plastic screws bolting his laser finger to his palm popped out.

And THE EXCORIATOR's laser finger fell to the ground.

That was all it took.

It wasn't much of a wound really, considering the Abhorrorghast had already bitten out half of THE EXCORIATOR's chest-section.

But, "WOW...," breathed Vorcxix, from underneath THE EXCORIATOR's shoulders.

He stared across at the furious little infant holding Theo's hand, wiggling her fingers, preparing for another attack, and reconsidered his options.

Vorcxix was desperate to eliminate this O'Hero family... when was he going to get another chance of them all being in one place together?

But he couldn't fight the Abhorrorghast AND Horizabel AND this who-knew-how-powerful baby at the same time, and risk the possible destruction of THE EXCORIATOR.

He had to live to fight another day.

With a scream of fury and a last stinging wail of

his whip, Vorcxix rode THE EXCORIATOR out of there, striking dead a few poor leopardsharks who happened to be in the way out of pure maliciousness.

The Abhorrorghast spat out the robot chest-section.

The confused plants and animals halted their attacks, turning their quivering heads toward their leader.

The Abhorrorghast limped forward, a pathetic sight now, for he was very wounded. Freya and the aunts lowered their spell.

The great Beast stopped at Mabel.

He collapsed in front of her and reached his giant head forward, an inarticulate sound trying to form in his throat.

"The Cure," whispered Mabel. "He wants the Cure."

Chapter 38
THE CURE FOR THE PLAGUE OF THE SILK TREES

Theo brought out the potion bottle and gave it to Aunt Trudie.

The limping Abhorrorghast turned and led them through the forest, and they followed him like kittens. A little way away, with one bleeding paw, the Abhorrorghast tore down a choking mess of cress and vegetation and thorn, to reveal, in the center...

...a tiny, ragged tree, twisted and pathetically small. The golden branches bore no leaves, and the tree was bent over, on the edge of extinction, desperately clinging to its last gasp of life.

The Abhorrorghast turned his great sad eyes toward the humans. He tried to say something, but the humans already knew.

This was one of the last silk trees.

They all circled around: the humans, Horizabel, the lions, leopardsharks, tiger-griffs, unideer, Flytraps, toothbrushes, Puck, blow-dryer...a quiet, solemn audience.

The blue monkey sat on his haunches and wrapped his tail around himself, staring hopefully at the tree.

Aunt Trudie stepped forward.

This was the moment.

Fifty-five years of searching for a Cure, all those late nights, the failed attempts, the false starts, and that was just *Aunt Trudie's* lifetime; for she had built on the research of her ancestors...generation after generation.

Aunt Trudie knelt down in front of the little tree.

Trembling, she took the stopper out of the bottle of potion.

One of the last
Silk trees ...

She poured one drop only
onto the roots and said some
words that made the green tips of
her fingers glow.

And she knelt back and *waited*,
her heart in her mouth.

Nothing for a second.

And then it was just like Magic,
really.

Astonishing.

The little tree quivered, like
it was catching its breath. The
watching audience gasped in
amazement as it straightened, like
a small golden animal. In front of
their eyes, it grew, up, up, until it
was taller than Annipeck, taller
than Mabel. Only when it was
taller than Theo did it stop. Tiny
leaves of unbelievable softness and

And it was just
like magic, really.

frail see-through
beauty sprouted from
the branches as it grew,
straight and strong, to the sound
of strange music that seemed to be
coming from inside the tree itself. Buds were
already bursting on the branches, filled with
seeds that would lead to more trees.

And where it grew, the cress died. It withered
in front of their eyes, until all around the whispering,
wondering audience there was a ring of the dying-
away cress, a circle of promise that this could be
repeated all over the planet.

Aunt Trudie tried to keep command of her
shaking voice as she replaced the stopper in the
little bottle of the Cure and put it in the hand of the
monkey. "One drop, three times a day, until the tree
grows to full size," she said. "Use it on all the trees
you have left, and the seeds will fly on the wind,
and before you know it, you will have your silk tree
forest back again. And don't worry about running out
of potion. This particular magic bottle is a 'cup that

Astonishing.

overflows.' The Cure will last forever; it never will run out."

Silence.

A long intake of breath.

And then the Abhorrorghast threw back his head.

"*ROOOOOOOOOOARRRRRRRRRRRR!*" he bellowed.

A rich, rude roar of truly wonderful loudness.

This was a roar of VICTORY.

And all around the clearing the plants and animals turned and roared in company with him.

"*ROOOOOOOOOOARRRRRR!*"

Louder still and louder.

"*Roaooorrrrr!*" said Annipeck, banging her fists joyfully from her vantage point on Theo's shoulders. "*Roarrrrr! Reooorrrr!*"

Chapter 39 TIME TO LEAVE

As all around the animals and plants stamped their hooves and clashed their leaves and roared and rustled in joyful jubilation, Horizabel quietly motioned to the family that this really *was* the time to depart now.

The Abhorrorghast roared and swiped his tail for his plants and creatures to follow, and even though he was wounded, he was moving with a lightness of spirit he had not had for many hundreds of years. Off he bounded through the forest searching for the other few remaining silk trees still clinging on to life, with the monkey racing after him clutching the potion bottle, followed by leopardsharks, lions, and Flytraps.

And the family and Horizabel ran back to the clearing and a patiently waiting Blinkers.

Horizabel firmly took K2's rescued Alternative Atlas off him to look for a Which Way, when she could perfectly well have looked in her own. She found an "X" just to the west of the desert, then put K2's Atlas in her backpack before he could object.

Annipeck joined Freya on her Hoover, and Daniel climbed on the back of Aunt Violet's, and Mabel on the back of Aunt Trudie's, and Theo and Izzabird and K2 followed on the Flymaster Homemade-O and the tree branches. Horizabel led the way, with Blinkers carrying the two prison pods containing Cyril and Everest, and in an untidy, wild, and snaking mess, the little family group flew up and out of the prison of No

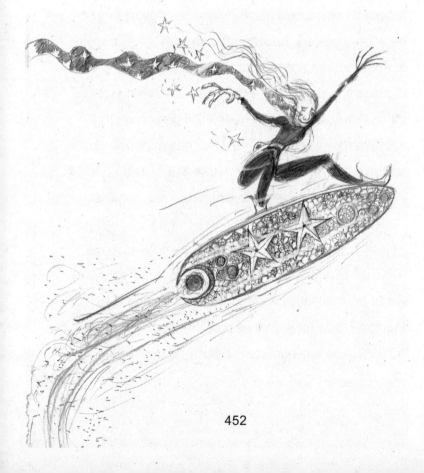

Man's Land, and toward the Which Way that led back to Planet Earth and the House of the O'Heros...

"WOO-HOO!" yelled Aunt Violet in delight, her Hoover honking rudely.

They kept looking back over their shoulders at the forest they had left behind.

To K2's delight, every now and then they would see sections of the forest light up with a strange gold-and-silver light and a vague noise of animal and plant applause, as another dying silk tree was brought back to life from the edge of extinction.

And then later, much later...

They had nearly reached the edge of the desert, and Annipeck had fallen asleep clinging to Freya like a baby koala, when something even more peculiar began happening. Something different.

Strange things were flying up and out of the treetops, in an explosion of leaves and joy, like the cork being taken out of a bottle of fizzy wine.

"What are those?" said K2, shading his eyes.

Theo got out the binoculars. "They look like flying centaurs...or flying horses? And look!" He pointed at the horizon.

An extraordinary sight.

The awe-inspiring approach of four, five, six floating cities, sailing slowly but surely through the bright evening Excelsiar sky toward the Prison of the Abhorrorghast.

"What's going on?" asked Theo.

Horizabel made a flashy, sweeping turn on her Flymaster above them. "Looks to me like in his joy, the Abhorrorghast may be releasing the prisoners he's captured from the cities," said Horizabel.

Everyone smiled to see the uncontained happiness of those flying, fleeing dormindrads, and the mighty cities coming to rescue their citizens.

And not a shot was being fired from the forest to stop them doing that. In fact, the vines reached up to stroke and welcome them.

Maybe it was their imagination, but traveling across the desert air from the distant floating cities, could that be the faint sound of cheering?

And as the sun went down over the big Excelsiar sky and the three moons rose, they had the truly incredible sight of one of those great cities actually *landing*, for the first time in centuries, to collect their fellow boggles, the elves, the cyclopes, and the gergashes who could not fly.

Slowly, slowly they watched the solemn descent of the great city, the citizens cheering from the walls, the juddering landing, the dust and sand rising all around in great clouds as the city finally settled on the sweet ground again.

And then the sun set, and they could see no more.

Aunt Trudie gave a sigh of contentment.

There's nothing like the satisfaction of a long, long mission, finally completed.

"Hundreds and hundreds of years in the making," she said. "But all worth it *in the end*."

She paused, adding wistfully, "I do wish we could stay and see those silk trees come back to life, though...

"...Legend says they are quite breathtaking when they are in full bloom."

So that was the story of the Great Escape from the Prison of the Abhorrorghast.

And I can look into the future, so I can tell you this will be a new beginning for the world of Excelsiar.

Although you can't always turn around centuries of warlike behavior in a heartbeat, however big the heart.

But the family have done their best.

And the silk trees are growing again.

And they will grow tall and they will spread fast and they will cover up the diamonts again.

And then the mines will shut down, the warrior-winds will die, the poison rivers will flow clean.

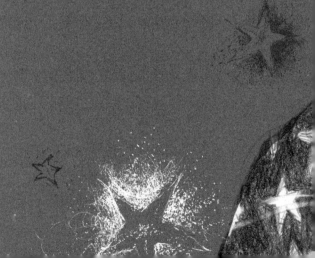

ALL the cities will land and plant their roots once more in the newly fertile soil of Excelsiar.

And the dream of a world where everyone can live and grow together in harmony will begin.

And this story could have ended here, when these ten human beings, some of whom were the first to escape from that prison for many hundreds of years, FINALLY reached the Which Way, tattered, torn, guided by the harpooned Alternative Atlas, stepping back through to Planet Earth with two great slashes of Horizabel's Air Stick, and a spritz of her Steri-gas.

But I can take you further.

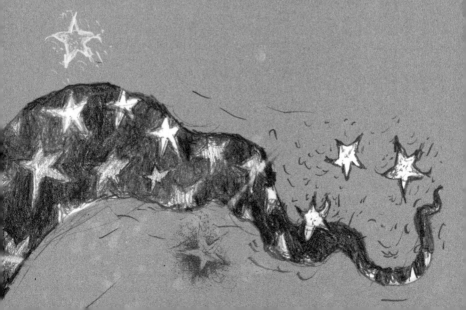

And so we are falling through space again.
From morn to dewy eve you will fall. From noon to
every eve, sheer over the battlements of time...until
suddenly you stop, hovering above where that small
blue and green planet is quietly spinning and, O stay
a moment, dear reader, to admire how beautiful it is,
gently glowing, like a perfectly round ball in the great
calm blackness.

   And from all that we have learned from what has
happened on Excelsiar, how carefully should we
look after it if we are lucky enough to be living there
awhile...

Chapter 40 WHEN THEY GOT BACK HOME

It was even more unpleasant going back through the Which Way than it had been before.

K2 had the same horrible feeling that he was going to suffocate as he pushed his way through the squeezing pressure of the space-between-worlds back to Earth at last. This time he lay on the ground gasping for at least two minutes, with Theo thumping him on the back to get more air into him.

That was an exhausted, bedraggled party that landed in the garden of the House of the O'Heros.

They staggered back into the house, with Blinkers dragging the prison pods containing Cyril and Everest.

They were home. They were alive.

Everyone was ravenous and extremely dirty, so they took turns to have baths, and Daniel and Freya and Aunt Trudie bustled about putting supper on even though it was one o'clock in the morning by the clocks on Planet Earth, with Clueless jumping all over them in her joy at their safe return.

Annipeck and her toothbrushes sat on the floor of the hall watching, fascinated, as Horizabel got Blinkers and Puck to tidy up the mess of the devastated front staircase. It was a magical sight as the tiny fragments reconfigured with the meticulous accuracy of an art historian, but about three thousand times more quickly due to the impressive speed of the little robot arms.

When Mabel opened the linen closet, there was no longer any sign of the sad, ghostly gentleman in the Viking helmet. But all the clean towels and the sheets had been folded very neatly while they were gone. As she closed the door, was it her imagination or did she hear the whisper of someone saying thank you?

Something's wrong, though, thought Izzabird.

She ought to be happy. They were home, they had rescued Annipeck and her father, and she was trembling with excitement at the thought that she was about to see him again. But in her heart of hearts, she knew they weren't safe yet.

Horizabel was looking twitchy and unsettled, as if she had something unpleasant to do and couldn't decide whether to do it very quickly and get it over with, or leave doing it until the last possible minute.

And something about Horizabel's fidgeting and tenseness was making Izzabird nervous.

What was the Grimm intending to do?

"Will you stay for supper, Horizabel?" said Aunt Trudie cozily, popping her head around the door of the kitchen, for all the world as if Horizabel was a perfectly ordinary visitor, rather than a bounty hunter from another world.

"No, thank you," said Horizabel. "I'll just finish tidying up, and then I really do have to get on."

"You need to release my father from his prison pod first," said Izzabird.

"I *need* to do no such thing," said Horizabel, with tight lips.

But, unfortunately, back in Excelsiar when

461

Horizabel had been sawing through the vine attaching Everest's pod to the tree, Everest had made a wish.

"Oh, how I wish," Everest had sighed, "HOW I wish that I could hold my children in my arms, just one last time..."

Wishes in the presence of an unseen Grimm have such power, particularly when they are made by a Hero from the bottom of their heart.

And although Horizabel was not absolutely *tied* by such a wish, she was honor bound to grant it if she could.

"I will release you, Everest, *for a moment*, to say goodbye," said Horizabel now, "if *you* promise, Word of a Hero, that you will come quietly with me, directly afterward."

"I make you that promise, Horizabel!" said Everest eagerly. "Word of an O'Hero!"

"Goodbye?" said Izzabird, her face falling, as Horizabel began working with her Air Stick on the prison pod containing Everest. "But why are you saying *goodbye*, Dad? You've only just come back!"

"I wish I had more time to explain," said the faint,

muffled voice of Everest from inside the prison pod. "I never *intended* to be a pirate, just an ordinary adventurer. But I made a friend or four when I was young who turned out to be bad'uns. And for a while there, wherever I put my footsteps, the pirates seemed to follow."

"Like Cyril?" wondered Izzabird.

"Indeed," said Everest ashamedly. "Though, ever after, I have been trying to make amends."

Both children were now sitting cross-legged beside the prison pod at Horizabel's feet as she worked on it.

Izzabird's heart was thumping in anticipation.

"Not long now, Everest!" Puck buzzed excitedly. "You're nearly out!"

Crack! Horizabel broke through the remaining layer of the prison pod.

Out staggered Everest. Blinking, unsure on his feet. He gave a gasp of joy and relief as he saw the light, for even a very Great Hero is worn down when they have been imprisoned in such cramped and deadening darkness that they think they will never see daylight again.

Maybe he was a little older than they remembered him.

A little more weary around the merry eyes.

But still the same beloved Hero of an Everest.

Their father.

And it was *out-of-this-world* wonderful to see him.

K2 and Izzabird threw their arms around him, and they held on tight, oh, so very tight, for they never wanted to let go.

"You're always going away, Dad," said Izzabird in a choked, impassioned voice. "Couldn't you stay *here* for once?"

"I have...er...Important Work to do elsewhere," explained Everest.

"Aren't *we* Important Work?" asked K2.

"Of *course* you are: You and Izzabird are much loved!" said Everest, squeezing them tighter. "But, unfortunately, Horizabel here is insisting that I spend some time in a...in a...in a reformatory confinement situation...belonging to the Evergods," explained Everest.

"By 'reformatory confinement situation' he means 'prison,'" said Freya dryly, emerging from the kitchen.

"Thank you, Freya. *I'm* explaining this to the children," said Everest testily. "Izza and K2..." Everest knelt, stroking their hair. "It's complicated, but long ago I crossed a line, so for now I cannot come back and look after you like I should.

"I love you very much, and I wish, beyond worlds, that I could turn back time, and make things right, and come back and be with you and your mother. But I can't, and I want her to be happy. That is what

True Love is. Loving someone so much that you want them to be happy...even when that means that you have to let them go."

He heaved a large sigh, then continued admiringly: "You did some wonderful Hero-work on that adventure, Izza. Considering you're a girl, that was pretty good..."

"Considering I'm a *girl*?" said Izzabird, in astonishment. "What do you mean, *considering* I'm a *girl*? Look at my mother and Horizabel! And, anyway, girls are the BEST!!!"

How long had her father been IN that prison pod, for the black holes' sake? Since the 1940s?

"Oh, ah, yes, of course," said Everest hurriedly. "And K2 was very impressive too, considering..."

"Considering *WHAT*?" yelled Izzabird. "You mean, considering his father is JUDGY and completely WRONG? K2 is *MARVELOUS*!"

K2 grinned proudly, but shyly, as his mom squeezed his arm.

"Yes, of course he is, I see that now," said Everest hastily, in a harassed sort of way. "Um...I still have a lot to learn..."

He certainly did.

Izzabird was looking very thoughtful.

"I wish I'd been a better father," said Everest wistfully, "and maybe in another time...another world...things could have worked out. But I'm happy that we were able to have this last journey together. And if it makes any of you feel a bit better, this adventure has taught me one thing...I have the most wonderful children."

"We all do," Daniel joined in.

Well, as it happens, that DID make things a little better.

"Look at me, Izza and K2!" commanded Everest.

Izzabird and K2 looked into his eyes.

"You need to know this in your heart, and I'm going to repeat it, because it's so important," said Everest. "I love you very much, and I would come back if I could. But I can't..."

Izzabird hadn't cried since her father left, just been angry, so she cried a *lot*, great gulping sobs.

"The universe is a wild and wonderful place, Izza and K2," said Everest. "But do not forget that the particular little spot where *you* are is wild and wonderful too. And Planet Earth needs you. Don't make the same mistakes I have made...don't wander the world looking always so far to the next horizon that you forget about the beauty that is right in front of you."

Grown-ups are always doing things like this. Giving you advice that they'd never dream of actually taking themselves.

"But know this, flawed as I am, I will be in your hearts forever. And I will be watching you from a faraway star...Use your gifts for good. That is all we can ever do: try our hardest to use our gifts for good."

Everest stood up and turned to his faithful robot, hovering in the background. "Goodbye, to you too, Puck," he said.

"But, Everest, I haves to go with you!" said the little robot, very distressed. "Who will be your helper?"

"I won't need helping in the Prison of the Evergods, and you were a little broken up by our last adventure. You must stay here and be mended," said Everest. "Aunt Violet is the best mender of robots I know. And, of course, you must look after Izza and

K2, and the rest of these children here will need your protection. It's a very important role."

"*Is it?*" said Puck in delight. "In which case, I *exclept!*"

"Grandpa?" said Annipeck, toddling over. "Worrr war ma Grandpa?"

"Cyril has some thinking to do," said Horizabel. "I'm taking him to a nice peaceful spot where he can do that."

Cyril had gone quiet. The Prison of the Evergods was sounding like a rather restful location after all that he'd been through. And Vorcxix and THE EXCORIATOR wouldn't be able to get him there.

Everest hugged them one last time.

He and Horizabel were about to set off when...

"One moment...," said Everest casually, holding up a finger, as if it were an afterthought. "Just before we go, Horizabel, I would love to see K2 draw in the Atlas, for one last time. So I can have something nice to remember when I'm whiling the long hours away in prison?"

Horizabel's eyes narrowed into slits of suspicion.

She was about to deny the request, and then,

for reasons of her own,
she changed her mind.
"Actually, that's a good
idea. Just to make a final
check before I..."

"Before you... *what*?" said Izzabird.

What was Horizabel going to do?

Horizabel ignored the question. "Quick! Bring out the pencils, get him some paper, here!"

K2 stepped forward.

"This is the last time, mind," warned Freya, her eyes sharp and anxious, her head roaring as if it were on fire. "We'll never let him do it again, will we?" She looked at the aunts.

"I'm sure you won't," said Horizabel. "But it would be good to see the boy do it...

"just...

one...

last...

time."

470

Freya, Aunt Trudie, and Aunt Violet surreptitiously moved their hands to their Spelling Sticks, looking at Horizabel warily.

"What world do you want, Father?" asked K2 timidly.

"Make it a good one," said Everest. "Somewhere to rest your feet awhile, before you get on with the journey. No Beasts, no Mortifer Flytraps. A quiet place, with the drowsy hum of gentle bees, and the slow growing of a marrow or two, that sort of thing. A kind old dog idling in the warm shadows to greet us, with a great waving flag of a tail. A distant horizon with a few suns going down. Somewhere wonderful."

K2 sat down.

He took his Alternative Atlas in his hands.

It was looking rather the worse for wear. The poison of the Abhorrorghast's harpoon had pierced it right in the center and it was smeared with moss. But it would do nonetheless.

There in the kitchen K2 settled down to draw a map.

And they all leaned in to see him draw.

Chapter 41 WHEN WE GET TO THE POINT-Y BIT OF THE STORY

Now this is where we get to the point-y bit of the story.

It is always important, readers and listeners, to think, who is telling me this story?

Who and why?

You have probably guessed, you clever people, that I, the Story Maker, and the beautiful, clever, BRILLIANT Horizabel, are one and the same person.

So yes, I, Horizabel, am the Story Maker.

And we have come to the prickly *point* of the story at last.

I am, among many things, a bounty hunter, and my mission all along has been to get rid of any illegal Alternative Atlases that are wafting about the universe, arrest any who use them...

...and, which I might not have mentioned before, to eliminate the One-with-the-Atlas-Gift.

It is a heartless task, but then Grimms are not supposed to have hearts.

I have nothing against K2 personally, but...

K2 has the most dangerous Gift in the universe,
and *bad people* want to use that Gift. Look at all
the disorder the O'Hero family has caused in the
universe already! If I just get rid of this one child,
the Universal Government can put a stop to all this
chaos and destruction, once and for all.

But as I look down at the small boy, so trusting,
so sweet, opening up the bedraggled remains of his
Atlas in all innocence, keen to impress his father,
I feel an unexpected pain in the chest area where
hearts are meant to be if you have them.

I hardened myself.

I readied my Spelling Finger.

Chapter 42 How THE STORY TURNS...

I *will just let him draw the beginning of the map,* thought Horizabel. *And then I'll do it.*

The Spell-Shot is invisible and it would not act immediately. Still time for Horizabel to do what she was supposed to do, no one would know, and she could leave without fuss, and with Cyril and Everest obediently in tow.

That was the *plan*, at least.

K2 settled down at the kitchen table, beaming shyly.

K2 had imagined this in his head so many times, hugged to himself the proud occasion of his family admiring what *he* could do for once.

Even Aunt Violet would be impressed.

And his father too!

What a moment this was going to be!

The entire family pressed in, crowding around him.

"Draw me a good one, son!" said Everest heartily.

"Something very, VERY complicated," suggested Izzabird.

"Um . . . you're not being very helpful," said K2.

"Show your father how *well* you can do it!" suggested Theo.

K2 had started drawing, but at these words his hand slowed.

"Are you certain *he* is the one who can draw the Atlas?" said Aunt Trudie. "Maybe it was Annipeck after all, did you SEE that magic coming straight out of her hands?!"

Now Aunt Trudie was joining in! *She* normally believed in him.

"Make sure it's neat," recommended Freya.

K2's hand stopped entirely, and the pencil smudged into an ugly, awkward mess.

Once, he had taken out that pencil and empires flew from under his fingers. Worlds sprang up at his command, islands grew warm at his direction, and the seas leaped with fish as he drew them into being.

Now his pencil stuttered awkwardly, and nothing would come into life beneath his clumsy hand. All his imaginings were stopped up, muted, closed off.

K2 started again. The pencil stumbled and broke entirely in two.

"Perhaps he's lost the Gift. Is that possible?" said Izzabird.

"I knew he was very unlikely to have it," sniffed Aunt Violet. "Funny little thing like him. Probably just had a very mild case of the Gift all along…"

"Worra!" added Annipeck.

I can do it… I know I can do it…

He's lost the Gift!

"Stop talking at me!" said K2, putting his hands over his ears. "I did well on that adventure, didn't I? I know I can do it!!!"

"Never mind, son," Everest patted him consolingly. "Maybe you have other Gifts."

"See, Horizabel, HE'S LOST THE GIFT!" cried Izzabird triumphantly.

"But, Dad, I really *can* still do it!" said K2, furious now.

"K2," said his father firmly, "YOU HAVE LOST THE GIFT."

"But *YOU* are more important than any Gift you may or may not have," said Freya.

Chapter 43 A SLIGHT CHANGE of PLAN

orizabel's eyes were harder than diamonds. "What you're saying is ridiculous," she said. "He can't have lost the Gift!"

"It must have been that bump on the head," said Everest, his eyes on the drawn Spelling Stick in Horizabel's hand.

"Yes, maybe the Gift left him when that happened?" agreed Theo. He was looking at the Spelling Stick too.

Curse these little humans! Nobody told me they were so acute with their senses!

"It can't disappear in a winking!" hissed Horizabel. "That's impossible..."

"I bet it happens sometimes, though," said Izzabird. "Has someone ever lost a Gift as a result of an accident, Blinkers?"

Blinkers rapidly searched through her memory systems. "Found one!" she said smartly. "Roughly two hundred twenty years ago, a small girl over in the second Galaxy to the left lost her Gift of Seeing Into the Future when she got a very high temperature with the urgle pox."

"There you are!" said Izzabird triumphantly. "So what just happened here, then?"

"Small boy lost the Atlas Gift because of bump on head," said Blinkers promptly. "Unlikely but not impossible."

Humph. That might satisfy the Universal authorities, if it ever came to that, for robots do not lie.

All the humans looked at Horizabel so pleadingly.

"I'm not as easy to deceive as Blinkers and *I* don't think K2 has lost the Gift," Horizabel said.

"Oh good," said K2 delightedly. "I didn't think I had!"

Horizabel was right: K2 had not lost the Gift.

"And that leaves me with a problem," said Horizabel, her icy eyes bleaker than frostdrops. "I am a bounty hunter who reports directly into the Universal Government. And in that role I am supposed to not only apprehend and imprison anyone using an illegal Atlas but also to ELIMINATE anyone who can create an Atlas themselves."

"*Ohhhhhhhhhh…*" K2 whitened and backed away from Horizabel, and the way that the friendliness in his eyes turned to fear when he looked at her gave her a pang that she found infuriating.

"Give me *one* good reason," said Horizabel between gritted teeth, "why I should break the rules? For the High Council of the Universal Government I serve would have no mercy on *me* if they found out I had left the Child-with-the-Atlas-Gift alive…"

"Because in your heart of hearts you are fond of him," said Aunt Trudie.

"I have no heart," said Horizabel.

But she didn't say that quite as convincingly as she ought to have done.

For Horizabel was making an unwelcome discovery.

She was finding, for the first time, the soft spot that one can have for humans.

Even their pathetic attempts to trick her were touching as well as exasperating.

But then…

Telling herself that this had really been her own

plan all along, Horizabel shook her lovely shoulders and was restored to good humor.

She smiled and put her Spelling Finger away.

The little family did not smile back.

"Why are you looking at me like that?" Horizabel said, when she saw their nervous expressions. "Oh, was it that little thing that just happened there?" she continued, waving the last five minutes away with an airy sweep of her hand. "You can't hold *that* against me. I'm a bounty hunter. I was only doing my job."

Horizabel raised her tree-branch hand and put it on her chest, over where her heart would have been if she had one.

"I never really *wanted* to harm K2," said Horizabel.

The family still looked unconvinced.

"I know I'm going to regret this," said Horizabel. "But you have one…last…chance. I will clear this whole thing up for you, and there will be no more unwanted attention from robot assassins or the Universal Government, and you can go right back to being the unnoticed little world that you were before this fiasco. BUT if I'm going to do that, I need some pretty impressive promises out of the lot of you."

Everyone nodded enthusiastically.

"Firstly, even if you're keeping your Magic secret from outsiders, the adults in this family are going to have to teach the children how to use it, for your own safety, never mind anyone else's."

"Maybe a little extra tutoring in 'Magic' and 'other worlds' on top of their regular school subjects would be a good idea...," admitted Freya.

"Brilliant!" said Izzabird excitedly. "FINALLY we can find out what my Gift is. Invisibility? Teleportation? Telekinesis?" she wondered aloud. "It could be *anything*!"

"What about Theo and me?" said Mabel wistfully. "Are we going to be left out? Just because we're ordinary Smiths?"

"Non-Magic people may not have 'Gifts,' but they can still perform Magic, Mabel," said Aunt Trudie, "if they use a Potion or a Spelling Stick or an incantation.

"And 'Smith' is no 'ordinary' name either. It's a wonderfully *creative* name!" she continued. "A 'smith' means a craftsperson, an ARTIST. It's really another word for 'Wizard.'"

"Is it?" said Mabel, her face lighting up. "Mabel the Wizard! *Thank you*, Aunt Trudie!"

"And while we're on the subject of Magic...," said Daniel, and then stopped. It was difficult to know where to start.

The robots! The Alternative Worlds! Secret missions to strange locations behind his back! The children with Gifts that got unexpected and unwelcome intergalactic attention!

"...I do feel that you might have not kept *quite* so many secrets from me," said Daniel at last, a little lamely.

"I'm sorry, I didn't want to scare you away," said Freya. "But know that I love you," she smiled, holding out her hand.

How could he be firm when she smiled at him so sweetly?

All his firmness dissolved, like a soufflé in a shower.

"And I love *you*." Daniel beamed. "For better, for worse, in this world or any other."

Everest gave a big wistful sigh.

Time to move on.

"And what about the rest of you?" said Horizabel. "No more arguing?"

No more arguing was a little much to hope for. But the adventure had changed everyone, as adventures will.

"Will you promise to stop trying to get rid of Daniel, Izza?" said Freya.

Izzabird was looking very thoughtful. Maybe the Stepfather wasn't *so bad* as an extra father. He was kind, he was brave, he tried to do the right thing.

He wasn't running out the door to different worlds all the time.

And he wasn't, and had never been, a *pirate*.

"All right then," said Izza. She hugged her mother. K2 gave a big sigh. Izza looked happier than she had done in a long, long time.

"And you, Theo?" said Daniel. "I'm sorry I didn't

believe you when you were trying to tell me about this whole"—Daniel coughed—"*Magic* business. You did wonderfully well out there, Theo. Your mother would have been so proud of you."

Theo smiled and his whole face lit up.

"Will you keep our secret?" pleaded Freya.

Theo's phone was still broken, but maybe he could ask Aunt Violet to mend it, after all.

This new family was messy and different, but perhaps that was kind of...

...exciting.

Theo nodded his head.

"From now on, you will be known as *the 'O'Hero-Smith' family*, which means 'Heros-in-the-Making,'" said Horizabel. "So next you must all SWEAR," she went on. "In the name of True Love and Beyond, in this world and the next, that you will use your Magic to improve life for all living things on this Earth, here, and you will never use an illegal Alternative Atlas again...

"For if you do"—and now Horizabel's voice reeked of menace—"you will draw down the wrath of the Great Ones upon you and your whole precious planet."

"PROMISE!"

They all shook on it in turns. Ten human hands, shaking hands with Horizabel's tree branch.

"Very good," said Horizabel.

She crossed her arms.

"And now you have to give up all the copies of the Atlas that you have in this house."

"I don't know what you're talking about. Do you, Trudie?" growled Aunt Violet, looking at Horizabel with big, innocent eyes.

"ALL of them!" said Horizabel firmly.

Copies of that Atlas were hidden absolutely *everywhere*. Some hand-copied, some photocopied, some a mixture of the two. Some of them covered single planets, some of them a multitude, some of them were just a couple of sheets stapled together.

Under Aunt Violet's mattress. Behind the picture of Everest rappelling down the Grand Canyon. Inside the old grandfather clock. Rolled up in Aunt Trudie's yoga mat. Behind the loose tiles at the back of the bath.

Horizabel made them find every...single...one.

And, finally, the biggie.

In a subterranean cellar, underneath Aunt Trudie's secret library, buried in Magic so complex that it took Aunt Violet and Aunt Trudie half an hour to undo...

...*The Ancestor's Atlas itself.*

The original Atlas, that the First Atlas-Maker had created so many centuries before, full of a mind-boggling amount of planets. It was a truly gigantic, crumblingly ancient book, compacted by Magic, of course, because otherwise it wouldn't have fit in the house, but still so wide you could barely get your arms around it. Contained inside were the exquisite drawings of impossible worlds quivering into life, and X-shaped Which Ways that flitted this way and that, the trembling yellow of the curled pages unfurling their secrets in front of your very eyes.

The first non-O'Hero hand to touch the Atlas in thousands of years belonged to Horizabel.

She put on gloves and her gas mask to remove it from the cellar, for it was the sort of thing that might have been booby-trapped. Aunt Trudie wept as Horizabel carried the Atlas solemnly through the hall as if it was nuclear material. (Which in a way, it was.) She locked it carefully in the belly of Bulk Mode Blinkers, who specially expanded to her utmost size to accommodate it, then compressed herself down again so she could fit through the door.

"It's the lifting of a Curse, Trudie, it's the lifting of a Curse!" growled Aunt Violet, giving her sister a hearty thump on the back to console her.

Mission completed.

That Atlas was going back to the Universal Government where it belonged.

And Horizabel was relying on the O'Hero-Smiths' word that K2 would never create another one and that would be the end of the story.

"Well done, everybody!" said Horizabel buoyantly, rubbing her hands together. *Finally* we'll be on our way! Quick! I hate long goodbyes..."

"Horizabel, why don't you stay?" said Theo.

"No room," said Aunt Violet and Aunt Trudie at exactly the same time.

That didn't seem very hospitable.

"Yes, do stay!" said Izzabird, surprised at the aunts' unfriendliness. "I need a positive female role model in my life."

Horizabel grinned. "But look! You have plenty of impressive women in front of you already."

"Aunts!" sniffed Izzabird dismissively. "*Mothers!* They don't count."

"Inventors, scientists, and teachers are worthy heroes," said Horizabel. "And, most importantly, they are your *family.*" Her voice had a hint of yearning in it. "I don't have a family, which is why I know how important it is. The life of a Grimm is a lonely one, Izza. Do not wish for it. But I cannot change who I am. The sky calls me like a fate I have to answer. My feet hear the cry; they have to dance."

"Hurry, now, Horizabel, the wind is in the right direction," said Freya, encouragingly shooing her toward the door, as Horizabel sorted out attaching Cyril's prison pod to Blinkers.

Casually, Izzabird draped Aunt Violet's duffel coat over Horizabel's Flymaster lying in the corner, in the hope that Horizabel would forget it and leave it behind.

Nonchalantly, Everest took out the burnt, tattered remains of K2's Alternative Atlas from Horizabel's backpack, which she had carelessly left unattended on the kitchen table.

"These are beautiful drawings, K2," said Everest, admiringly leafing through the pages.

"Thank you," beamed K2 proudly. "I wish you could have seen me draw in it."

"Maybe next time," said Everest.

"But...should you be taking that from Horizabel, Dad?" K2 whispered.

"This doesn't belong to Horizabel, though, does it?" said Everest. "It's *yours*. Will you lend it to me? I do miss having one."

"Of course," said K2, and then he grinned. "It's not a loan though, Dad...It's a *GIFT*."

Father and son smiled at each other.

"Put that down!" said Horizabel sharply as she turned to see Everest tucking the Atlas in his pocket. "That's confiscated Universal Government property! You won't need *that* in the Prison of the Evergods!"

"Yes, about that," said Everest, standing up. "There's been a slight change of plan. I think I may

It's a gift.

not go to the Prison of the Evergods *quite* yet, after all."

"Whaaaaaaat?" Horizabel's eyes were now as pointed as the scarily pointy bit of an Air Stick. "You made the Promise of a Hero!"

"I made the promise of an *O'Hero*, not *a* Hero," said Everest. "It's a slightly different thing."

Horizabel reached for her Spelling Stick.

It wasn't there.

Everest had pickpocketed it, the rascal!

491

And when she pointed her robot hand at him, he pointed the Spelling Stick at his own chest and muttered some chant-words to himself.

K2, Izzabird, and the others gasped as there was a blinding flash, and in front of their eyes Everest disappeared into what looked like an Everest entirely made out of stars.

Curses! Horizabel would need a moment to adjust her robot hand to make it work on him in hologram mode...

"I'm afraid you're not going to have enough time, Horizabel. Clever of me, don't you think?" said Everest, charmingly regretful but unable to resist showing off. (Conceit was another thing that Everest O'Hero had to work on.)

Everest winked at K2 and Izzabird, and in one, two, three bounds, he reached the door, and in his hologram state he stepped right through it as if it weren't there.

"Sorry, everyone, and thank you for all your help!" he shouted back through the keyhole.

Was it K2's and Izzabird's imaginations, or could that be Everest's hologram arm, thrust back through the door a moment, with the shining hand waving goodbye?

But by the time Blinkers and Horizabel had dragged open the door, the hand had disappeared, and in the dark rectangle of the doorway there was only a night sky filled with stars.

Everest was gone.

All that remained was a faint echo of his voice, calling through the empty air:

"Catch me if you can, Horizabel! *AN O'HERO KNOWS NO LIMITS!* THE SKY IS JUST THE BEGINNING. NO RIVERS CAN STOP US! NO MOUNTAINS CAN STAND IN OUR WAY!"

Chapter 44
THE CROSSING OF THE WAYS

Where is he?" hissed Horizabel.

"This house is built on a Crossing of the Ways," said Blinkers. "And Everest has an Alternative Atlas. He really could have gone anywhere. The options are as numerous as stars in the sky."

Curses and irritations and little fiddly fingernails of the great goddesses of the galaxies!

"After him! Before the Which Way he used heals up and we can't see which one he took anymore…" Horizabel ran out of the porch, looked left, right, down, and up. "There it is!" she said excitedly. "I can still see it!"

"But hang on, that's in the—" Izza gasped.

"—SKY," said Annipeck, toddling after them all and pointing upward.

"Impossible," said Theo.

As if Theo were giving her a dare, Horizabel ran out onto the lawn.

She was followed by Blinkers in Bulk Mode, carrying Cyril's prison pod slung underneath her.

The rest of the family came after: Freya scooping Annipeck up into her arms, Daniel moving stiffly still, the four children, the two aunts, a small black-and-white dog, and a tiny robot called Puck.

Horizabel took out her official Alternative Atlas and punched away at the touch screen until the map of the O'Hero-Smith house and garden came up, with the calm night above it, and the dark shape of the "X" that marked the Crossing of the Ways hovering somewhere above one of Everest's telescopes.

Horizabel tapped again, and the map flipped over.

"Vercivon," she breathed. "Brace yourself, Blinkers! Next stop, the distant planet of VERCIVON!"

Horizabel pointed her hand up toward the sky, and out of the twiglike fingers shot a lightning bolt of Magic and it highlighted a great tear up in the sky above, in the shape of an "X."

X marks the spot.

Horizabel stamped her foot and seemed to grow

in front of their very eyes. She looked no longer human. She hardened, like wood, and then metal, and then stone, and burned as if she were mercury on fire, unlikely and so bright it was hard to look at her.

Stamp! Stamp! Stamp! Like the foot of Rumpelstiltskin.

There was a strange, soft rustling noise from underneath her star cowl.

Something had been hidden there all along.

Slowly, slowly, from underneath the star cowl of Horizabel the Grimm, two dark wings gra-a-a-dually unfolded.

The wings of the Story Maker are a glorious sight.

Horizabel bent her knees.

And UP she leaped, Blinkers following after, trailing stars like the pathway of a rocket.

Shaking the dusty stars from under her feet. Leaping from impossible planet to impossible planet.

"I wish she could have stayed," sighed Theo, watching Horizabel go. "I think I might be in love."

"You're way too young to be in love, she's completely unsuitable, and I bet human beings aren't allowed to fall in love with Grimms of the universe," said Izzabird.

There was a pause.

"If I became an intergalactic hero, do you think that she might love me back, then?" asked Theo.

"No chance," said Izzabird.

Horizabel glanced down a moment, longingly, at the faces of the family looking up at her.

And then she shot on.

"Fly fast, Dad," whispered K2.

"Don't let Horizabel catch you," whispered Izzabird.

They all watched for as long as they could, till they had cricks in their necks and remembered that they were very tired, and there was more chatting and eating to be done, and further in the future their beds were calling.

The O'Hero-Smith family walked slowly back into the house.

You already know the end of the story.

The storm had lifted.

The winds had died down.

The friendly old house in the middle of that boggy little part of Planet Earth was only just a little bit less messy and falling-down and unsatisfactory than it ever was or had been.

And everyone had made promises that they would find hard to keep.

But there was joy in the kitchen that night.

EPILOGUE

s I told you before, I, the Story Maker, and Horizabel, are sort-of one and the same person.

This *ought* to have been the story of how I got rid of a terrible threat.

But stories are so hard to pin down.

Instead, it turned into the story of how I was tricked by nine little humans and a baby into leaving the one with the Atlas Gift alive.

It is our hearts that get us into trouble.

For was I right to be merciful in this case?

K2 himself was not the problem: I knew he could be trusted with the Gift. It was the others who would *want* that Gift.

I could have eliminated K2, and with that one stroke, all the problems and heartaches and messiness of the future, of having such a dangerous Gift alive in the universe, would be avoided.

But could *you* have done it, to well-meaning, well-deserving, and clever little K2?

I ask you that. Search your consciences, dear readers.

In the meantime, I have left the children in the chaotic hands of the aunts, with all their good intentions; and their parents, who have promised to educate them. I have flown away, hoping, as the Great Ones have always hoped, that the humans will keep their promises, and that their cleverness and their love and their ingenuity will lead them out of the problems of their own making and make a world for all living things on their

one

precious

planet.

But only time will tell.

And so many more questions are bothering me in the quiet watches of the night.

Is it really only K2 who has the most dangerous Gift in the universe? (Because of course, K2 never lost the Gift. The family were just pretending he had to protect him.)

That little baby Annipeck ALSO has a unique Gift, one I've never seen before.

Is it a coincidence that they are both living in the same house?

Could one of those other children have a Gift *even more powerful than K2's*?

Izzabird has an aura so fiercely scarlet it pierces the eye to see it.

And Theo and Mabel may *think* they are not Magic, but I know better.

I have seen their auras.

Theo's is a yellow brighter than gold.

And Mabel's is greener than the most emerald forest.

Is the House of the O'Hero-Smiths shielding an even bigger secret than the Atlas-Maker himself?

Vorcxix the Vile will have seen their auras too.

And now he knows where the O'Hero-Smith family are hiding…

Oh, another Story is coming; I can feel it in the twitching of my tree-branch fingers.

So, Watch Out, O'Hero-Smiths.

There will be people coming to get you.

And it won't just be me.

MUCH LATER, IN ANOTHER WORLD

The bleeding figure of Vorcxix, in the middle of a sandstorm and a desert of his own making, riding on the back of an exhausted, dented EXCORIATOR.

Opens up the home page of his Alternative Atlas.

Reads the message that Horizabel has kindly transmitted to him just before she left Excelsiar:

"I CAN KEEP A SECRET IF *YOU* CAN…"

He thinks about the slippery bounty hunter and the family with the Atlas Gift in their grasp. Vows, as THE EXCORIATOR limps across the long and lonely sands:

"I AM GOING TO *GET YOU*, O'HEROS AND SMITHS AND HORIZZZZABEL THE GRIMM! *IF IT'S THE LAST THING I DO…*"

Bounty Hunters Have No Hearts

I don't care for Mothers
And Mothers don't care for me
The stars make lonely parents
But at least you can be free

Swim hard enough and deep enough
And your arms turn into fins
Fly hard enough and high enough
And your shoulders shall grow wings

SO…

DANCE, Horizabel, DANCE!
And I'll tell you a story or two
That'll keep us warm till Andromeda
And pass an eon or few…

On the Witching Hour of Nowhere
When the Stars were shining full bright
Someone took a little child
And left them out that night

It's a cold old Life, the Traveling Life,
But at least that set me free!

For I'll tell you an ancient secret;
That little child was ME...

AND...

    You need loving hands to grow a heart
      Loving eyes for the heart to form
        You need loving words for a heart to start
      Loving breath to make it warm

      Gentle words, and the heart begins to tick
    Songs and stories set the beat
But it's hard to make a heart pump quick
When you've got no food to eat

SO...

DANCE, Horizabel, DANCE! Whirl your cowl
and SING!
    At least you've got your freedom, let freedom
be your thing!
    Toss your hair and surf those storms
    Dive deep into that sea
    I don't care for Mothers

    No Mother ever cared for me...

The Making of an O'Hero-Smith

No heart is born a Hero
Your Atlas sets your Quest
You'll take the Which Way Star-Cross
You'll do your very best

You'll travel the dusty space miles
A gazillion years or two,
And it's a cold old Life, the Traveling Life
The frost turns your toenails blue

But once you've braved the fearsome Star-Cross
And faced a Beast, and a Rider or two
You'll return a wiser Wanderer
And the Hero could be YOU

Use Your Gifts for Good

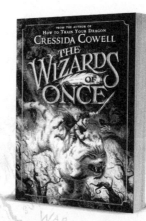

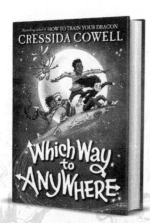

Watch Out for the next
adventure,
Which Way
Around the
GALAXY

Discover the Magic of Cressida Cowell

visit
cressidacowell.com
to find out all about her books,
events, and lots more!

/CressidaCowellBooks
@CressidaCowellAuthor
@CressidaCowell

Lots of thank yous are in order here

I'd like to extend a huge thank you to the lovely Helen Cosgrove, who inspired me to make my first cake and who told me how to go about it. ('You need to buy a tin,' she said.)

Thank you to everyone who contributed recipes: John Baines, Shirley Baines. Himself Baines, Sean Ferguson, Mam Keyes, Zaga Radojčić (and thank you Ljiljana Keyes for translating them from Serbian), Beth Nepomuceno, and Zeny Perez.

I did a couple of great day courses in baking at Cooks Academy in Dublin and I learnt magical stuff about cake decoration in Cakes 4 Fun, Putney and the Cake Box, Dún Laoghaire. I'm very grateful for the expertize they shared with me.

The books and recipes of several famous bakers have inspired me and I'd like to give a special mention to the thrillingly innovative Dan Lepard, the lovely, lovely Nigel Slater and, my very favourite, Catherine Leyden (check her out on Ireland AM).

Thank you to all the people I forced cake on and who gave me their opinion – too many to mention.

Thank you to all the people at Michael Joseph who embraced the idea for this book so enthusiastically and who worked on it – and with me! – with such diligence and patience: Lindsey Evans, Louise Moore, Liz Smith, Nick Lowndes, Lee Motley, John Hamilton, Sarah Fraser and the copy-editors. Thank you to Louisa Carter and the small army of people who 'test-baked' all my recipes to make sure they worked. Thank you to my ever wonderful agent Jonathan Lloyd, and all at Curtis Brown.

Thank you to Alistair Richardson for the beautiful photography, and to Barry McCall, his lovely assistant Paul and my stalwart hair and make-up pal Tish Curry, for making the cover-shot so painless.

Finally, the biggest thank you goes to Himself, who puts up with living in a house where everything is coated in a thin film of icing sugar, and who photographed every single thing I baked and encouraged me every step of the way.